DRAMA!

A SOUTH ROCK HIGH NOVEL

A.J. TRUMAN

Cover by Bailey McGinn

Proofreading by Heather Caryn

❀ Created with Vellum

1

EVERETT

Today was the day I'd been dreading.

I opened the envelope to the wedding invite with one hand and spooned another scoop of double chocolate fudge caramel swirl ice cream into my mouth with the other. Fact: the more words in an ice cream flavor, the more delicious it tastes.

Jordana and Bethany were cordially inviting me to their nuptials next month. It was going to be the lesbian event of the year, and I was excited for them. We were theater nerds in college, spending every available free moment putting on plays in basements that nobody saw and getting drunk on off-brand alcohol at off-campus parties.

But two dastardly words embossed on the RSVP card were staring me in the face, sticking their tongue out at me. Assuming words had tongues.

Plus. One.

Had two words ever held such double-edged meaning? "Plus one" was wedding speak for "Oh, you're still single?"

"Plus one" meant I had no husband, no serious boyfriend, no casual boyfriend, no partner. Christ, I didn't even have a fuck-buddy. I hadn't had sex in months. I forgot the actual month. I should've kept track the way prisoners scraped tally marks into their jail cell walls. It'd been so long I Googled *Can testicles dry up if not used?*

And I was only half kidding.

I didn't want to call myself unlucky in love because a) that was depressing, b) romance wasn't a lottery, and c) love was utter bullshit.

Surely if there was anyone worth mentioning to Jordana and Bethany, they would've heard about him.

But there wasn't.

The thing was, while I was definitely down for a good dicking, I wasn't feeling the need to add a plus one to my life. The last time I did the plus one thing, it ended in tears. My tears, not his.

His name was Noah Paxton, the star of our college theater program. Like everyone else at school, I was swept up in his orbit. Every theater program or production had a guy like that, a guy who you know was going to make it. It was inevitable.

Noah was the gorgeous, charismatic sun around which we all revolved. When he chose me to be his boyfriend, I felt like I'd... fine, won the lottery. That should've been my first sign things weren't going to work out. People win the lottery and go broke all the time.

He dumped me after graduation. Like, *right* after graduation. Like, we were still in our caps and gowns, and I dabbed at my tears with my rolled-up diploma.

It was relationship whiplash.

"We were never built to last," he told me which, as a heart-broken twenty-two-year-old, I considered remarkably profound. Translation: I wasn't proper boyfriend material.

Noah fulfilled his potential as star of the theater program. He was currently starring on Broadway in the biggest hit the Great White Way had seen in years. He'd won a Tony, a Grammy for the cast album, and then when he performed songs from the show on *Good Morning America*, he won an Emmy.

Meanwhile, I couldn't get more than a half-dozen kids at South Rock High to audition for the fall musical. I loved being a drama teacher, but it was a constant uphill battle in the face of SPORTS!, which our whole school worshiped.

Maybe there was a reason why Noah dumped me so easily, and why in the years since, I'd been unable to make it work with any other guy. I just wasn't boyfriend material.

Shaking myself out of my funk, I texted Jordana and Bethany back. *The invites are gorg! OMG so excited for you!!* I'd watched them fall in love during college and was happy that some relationships were built to last.

Jordana responded with a string of heart eyes emoji. Despite her being a playwright, I couldn't recall the last time she'd texted actual words. She was reverting back to hieroglyphics.

Will you be in our wedding party? Bethany asked.

I'd love to! I added a bunch of girl-girl emoji. Asking was merely a formality. If they wanted me to walk over hot coals as part of their ceremony, I would've said yes.

We're getting the whole gang back together for the wedding, Bethany texted.

The whole gang? I wrote back, my palm becoming very sweaty all of a sudden.

Yeah... Bethany sure knew how to crank up the tension, both while directing plays and in everyday communication.

The ellipsis was as dreaded as seeing "plus one" on a wedding envelope.

Noah is coming, she wrote.

Jordana texted a string of cringe face emoji to follow her fiancée's text.

That's cool, I texted. In reality, I paced around my apartment, as a familiar lump hit my chest.

He's bringing Gavin, Bethany texted.

Jordana texted the boy-boy emoji, digital salt on a still open wound.

How will you tell them apart? I texted with a smiling emoji to show them that I was totally cool with it. Cool as a drink with ice in it. Some ice. Not a lot of ice or else I'd be cold, and I'm not going to be cold to my ex-boyfriend and his twin boyfriend.

For the past year, the internet had been all abuzz over Noah dating his understudy in the play, Gavin Blanchard. Yes, we all knew it was a thing that gay couples looked like each other. But to date his understudy, who looked like an off-brand version of Noah —hair not as curly, eyes not as intense, voice not as silky—seemed like the height of self-absorption. Noah was quite literally fucking himself.

But the public ate it up. They were the cute gay couple du jour, launching a thousand OMG squee memes and lighting up Instagram.

And I was...practically *begging* students to audition for the fall musical.

It'll be good to see him, I texted, mustering all my bigger person energy.

Reunion time, Bethany texted back. *The whole crew back together for one weekend.*

Life was one constant performance, but our roles were always changing. In one month, I had to play the part of the chill, suave ex-boyfriend.

No problem.

Jordana texted one more cringe face emoji.

Sorry, that was for someone else, she texted right after.

Okay, so maybe a slight problem.

I couldn't face this wedding alone.

I was never good at one-man shows. I worked best when I could bounce off a scene partner. I couldn't show up at this wedding alone while Noah and Gavin waltzed in and soaked up all the attention. I didn't want to give them the satisfaction. I didn't want Noah to believe he was right, that I wasn't boyfriend material.

And I needed someone I could roll my eyes at and make bitchy under-my-breath comments to.

I needed a plus one.

————

UNLIKE MANY OF those "if you can't do, teach" people, I was the weird unicorn that loved being a teacher. I got off (metaphorically!) on helping students realize their acting potential, watching them transform into new characters, and gain a new understanding of the world through plays. Even in the twenty-first century, theater was still a radical act.

Unfortunately, though, drama was becoming an endangered species at South Rock.

When I started at South Rock High, I was brought in as the drama teacher who could also teach a public speaking class, which was a requirement for all freshmen. But with each year, the administration added another public speaking class and removed another drama class due to lack of enrollment. This year, I was down to one drama class per day.

I entered the school from the teacher's parking lot and beelined to the fall musical sign-up sheet hanging outside the auditorium. South Rock used to put on two productions per year, a fall play and a spring musical. At the end of last year, Principal Aguilar unfortunately broke the news that because of budget cuts, we were now down to one.

But of course, SPORTS! got brand new equipment and a shiny new locker room.

I did my usual tradition of closing my eyes just before I

rounded the corner to the auditorium. I prayed for more sign ups in those precious seconds. I supposed I couldn't blame the school for cutting theater since in the past, we could barely wrangle enough students for a decent production.

It was a new school year, though. New year, new you?

My heart lifted at the sight of multiple audition slots filled in. Names! So many names! Yes, the show would go on!

Yet as I ran my finger down the list of names, my elation curdled into despair. My hopes sunk like the actual Titanic. (not the 1998 musical *Titanic*, which infamously couldn't rig the titular set piece to pretend sink)

Hugh Jass

Ophelia Balls

Phil McCrackin

Pat Mysak

Seymour Buttholes

I looked to the left, then the right. The hall was empty, so I rested my head against the wall and heaved out the most crestfallen sigh I could muster at seven in the morning.

"Will there still be a fall musical?" Rhiannon asked me a half-hour later in South Rock High's sole remaining drama class. The girl had the presence and pipes. She could've been my Gypsy Rose Lee, my Anita in *West Side Story* if we had a robust theater program.

She and the five other kids in class, the core drama nerds at South Rock, sat in a circle on the stage. They looked up at me with those big, pleading eyes. I was grateful for every single one of them. Drama nerds were a rare breed.

"Of course there will be." I scoffed at her question. "There's always a musical."

"There was always a fall play, but now there isn't," said Jimmy, a fabulous, openly gay kid wearing a vast assortment of rainbow bracelets. I didn't have the balls to come out in high school. He did it in fifth grade!

"It's just a one-year suspension of the play while the administration deals with budget cuts." I didn't consider this lying. It was a down payment on a future truth. "Let's focus on delivering a smashing fall musical!"

Jimmy played with his bracelets. "But if we don't have enough people to audition...unfortunately, Hugh Jass et al aren't real people."

"Just jocks in disguise," said Rhiannon with an eyeroll. The other drama nerds nodded in resentful agreement.

"There's still time." I had to keep things positive. As a leader, if I showed any defeat, then it was game over for the fall musical.

"What play are we doing this year?" Rhiannon asked.

"Good question. We're going to do *You're a Good Man, Charlie Brown*." I turned away to rustle up papers for today's class—and to avoid their reactions.

"Again? Seriously?" Rhiannon asked.

"Actors, it's a great play!" I said.

"We did it last year." Jimmy twirled a bracelet on his wrist more forcefully.

"And now we can perfect our performances."

I looked out on my circle of six theater acolytes. The disappointment in their eyes crushed me. Being in the theater meant a lifetime of disappointment: rejections, low pay, plays closing down, not to mention facing a world where ninety-eight percent of people were indifferent to this thing that you held life-affirming reverence for.

This should've been the happy times. I had an absolute blast in my high school theater program, and I refused to watch their dreams die before they'd even had a chance to experience that awesomeness.

So I gave another down payment on a future truth.

"Just kidding!" I chucked the *Charlie Brown* scripts in the trash with a flamboyant whoosh. "We're not doing *Charlie Brown* again. I had you fooled. We're doing *Into the Woods*."

The title popped from my lips before I could course-correct, like it'd been sitting on the tip of my tongue for years.

Their moods immediately flipped. It was as if I'd given them each one million dollars.

"Are you serious?" Jimmy asked, on the verge of hyperventilating.

"Oh my God." Rhiannon's big eyes bulged from her face. I hadn't seen her this excited since that time she won the *Hamilton* ticket lottery. "We're really doing *Into the Woods*?"

"Yep."

"Can I play The Baker's Wife?"

"You'll have to audition at the end of the month like everyone else."

Into the Woods had parts for over a dozen cast members, which we didn't have, unless some parent was cruel enough to name their child Ophelia Balls.

It required elaborate sets and costumes, which we couldn't afford.

To perform the beautiful songs composed by the great Stephen Sondheim, we needed a full orchestra, which we also didn't have.

In summation, we were fucked.

I raised a fist in the air. "Get ready. It's going to be great!"

2

EVERETT

I had the back-to-back crush of public speaking classes to distract me from the back-to-back headaches of having no plus one and no chance to pull off *Into the Woods*. There was nothing like watching kids panic and freeze in front of their fellow classmates to put things in perspective.

Public speaking wasn't theater, but it still accomplished the same goal: giving people confidence by letting them step outside themselves for a moment. I gave notes to the brave students who practiced giving extemporaneous speeches and couched in lots of positive feedback.

During seventh period, we were one speech in when Principal Aguilar came on the loudspeaker and instructed us to head down to the gym for yet another pep rally. I'd never seen such relief on my students' faces.

The crush of two thousand students and faculty cramming through the halls and into the gym gave me cover to whip out my phone.

Everett: Good afternoon, friends! Meet at our usual spot?
Julian: Yep.

Chase: Just got here.

Everett: I can't wait to see you guys.

Amos: What do you want?

Everett: Uh...to sit next to you?

Amos: Funny.

Amos: What do you want?

Everett: Jesus. Can't a guy wish his friends a good afternoon without said friends thinking said guy wants something?

Amos: What do you want?

I shook my head and avoided barreling into a pack of cool kids.

"Seriously?" I asked my so-called friends when I sat down at our spot on the bleachers. Long ago, we'd staked out aisle seats at the far end which were partially blocked by speakers. That way, we could chitchat during these inane assemblies that were a blatant waste of time.

I thought I would understand the point of pep rallies when I became a teacher. I was wrong. They were useless time sucks. We weren't sending our athletes into battle.

I took a seat next to Amos, while Chase and Julian sat in the row behind us, making it easier for us to stealthily schmooze.

"Good afternoon. You guys look great," I said.

"What do you want?" Amos asked, not missing a beat from our text convo. We were all nerdy teachers, but Amos had the cute dork look down with a mop of brown curls and boyish smile.

"I don't need anything...per se."

My three best friends rolled their eyes in unison. We all met as teachers here at South Rock High, connected by our love of teaching, our camaraderie, and the fact that we were all gay nerds of different varieties. We'd gone from co-workers to friends to me drunkenly calling them my brothers one night and nobody blinking an eye.

But currently, they were being major buttwhistles.

"I don't have the data handy, though it is available as a PDF or CSV file," Chase said, pushing up his thick glasses, really going for the nerdy scientist aesthetic. "But whenever you wish us a good morning or good afternoon and compliment us, there's a sixty-five percent chance that it's a preamble to you asking for a favor."

"Thank you, Chase," I deadpanned. I wasn't one of those people who refused to believe science, but Chase loved to test my limits.

"In fact, you'd actually save us all time by not buttering us up. Approximately thirty-six minutes per person per year."

"Oooh, think about all the gay porn I can watch with that free time back." I arched an eyebrow at Chase, signaling that the numbers part of this conversation was over.

"So what do you need?" Julian, the sweetest one of our group, asked.

"I need a date to a lesbian wedding."

"Do they need to be a lesbian?" Chase blinked at me.

"No," I shot back. "Preferably a date with a...pocket calculator. Maybe even an extra-large calculator if I were to be so lucky."

We'd devised a code to talk about sex, or anything sex adjacent, in the presence of students. (I'd broken that code by mentioning gay porn a second ago. I was a work in progress.) Fortunately, the gym was loud with the cacophony of students milling about before the pep rally officially kicked off, drowning out our voices.

Though let's be real: These kids were having a lot more sex than any of us. Well, save for Amos who recently began dating the new gym teacher, Hutch.

"It's in one month," I continued. "Noah and Gavin are going, and they're gonna be adorable and everyone's going to fawn all over them. I can't be the sad single spinster in the corner."

"Technically you'd be a bachelor," Julian pointed out.

"That doesn't make it better."

"I can be your date," he said.

"In any other universe, I would take you up on that, J-Money. You'd knock 'em all dead." Julian was a cute bear of a guy with flowing hair and delicate features. He had a little extra cushion that filled out his face and he wore it well. "Unfortunately, my college friends know you guys. They'd know we weren't really dating."

A flash of relief crossed his face, but I appreciated him offering.

"They'd know you were only a plus one. I can't go with a plus one."

Just saying those two words made my skin crawl.

"I need to go with a boyfriend, or someone who could believably be my boyfriend." I heaved out a sigh. "Any ideas?"

Silence descended upon our foursome. A deafening, depressing silence. This explained why three quarters of us were single.

It was hard to think with the noise. The sounds of cheers and applause bounced off the walls as Principal Aguilar took the stage to introduce the football team. Cheerleaders danced around the players in a sign that gender roles hadn't really changed in seventy years.

And in the center of the fracas was the coach, Raleigh Marshall, soaking in the adulation with that cocky grin of his. Raleigh was a Ken doll in two ways:

1) He had the body: golden complexion, sun-kissed blond hair, tall, broad shoulders and slim waist.

2) Like a Ken doll, there was nothing but plastic and air between his ears.

"Do they have to shout?" I turned to my friends, hand covering my ears to shield me from the blaring.

"Yeah. It's a pep rally." Amos had tiptoed to the pro-sports dark side since dating Hutch. "That's the point."

"Chase, is there any scientific correlation between pep rallies and victories?"

Chase gulped at the sudden spotlight. He tucked a lock of wavy, blond hair behind his ear. "I don't know. We'd have to set up an experiment with a control group."

"I'm going to take that as a no. Isn't our football team having a so-so season? Yet they insist on pulling us out of class, which we have to make up somehow." Thanks to previous pep rallies so far this year, my seventh and eighth period classes were falling behind in the curriculum.

I could tell that my friends were getting annoyed with my usual anti-sports rant, but the train had already left the station.

"Why are we so obsessed with sports? This is school. We're supposed to value education and knowledge, not students who run head-on into people for the pursuit of an oddly-shaped ball."

I was self-aware enough to know that my beliefs were in the minority. But these football players roamed the halls like they owned them, and everyone else was supposed to bow down. It was like that when I was a student, and things hadn't changed. Anything that wasn't sportsball was mocked.

I was also certain a football player was the one who defaced the signup sheet. Athletes at South Rock treated the drama program like a joke, like we were just a bunch of theater losers.

The football team were the worst offenders. Guys would poke their head into the auditorium during rehearsal and shout obscenities. Last year's *You're a Good Man, Charlie Brown* poster had to be taken down because so many dicks had been drawn on that it looked like poor Charlie was at the center of a gangbang.

Over the years, I heard rumors of a longstanding, unwritten rule set by the football coach that players were strongly cautioned against auditioning for plays. Too dorky. Too gay. Since the football team was at the top of the social hierarchy, that scared off other kids from getting involved, leaving my theater program to wither on the proverbial vine.

All these roads led back to Raleigh. He was King of King Shit Mountain. His alpha grin beamed from center stage. And why wouldn't it? He received unlimited funds, unlimited praise, and unlimited power from the school.

Aguilar pointed to the man of the hour. "Let's hear from our fearless leader, Coach Marshall!"

The crowd roared with excitement as Raleigh strutted across the gym floor. Even my friends clapped for him. Traitors.

He knew how to charm everyone. I was one of the few who refused to fall under his spell.

He took the microphone from Aguilar and flashed a grin to his loyal subjects in the bleachers.

"Wassup, South Rock! Is that all you got for the Huskies? Let's try that again. And like you mean it!"

The bleachers erupted in screams.

Ugh.

I leaned into my friends. "If you're thinking of a fake date for me to bring to this wedding, imagine Raleigh, then run in the opposite direction."

3

RALEIGH

R eal talk: Pep rallies were kinda weird.

It was a lot of standing around not saying anything, listening to other people speak while the entire school stared at you. First, the principal said something, then the assistant principal, then the athletic director for the school district, then the captain of the cheerleading squad, then the quarterback. Why not have the janitor say a few words, too?

By the time I gave my spiel, I basically repeated what everyone else had said. How many different ways could we say *Go Huskies!* and *We're gonna kick some ass!*

I kept the spotlight on my players as much as possible, highlighting how hard they'd been working and how dedicated they were. My guys deserved every ounce of praise because they were incredible athletes who worked ridiculously hard.

Eddie, one of our defensive linemen, took the mic and talked about how much South Rock meant to him, and how the Huskies wouldn't let the school down. It was a spontaneous, heartfelt moment that underscored what kind of impact sports could have on these students. I looked out on the sea of adoring faces, everyone hanging on his touching words.

All except one.

I shouldn't have gotten off on Everett Calloway's stink face, but getting under his skin had become a weird kind of fun lately. We were around each other more since our friends were dating, and everything I did or said – my very essence – seemed to piss him off.

At first, it was annoying. Then it became entertaining.

Anything I said, anything I did. Hell, sometimes just seeing my face brought out the Red Hulk.

Everett was a redhead with creamy, pale skin. His face flushed an uncontrollable shade of red, almost cartoon-like, when he was frustrated. Watching him try and keep a neutral expression while his face was giving him away was free entertainment.

I might have egged him on from time to time to bring out the Red Hulk, asking him if he caught the latest NFL game or who was in his Fantasy Football lineup. It was too easy.

Sure, I seemed a little mean, but it was all in good fun. I playfully teased all my friends. Everett was the one who was incapable of taking a joke.

He was...kind of a snob. He thought sports were beneath him and his precious theater. Oh, if only everyone could love the theater as much as he did, then there'd be no war.

I had to watch a performance of *Long Day's Journey into Night* in high school. The word long didn't do it justice. For me, it was a short journey into sleep.

Just because I wasn't a nut about the arts, Everett looked at me with constant disdain, like I was a rube. He preemptively rolled his eyes at everything I said. *I went to college, too, dude.* I watched every *Fast and Furious* movie. I knew all about art.

So what if I didn't live and breathe theater? So what if I didn't spend every free moment going to museums and opera houses and botanical gardens? Because of that, did I and all other athletes deserve to be looked down upon?

Fine, so *maybe* he got under my skin a tad, too. At least I didn't turn into a tomato.

Every student and teacher in the bleachers shouted and cheered at the rousing speech Eddie was currently giving. Except for Everett, whose flat smile said he couldn't be more bored. Frankly, it was obnoxious. Sports were psychological, and if any of my players caught a glimpse of a teacher giving them the stink face, it could mess with their heads at this crucial juncture in the season.

"Any final words, Coach?"

I took the microphone from Eddie.

"South Rock. We couldn't do this without you." My voice echoed through the PA system. "The support that each and every one of you gives us lifts us up. We wouldn't be half the team we are without the amazing banners painted by our art students that we run through each game, without the call-and-response cheers led by these remarkable athletes in our cheerleading squad, and without the personal support of every student and teacher in this gym. Teachers like you, Mr. Calloway, whose enthusiasm for the Huskies we carry in our hearts every time we run onto that field."

I pointed to Everett and winked, giving him the spotlight a theater snob craved.

"Mr. Calloway came up to me before homeroom. He said, 'Coach Marshall, I've been saying a prayer for the Huskies every night before I go to bed. There's nothing in this world I love more than seeing our players win.'"

The school gave him a rousing round of applause.

I put my hand on my heart, really letting myself enjoy this moment. "Thank you for cheering us on."

Everett turned ghost white, but only for a second before the Red Hulk emerged.

Hilarious.

"Let's go Huskies!"

———

AFTER THE PEP RALLY ENDED, I turned to my players and put my game face on. "Okay, guys. Praise is nice, but we gotta earn our W's the hard way. I'll see you on the field for practice in twenty minutes."

I had us put our hands in and shout *Go Huskies* on the count of three.

Before joining them on the field, I swung by the faculty lounge for a not-half-bad cup of coffee. I needed that midday caffeine jolt, as practice would go into the early evening. My guys were tired after a long day, and the last thing they needed to see was their coach yawning.

On the way to the lounge, random students shouted *Go Huskies* at me in solidarity. When I got to the lounge, a teacher stopped me in the doorway, but there was no *Go Huskies* cheer from him.

"Nice pep rally, Raleigh," said Mr. Zepowitz, old and gruff, a teacher lifer. "Hopefully it actually translates to a winning season this year. We're two-for-two so far. You need to get more aggressive on offense."

He continued to give me some "constructive feedback" on what I could be doing to improve my coaching. Lots of people had an opinion on what I should be doing. I took it on the chin, holding back my feedback for him. No way could I bring that kind of energy into practice.

"Have you seen North Point this season? We can't let them win again."

"Thanks for your support, Mr. Zep." I clapped him on the shoulder, then pushed past him into the lounge, maybe a little stronger than I should have. But hey, I was just being aggressive, right? That was the thing about coaching the most popular sport in school: more attention, good and bad.

I definitely couldn't be bringing bad juju about North Point High into practice. They were our rival, and I one-million-percent hated them, for several reasons.

"It's the man of the hour!" Hutch held his arm up for a hi-five, which I happily slapped. Mr. Zep's and North Point High's bullshit faded to the background.

Hutch joined the athletics department last year and quickly became one of my best friends.

I put a new coffee cup into the Keurig. The lounge was fairly spacious, and it was the best place to be at the moment.

"I just got some pointers from Mr. Zep." I rolled my eyes and scanned the selections in the vending machine.

"Oof. Ignore, ignore."

I selected a bag of potato chips and watched them tumble down. "Apparently, North Point is undefeated so far this season."

"Fuck them. You'll get 'em on Thanksgiving."

"We said that last year, and the year before." It was tradition that old rivals South Rock and North Point faced off on Thanksgiving day. The losses over the past two years were extra salt in my wound; the literal Monday morning quarterbacking from the administration put more pressure on us to win. "Whenever someone mentions North Point to me, I immediately think about Donovan Heller's pale ass first."

"That's a hard visual to get out of your head."

"I can't wait to wipe that smirk off his face this year." I could feel my neck boil like my coffee. It was one thing to have a football rivalry with another coach and for that coach to be an asshole. But it was quite another to walk into your house and find that coach's pale ass cheeks thrusting as he fucked your fiancée.

"Hey Coach. Are you sufficiently full of pep?" Amos walked over and gave me a light punch on the shoulder. He was Hutch's boyfriend, and his best friend stood at his side with a typical eye roll that brightened my mood.

I puffed out my chest. "I am full of pep." I wrapped a congenial arm around Everett's shoulder. I could feel the seething dislike coming off him. Glorious.

"Ev, I hope you don't mind me shouting you out today."

"Yeah, thanks for that." He shucked out of my grip, which was a shame since he fit so well in my arm. Maybe being Red Hulk gave him extra strength.

Hutch shot me a look not to get him started.

"I don't understand why your team needs people shouting at them to do their job. In the theater, we work best in silence."

In the theater. Ugh.

"Y'know, Ev. We need a new mascot. The guy who usually dresses up as Horton the Husky sprained his ankle. It could be like a performance for you."

"Pass," he said with his bitchy deadpan. "Amos, can we go?"

"What happened to us, Ev?" I asked with full sarcasm deployed. Who needed coffee to perk up when I could spar with Everett?

"Raleigh, your coffee's ready. Don't spill it on yourself."

I caught a whiff of his mix of deodorant and clean Everett scent and, for a moment, wished he hadn't squirmed out of my grip.

"Remember last spring when we teamed up for cornhole?" I asked.

"So we played a game of cornhole once."

"We made a good team." I was still being a sarcastic shit, but I did mean it. When we paused hating each other and united to defeat a common enemy (Hutch and Amos) at the end of school party, we had good times.

I tried building bridges. "How are things going with the fall play? I heard you're doing a musical. That's cool!"

That only made him more frustrated. The red climbed on his face. What did I say?

He turned to Amos. "I'll meet you in the parking lot."

Then Everett was gone.

"Hey, are you coming to our housewarming party this Saturday?" Amos asked me, quickly diffusing the awkwardness of his friend's exit.

"Absolutely!"

"Is Mimi coming?"

"No. I'm breaking up with her tomorrow."

Hutch blinked and shook his head, more surprised than I expected from him. He knew Mimi and I weren't serious. Amos's shock was right on the money.

"You have a date scheduled to break up with her?" Amos asked.

"I would do it tonight, but I have to get an oil change after practice."

"You're keeping this poor girl in relationship limbo so you can get an oil change? I thank God every day I wasn't born a straight woman," Amos said.

Hutch pulled my arm to look at me. "Dude, why are you breaking up with Mimi? I thought things were going well and you liked her."

"She's nice, but she wants me to have dinner with her family on Sunday night."

"What's wrong with that?" Amos asked. "Are they the Manson family? Mimi is the first woman you've dated who can string a proper sentence together. She's beautiful, smart, and kind. We had so much fun on our bowling double date, and you're now casting her aside because why? Not enough cleavage?"

Hutch put a hand on his boyfriend's forearm to calm down. Amos had some Red Hulk tendencies himself. "Hey Famous Amos, Everett's waiting."

Amos and Mimi hit it off on our double date. He was a history buff, and Mimi's stories of her recent visit to the Smithsonian were catnip to him.

Amos took a deep breath. This was decent practice for my future break-up with Mimi.

"Raleigh, maybe you'll do some soul searching during your oil change and reconsider, and I'll just leave it at that." Amos kissed Hutch goodbye. I held out my fist to him, and to my relief, he gave me a bump.

Hutch watched him go, then spun around to me before I could even take my first sip of coffee.

"What the hell, man?"

"What did I do?"

"You're breaking up with Mimi?"

"Shit. You too, man?" I took a hearty gulp of my drink and wished I'd had the foresight to spike it. "I didn't know y'all were so obsessed with Mimi."

Hutch leaned against the counter and stared out at nothing in particular, just lost in thought.

"I didn't know my sex life was so perplexing."

"I thought things were going well," he said.

"I don't want to meet her parents. We've barely been dating a month."

"Meeting the parents means it's getting serious, and God fucking forbid that happened."

My jaw tightened. Just because Hutch was madly in love, he thought I had to follow suit. "The last time things got serious, I walked in on pale ass cheeks..."

"That was three years ago. It's shitty what happened, but you have to move on."

If only moving on was that easy. I heaved out a breath. "Tampa Bay and St. Louis."

"What about them?"

"November 8, 1987. Fourth quarter. Tampa Bay was crushing St. Louis by twenty-five points, 28-3. But then it all unraveled. St. Louis scored a touchdown, then another, then Tampa Bay fumbled a crucial pass. St. Louis won, 31-28."

"What does a football game from before we were born have to do with Donovan Heller screwing your fiancée?"

"Because things can change on a dime. I could be serious with someone. I could meet their parents and charm the fuck out of them. Everything could be going perfectly, and then just as quickly, it could all unravel in the fourth quarter. The clock runs out and you're left staring at pimply, pale ass cheeks in your own goddamn bed."

I chose to believe that people were fundamentally good...until they got into relationships. Being that emotionally connected to someone could flip a switch and make them do evil things. Being that connected to someone made you vulnerable. When you opened up so completely to another person, they could use it as ammo. Tori knew how much I hated Donovan, how much I wanted to beat our rivals and prove myself as football coach. She knew exactly which knife to use and how to twist it.

So no fucking way was I going to subject myself to a serious relationship again. There were hookup apps, sex workers, my right hand, and my left hand when my right got tired.

And for the record – my knife was definitely bigger than his.

Hutch looked down at his feet, scared thoughts swirling in his eyes.

"That won't happen to you and Amos. I promise. You two are the real deal. Not all of us have The One. Some of us are meant to walk the earth alone and have sex with lots and lots of hot people while doing it."

I kinda wish Everett was still in this conversation so I could watch him roll his eyes at that comment. Why did I love having that guy as an audience so much?

That managed a slight smile from Hutch. I meant it. Love wasn't for me, but I loved watching my friends in love. He and Amos were a great pair.

"I bet Donovan's ass is nice." Hutch flashed me a shit-eating grin that told me we were good. "Supple."

"Fuck, no. It's flat city. You'll never look at a pancake the same way again." I finished off my coffee and tossed it in the trash. I made the field goal sign when I sunk the shot. "I gotta run to practice. Thanks for being a concerned friend, but you don't need to worry about me. I'm looking forward to the party on Saturday."

"Cool. When you're there..."

"What?"

"Try not to piss off Everett. We don't want any drama."

4

EVERETT

Tonight was Amos and Hutch's housewarming, a night for them to rub their wonderful relationship in our faces.

Kidding.

They were an extremely cute couple. Amos had been lonely for so long; I was happy he found a great guy. Well, re-found technically, since they'd secretly dated in high school.

They almost made me believe in finding love.

Almost.

Speaking of, I was running out of time to find a suitable plus one.

I made an important call before heading over. The setting sun slashed through my blinds.

"How are you doing tonight?" a deep voice asked me over the line. "Looking for some fun?"

"In a manner of speaking, yes. You're a sex worker, correct?" I scanned his listing online. "Brandon. Is that your real name?"

"Yes."

"That's a great name. My older sister was a huge *90210* fan, and

I had a crush on Jason Priestley who played Brandon Walsh, before I fully realized I was gay. Did you know he's Canadian? Anyway, I'm rambling..." I paced in the tight quarters of my apartment. This Brandon didn't look much like *90210* Brandon, but I was an actor. I was used to making up new realities for myself.

"Were you looking to meet up tonight?" His deep voice was no nonsense and registered in my gut. "I'm pretty booked, but I could squeeze you in at 10."

"Or I could squeeze you in. I'm versatile," I spat out, then shook my head at that terrible joke. I'd officially lost all sense of sense. "Not tonight. I have a housewarming party."

"Congratulations."

"It's not my house. I've been in my apartment for about three years. It's all right. The building is managed by this adorable old couple. Unfortunately, they're raising the rent next year, though not by much. And I understand. As property values rise and what with inflation, it's not a renter's market...anyway, I'm rambling again." I sucked in a deep breath, finding my nerve amid my desperation. "I have a proposition for you, Brandon. In three weeks, I'm going to a wedding, and I'd like for you to be my plus one. It wouldn't involve the sex part of your job, just the worker."

"How long of an event would this be? Overnight?"

"Two nights. Get there Friday night, leave by Sunday morning. We'd stay at a hotel with two beds."

"What would you want us to do?"

"Pretend to be boyfriends. Boyfriends who are madly in love. Especially in front of my ex and his new main squeeze." His new main squeeze? Why did I start talking like my dad when I got nervous?

"What kind of sexual activity were you expecting? Intercourse each night?"

"Oh, no. No sex. I'd be hiring you for the worker part of your job, not the sex. Just some kissing. Do you do kissing? Or is this a *Pretty Woman* thing where you do everything except kiss on the lips?"

"No, I kiss on the lips," he said matter-of-factly.

"Great. With tongue?" I was trying to plan for all scenarios.

"If you'd like."

"Excellent." Maybe I could stage a casual run-in with Noah and Gavin while Brandon's tongue was down my throat. "It wouldn't be more than that."

"Okay. Give me a second."

I heard Brandon breathing over the phone. Was he doing a quick background check on me? How did one screen to make sure they didn't have sex with a serial killer? I supposed that could happen to anyone. Many serial killers lived normal lives. Their friends and family would be shocked to discover they were serial killers. Anyway, I was rambling again. Wait, I was okay. I wasn't saying any of this aloud.

"So for one weekend, which includes Friday afternoon and night, all day and night Saturday, and Sunday morning and possibly afternoon, the total due would be twelve hundred."

"Twelve hundred dollars?" I ran through the sorry state of my savings account.

"Correct. I prefer Venmo, but we can work out a cash situation, too."

My bank account was seriously depressing. Like Eponine-in-*Les-Mis* depressing. And that was before having to book a hotel and buy a gift. Having friends was expensive!

"Um, Brandon, could we work out a discount?"

"A discount?"

"Isn't there a special teacher's discount or something?" I tried to laugh, but my mouth opened and closed with only a squeak coming out.

"A teacher's discount?" Each word was a deep-throated question.

"Yeah. I'm a drama and public speaking teacher." Was I not supposed to tell him my occupation? Could he track me down? "Teachers get discounts at lots of places. Bookstores, office supply stores, Target."

"Isn't that for items for your classroom?"

"Technically, but sometimes I use my Target discount to get some notebooks for myself. I've tried journaling because that's supposed to be good for goal setting and my general mental health."

"You're rambling again."

"Look at us. We already have witty banter." I let out another nervous fake laugh.

"I can do teacher role play, but I don't do teacher discounts."

I pressed my head against the cool wall, next to a framed program from a production of *Waiting for Godot* I directed in college. Noah was my Vladimir, and he was very sexy waiting on that bench. Now he had his perfect boyfriend, and I was the one waiting for a miracle.

I mustered up the last traces of gumption inside me and made my final pitch to Brandon the sex worker. "Here's the thing. I don't have the money to pay your fee, and I do believe sex workers should be paid for your sex work. I'm trying to get by on a teacher's salary." I closed my eyes and found my zen place. Or zen adjacent. "I have to go to this wedding in less than a month and face my ex-boyfriend and his new boyfriend, and they're like hashtag couple goals. One understudies for the other. It's obnoxiously cute."

"Is your ex-boyfriend Noah Paxton?"

I blinked my eyes open.

Shit.

"Did you see the Instagram Live he and Gavin did where they tried to use their new air fryer to make French fries?"

"You're not helping, Brandon. I can't show up to that wedding alone. Can we work out a deal for the weekend?"

I gripped the phone against my ear, waiting for a response.

"What number were you thinking?"

Again, I scanned through the pitiful state of my bank account.

"Would you take fifty bucks?"

"Please tell me you're joking."

"What if I paid you in installments?"

"I'm hanging up now."

"How about this: I will do sex work to you for the weekend. You can use my body however you want when we're not doing wedding stuff."

The line clicked off, leaving me in an empty apartment filled with silence and singledom.

I slunk into my couch, which had seen better days even before I bought it off some college students. I promised myself that when I was an adult, I'd never split my space with anyone who wasn't a boyfriend. Growing up, I'd shared a bedroom with my brother and his unrelenting flatulence.

Even though I could've saved money having a roommate or two, I gave myself the treat of having my own place. I made it work, budget be damned. But in moments like this, when I watched Noah and Gavin's stupid cute Instagram Live on my phone in the darkness of my empty apartment, I realized how alone I felt.

My phone buzzed, stopping me from falling asleep on my couch. Could it be that Brandon wanted to give my offer a second chance?

My spine straightened and nerves surged up one vertebrae at a time when a text from Noah popped on my screen. He must've seen that I watched his video. Goddamn social media surveillance state.

We still had each other's numbers even though we never talked. People's cell phone numbers were like old clothes. Yeah, we always said that we'd take unused items to Goodwill, but when it came time to pack the trash bags, we couldn't bring ourselves to do it.

Noah: Hey, long time no talk. Are you going to the wedding?

I racked my brain for a suitable response.

Everett: Yeah.

I'd let him decipher that as he chose. Leave him wondering.

Noah: Cool. Should be fun. I'm looking forward to seeing you.

A wisp of nostalgia fluttered in my stomach. I chastised myself for being such a hollaback girl.

Everett: Same.

Noah: Gavin's excited to meet you, too.

My heart deflated like the one sad balloon that gets trapped on the ceiling after a party.

Noah: He's a really great guy. His soul is magnificent.

Noah had a thing about people's souls. It was another quirk of his that I found super deep in college, but in my hardened adult years, just made me roll my eyes.

Noah: Is it weird that I'm falling in love with him?

Noah: Sorry.

Noah: Overshare.

Everett: Cool. I'll see you guys soon.

No way could I attend this wedding solo and subject myself to pity looks as Noah intro'd me to his soulmate clone.

I shoved my phone into the space between couch cushions. Was there room in there for me, too?

———

I WAS happy to leave my too quiet apartment and head to Amos and Hutch's housewarming party. Technically, the house had already been warmed for a while. Amos had owned his condo for years. Hutch moved in over the summer, further solidifying their relationship. None of the furniture was changing, making house-warming merely an excuse for a party.

I wasn't one to turn my nose up at a fiesta with friends.

Amos, and now Hutch, lived in a condo that had partial views of the Hudson River, depending on where you positioned yourself on his tiny balcony. Friends and other teachers gradually tight-ened the space.

"You tried to bargain with a sex worker?"

Julian and I leaned against a living room wall interspersed with framed pictures of places Amos had traveled to along with a few cute snaps of him and Hutch. I knew they were saving up for a grand trip to Italy, hoping to add more pictures to their wall.

"Everything is negotiable," I told Julian. As a teacher with a piddling budget to put on grand productions, I had to master the art of making a dollar stretch. For last year's production of *You're a Good Man, Charlie Brown*, Lucy's lemonade stand had product placement.

"I tried to be fair." I gulped down my vodka and Sprite. "I didn't have twelve hundred bucks."

"Don't worry, Ev. I'm asking around, putting feelers out for you." Julian was too sweet to be a pimp, but I appreciated the effort.

"Thanks, pal."

"There he is!" Hutch yelled from across the room in his roaring voice, forcing all of us to crane our necks and watch Raleigh enter the premises.

The two jocks slapped hands in a raised hi-five. People let out whoops and clapped his back. Raleigh soaked it in with his calm, entitled charm.

"Why are we making a production of Raleigh showing up?" I checked my phone. "And a half-hour late at that."

"The Huskies won a nail biter of a game last night."

"Doesn't a nail biter mean that we almost lost?" A blowout would've been more impressive, but what did I know?

Julian laughed me off and slapped Raleigh on his back when he passed by us. "Nice job last night. That was quite a game."

"Thanks, Jules. I could hear you cheering in the stands." Raleigh ribbed Julian in the side. "We couldn't do it without the support of everyone at school, teachers included."

Julian shrugged modestly and blushed a little. Traitor!

Raleigh tilted his head to me, and an impish smile cracked his lips. "Ev, I didn't see you in the stands last night."

"I was busy. Couldn't make it. But amazingly, you still won."

"Maybe next game."

"I'm busy Friday nights." Busy watching TV and ordering pizza and falling asleep on my couch, which was a million times more fun than sitting on the hard, cold bleachers in the gusty wind to watch teenagers run into each other for three hours.

"That's a shame. Your sunny attitude and cheer could really lift the team's spirits." He gave my shoulder a squeeze. Why was he always finding ways to touch me? And why did it always leave me with a warm tingle?

"Raleigh, I'd hate to fake my enthusiasm. But you're probably used to people faking their enjoyment in your presence."

"Ev, I'm like a McDonald's. All of my customers leave with their happy meal. Trust me."

He shot me a wink.

"Gross. Go crush some beer cans on your forehead." I shucked from his strong grip and nudged him to a group of fawning party guests.

"Football is not the end all and be all," I said to my traitorous friend once Raleigh was gone. "What would our society be like if a math teacher or a French teacher walked into a party and received that kind of celebratory welcome because their students won a quiz bowl? Isn't that the kind of excellence we should be celebrating?"

"Or a drama teacher coming off opening night..." Julian raised his eyebrows at me.

"Well, that's another random example." I wouldn't kick it out of bed. I shuffled my ice-filled cup. "I'm getting another drink."

"Raleigh's still at the bar."

His tall, broad frame was a study in manspreading. Arms stretched from one end of the bar to the other as he leaned in to chat with Charlie, the bartender. Raleigh was like a giant hunched over a human-sized breakfast nook. Though the position did cause his round, tight ass to pop out.

So he did have one redeeming quality, it seemed.

"Everett?" Julian snapped me back to reality.

"I'm getting another drink. I'm not letting him interrupt my enjoyment of this party."

I weaved around furniture and pockets of people. Amos was picking a partygoer's brain about her recent honeymoon in Italy. Chase chatted about neutrons (yes, literal neutrons) with the other chemistry teacher.

When I got up to the bar, Raleigh was shooting the shit with Charlie, Amos's old roommate now shacking up with a rugged bear twenty-five years his senior. I needed a drink more than I needed to avoid him, so I pressed forward. I didn't put on my game face. I put on my drama mask.

"Hey, Charlie. Amos is still making you bartend these parties?"

"It's my pleasure. This is where I first practiced pouring drinks. It all comes full circle." Charlie was short and lovable, impossible to hate, like a puppy dog.

Raleigh was quite literally his polar opposite. He smirked at me, with a lot going on in his head that should stay there.

"Evening, Everett. Do people ever get that confused and say Everett evening?" Raleigh asked.

I sighed, already bored with this conversation. "No."

I focused my gaze on Charlie and tried to block Raleigh from my eyeline. "I'll take another vodka and Sprite."

Raleigh blocked my cup from passing across the counter with his thick, determined hand, a hand that in any other universe I would not mind skimming over my naked body.

"Vodka and Sprite? That's what you're drinking?"

"It's a perfectly valid drink."

"Yeah, if you're sneaking booze in your parents' basement. We have a master mixologist on duty here, a conductor of the cocktail orchestra." He gestured to Charlie, who blushed for a moment at the praise. Why did everyone fall under his spell like he was the Music Man? "Charlie, whip up something fresh for my guy."

My guy? What? No. I objected to every word in that sentence, though my body was having some weird heat-filled reaction I couldn't pin down.

Raleigh patted me on the back. More touching. More warm tingles. Why was his sole purpose in life to either get under my skin or touch it directly?

"Charlie, I'll just take the vodka and Sprite."

"C'mon, Ev. Live a little. Charlie has something good up his sleeve, just for you."

My curiosity was getting the better of me, but I refused to be told what to do by Raleigh.

"Have you ever had a Screaming Orgasm?"

If I had my vodka and Sprite like I wanted, I would've spat it out in shock at Raleigh's question. "I beg your pardon."

So now he was attacking me for my lack of sex life?

"It's a drink. Vodka-based." Raleigh looked to Charlie, who nodded in confirmation and then listed off the ingredients. But there was a look on Raleigh's face that didn't have me convinced he was referring exclusively to the drink.

"It's really good," Charlie said.

"I'll stick with vodka and Sprite." I couldn't give Raleigh the satisfaction of being right.

"C'mon, Ev. Don't let your hatred of me stop you from leaving your comfort zone."

"I don't hate you."

"Oh, you hate me."

"I hate homophobic politicians and people who leave their cell phones on during performances. I have a casual dislike of you. You're like a piece of food perpetually stuck in my teeth."

"I get major hate vibes coming off you. Like at the pep rally when you give me the evil eye."

"The evil eye? What am I, a witch?"

"Just calling it like I see it."

I didn't like being called out like this. Raleigh wasn't some innocent victim. If he was food in my teeth, I was a scab on his knee he couldn't stop picking. Casual dislike was a two-way street.

"Well, you hate me, too."

"No, I don't," he retorted.

Why the *hell* did that produce a flutter in my belly?

"I wasn't giving you the evil eye. I was giving the whole concept of a pep rally the evil eye."

Charlie held up an empty glass, my guess to ask whether he was giving me an orgasm or my usual. I gave him the "one minute" finger gesture.

"Can you pinpoint any part of the pep rally that clinched this most recent win for your team?"

"It's an art, not a science."

"Uh, no. It's football, the exact opposite of art."

Raleigh chuckled at that. The one benefit of him laughing at my pain was that he looked good doing it. His face brightened and lifted, showing off that gleaming smile. Why couldn't Raleigh have gone into a more useful profession like gay porn where I wouldn't have hated him?

I meant, casually disliked.

"Charlie, vodka and Sprite. Thanks."

"You got it." Charlie handed off drinks to other guests then got to work on mine.

There was still the issue of Raleigh looking at me and smiling with amusement, making my blood boil in record time—for multiple reasons.

"What?" I asked.

"You should check out a football game. You might like it."

"That's what my dad said to me about women when I came out to him."

Charlie slid over my fizzy drink of choice.

"What does vodka and Sprite even taste like?" Raleigh asked me, elbowing me in my side. Another heat-filled reaction from my mutinous body.

"Like Sprite. That's the point."

And then, in a swift move of jock entitlement, he took my glass and tasted my drink.

"Are you serious right now?"

"Relax. I don't have any communicable diseases."

"That you know of. Maybe one of your rocket scientist girl-friends gave you something."

He handed it back. I made sure to drink from the untouched side of the glass. Charlie watched the whole scene, biting back a laugh.

"Thanks, Charlie. Are you sure you're not taking tips?"

No matter how broke I was, I never skimped on tipping.

"No tips tonight. I'm here as a friend. If it wasn't for Amos, I never would've become a bartender or met Mitch."

I followed his eyes over to Amos and Hutch, being flirty and cute in the corner. They were a cute couple, but I didn't have the stomach to swoon over them. Raleigh's stern look seemed to have the same feeling behind it too.

"It's over-rated," he said, his cocky attitude vanishing for a shocking moment. "It starts off cute like that..."

"But then implodes in a supernova of shit," I said, finishing his sentence.

I cut my eyes to Raleigh, who broke into a small smile, the kind that looks like a sliver of sunshine in a rainstorm. And then I remembered what happened with his ex-fiancée. She was now dating some other high school football coach. Something like that. I wasn't that invested in gossip about heterosexuals. I got the feeling that the scar tissue hadn't formed yet.

"How are you..." I started, not sure how to tread. I wasn't used to asking Raleigh about his well-being.

"Shit happens. Engagements end."

There was a hard edge to his voice. I was never engaged to Noah, but I knew what that edge felt like. "The problem is the shit lingers. Festering."

Raleigh cut his eyes to me, a flicker of commiseration in them. A portal to a world where we were allies. Or more.

"Hey guys. Smile!"

We turned around to find Chase holding up his phone to take a picture.

"Pics or it didn't happen," he said.

"The party?" Raleigh asked.

"That, and you two having a normal conversation."

Well, I just wanted to curl up and die. I glanced at Raleigh, wondering what he was thinking. I didn't want the world to think we were friends, but I also didn't want to be the prick who refused to take a picture with someone.

"Let's do it, Ev." Raleigh roped a strong, heavy arm—one loaded with muscle—around my shoulders and lassoed me closer to him, as if we'd done this a thousand times. "Give the people some primo content."

It did feel nice inside the warmth of his embrace. Safe. Protected. And the man smelled good. Whatever skank-attracting body spray he was wearing was doing its job with me.

Once the camera flashed, I pulled myself away, lest I get any more ideas about Raleigh and his warmth.

5

EVERETT

The days marched on, but the countdown didn't stop. Exactly three weeks until the wedding remained, and I still had no date.

After two back-to-back classes listening to awkward speeches recited by very embarrassed teenagers, I found refuge in the faculty lounge. It wasn't anything fancy. Some old couches and chairs with a small kitchen area, but it was an oasis at school. I had to laugh when students speculated on what was inside, as if it were a speakeasy.

I texted Jordana and Bethany an excited *Three More Weeks!* message. Even though I dreaded going stag to their wedding, I was excited for their nuptials. They were hashtag couple goals.

Not *my* hashtag couple goals because none of my goals revolved around getting yoked in a relationship again.

Bethany called me soon after seeing my message.

"How would you feel about performing at our wedding?" she asked.

"That...sounds cool. What would I be performing?"

"We wanted to spice up the wedding service, make it more us.

Jordana was up until four this morning writing a play for us to perform instead. I figured, being up there reciting vows and prayers, was essentially a staged reading. Why not jazz up the dialogue?"

Besides being hashtag couple goals, Jordana and Bethany were a formidable theater power couple in off-off-Broadway circles. Jordana was a talented playwright, and Bethany directed everything she wrote. Jordana's play that revolved around the Disney princesses helping each other through group therapy was the buzz of the Lower East Side last year. For anyone else, I would've thought scripting their own wedding service would be a horrendous idea.

"That sounds cool!"

"The play won't have much of a plot. We'll still have the basic elements of a wedding service, but peppered in will be a few scenes and some monologues."

Monologues! I loved monologues!

But performing in front of all of my old friends and boyfriends when I was trying to keep a low profile...

"I'm writing a part for you, Everett."

There was no sentence more seductive to an actor. I officially couldn't say no.

"I'm in!"

"Awesome! The scripts won't be ready until the wedding weekend, but you won't need to be off-book."

"I love this. It reminds me of when we all did the twenty-four hour play contest sophomore year." Imagine six college students conceiving, writing, directing, and performing in a play all in the span of one day. It was exhilarating, the true essence of theater. And thank God for Red Bull.

Bethany radiated excitement and happiness through the phone. I was going to kick ass with my part and give my friends the proper sendoff into married life. And if I happened to upstage Noah and Gavin, that was just an added benefit.

"I can't believe I'm getting married in three weeks! At least I have a play to focus on. Jordana's family is dealing with all the logistical shit like flowers and the band."

Part of why Jordana and Bethany could be the darling power couple of off-off-Broadway was because Jordana's family was very, very rich. It was an open secret that many alleged starving artists in New York were funded by the Bank of Mom and Dad. The people who were actual starving artists couldn't survive on what the theater paid.

"Less than a month to go." Other teachers filtered into the lounge. I hung by the windows for the best cell reception. "I can't wait to see you two."

"And we can't wait to meet your boyfriend. You've been holding out on us, Everett!"

My breath caught in my throat. "Boyfriend?"

"Don't act so coy. Raleigh. The hot, jacked Nordic-looking snack."

And now came the dizziness. I gripped a nearby chair for support. "How do you know about Raleigh?"

"I'll be honest, he doesn't seem like your type. Like at all. You were never into jocks with muscles."

And I still wasn't! And definitely not Raleigh.

"What are you talking about, Bethany?"

"Your secret's out. I saw the pics. Your friend Amos tagged you two at someone's housewarming party."

My fingers dashed to Instagram. There was the picture of us from the party, Raleigh's arm around me. The warm, unabashed smile lighting up my face was alien. I didn't know I could have that kind of reaction around him.

Two of my favorite guys together at last, read the caption.

Oh no.

We were together at last because we agreed to be in the same picture without fighting, not because we were...

Oh no.

"I had a feeling something was going on. I remember a few months ago, there was another picture of you two together where you guys played cornhole. I chalked it up to you working at the same school."

"We do!" I spat out defensively.

"That's so sweet. Two teachers who fell in love. That's just like *Clueless*."

Did that make me the short, bald Mr. Hall?

I had to go to the evidence before I could respond. I scrolled and scrolled until I got to last June when Raleigh and I were stuck teaming up for cornhole. We couldn't agree on a strategy (surprise, surprise) and promptly lost. But not before another picture was taken, him with his arm around me like it was the most natural thing in the world. And me, enjoying being held.

"Please tell me you're bringing him to the wedding."

"What? I..."

"He's hot," she said.

Those two words were all it took for the lies to spill out, as naturally as Raleigh's arm had spilled over my shoulders.

"He wants to come. He's heard so much about you and Jordana. But he coaches football, and it's the football season. These next few games are crucial in order for the team to make it to state."

Was making it to state a real thing? I thought I'd heard that during one of the pep rallies.

"Everett, I can't believe you're dating a football coach. This is hysterical."

"You know what they say. Opposites attract."

"If I remember correctly, high school football games are on Friday night. Our wedding is on a Saturday night."

"You are correct on that but..." I regretted not taking an improv class in college. "They start practicing after each game. Raleigh runs a tight ship."

I darted my eyes around the lounge to ensure the other teachers weren't listening.

"Maybe it's for the best. I don't want any drama at the wedding with you and Noah."

I did a double take at her comment. "Drama? What do you mean?"

"I didn't want things to be weird with you and Noah both there. Especially...he kept asking me if you were coming, and if you were bringing anyone. It was a little weird. It's probably for the best that he doesn't meet Raleigh."

Noah was asking about me? And my plus one? And things got weird? These were sentences in English, yet I could not process them.

But why the hell did Noah get to call the shots? I had to go to this wedding solo for Noah's sake?

Fuck to the no.

"Raleigh's coming," I said with fierce determination.

"You just said that he couldn't–"

"He'll be there. This is your special day, and you and Jordana are two of my oldest, closest friends. We will all be there to celebrate together, and the only drama present will be occurring on stage. You have my word, although I can't speak for Noah."

"We can't wait to meet him!"

"You're gonna love him."

I hung up and pressed the phone to my chest as the panic rose in my body. What the hell did I just do?

6

RALEIGH

What the hell was he doing?

I blew my whistle to stop practice and jogged onto the field. The players parted, their teenage frames hidden behind heavy layers of equipment.

The QB dug his heel into the grass as he caught his breath. He avoided looking at me.

"Jackson, who were you throwing to just now?"

Jackson took off his helmet. His hair was flat as a placemat. "Rivers."

"Rivers had a man on him, a man who intercepted your pass. Dominguez was open."

"Sorry, Coach." Jackson tried making eye contact but couldn't hold it for more than a second. His usual assuredness on the field was missing today.

I clapped my hands twice and faced the rest of the team. "That's good for today. Go and hit the showers." I stopped Jackson from jogging off the field with his teammates. "Hang back."

The field felt massive when it was just the two of us there. I turned to my QB. He had that unsure hunch prevalent in all high school guys, the mix of bravado and insecurity.

"Let's check in. How are you doing?"

"Fine." Chattiness was not a quality found in most athletes. But I knew there was something bothering him. I didn't mind working for it.

"Things didn't seem fine out there. Seems like you were having an off day. Wanna talk about what's on your mind?"

He shrugged and grunted something unintelligible. "Like you said. An off day."

Jackson had a stoic face, but the swirling of something in his eyes was clear as day. Being a high school athlete was not for the weak of heart. These kids went to school all day, then had two hours of practice before heading home to do a full load of home-work, all while dealing with the social and emotional pressures of being a teenager. I wanted my guys to win so that all the sacrifice was worth it.

"I remember when I was QB in high school. A long time ago. Well, not *that* long." That got the tiniest smile out of him. A step forward. "People think it's all glory. King of the School, BMOC, all that bullshit. But I had to keep up morale, learn plays, and be a leader for the team. Being a leader is hard. If it was easy, everyone would do it. "

Jackson gave a quiet nod. He wasn't the type who crumpled.

His parents were immigrants and worked cleaning office build-ings. He had to be their translator in meetings; I had Seamus Shablanski, who taught Spanish and also coached baseball, teach me some basic phrases to communicate with them. Getting an athletic scholarship to college would be life-changing.

"We almost lost last week," he said, a crack in his dam.

"But we didn't."

"It was close. I should've passed to Atchison in the second

quarter. He could've run it in for a touchdown, and it never would've been that close."

"Hey, don't do that. We don't have a time machine around here. Take what you've learned and bring it into future games. Don't play what if with past games."

"We've been doing well, Coach. I don't want us to lose momentum."

Jackson wasn't the most talented player, but he worked the hardest. Hard work beat talent any day of the week.

"You're scared of shitting the bed."

"The whole school...the whole town is watching."

"Like I said, if this was easy, everyone would do it. Some people like to think that we're all a bunch of dumb jocks running into each other." A certain redhead came to mind. "Football is the most challenging game to play. And being a QB is the most challenging position. You're having to make split-second decisions over and over."

"Is this supposed to make me feel less stressed?"

Another crack of a smile. I'd take a sarcastic comment over sullenness.

"Funny," I deadpanned. "Trust the process. Trust the plays that we're practicing. Use your fear and channel it into the game. I'm behind you one hundred percent. So are your teammates, and so is Sourwood. You are a great quarterback."

I patted him on the shoulder. Under the hulking protective gear was a kid, a fact I never let myself forget.

"Thanks, Coach."

Jackson retreated to the locker room, walking taller than before.

"Hey, Mr. Calloway." I heard him say as he passed the bleachers.

Mr. Calloway? Sure enough, Everett sat in the front row, his red hair a bursting contrast against the industrial metal of the stands.

I strolled over, trying to process the image of Everett willingly in the vicinity of a football field.

"Did you get lost looking for your car in the teacher's lot?" I asked.

"Hey, Raleigh." He stood up and leaned forward against the railing. It was here that football players would jump up and kiss their girlfriends after a game. That would not be happening today.

"I never thought I'd find you here. Or should I say, I *neverett* thought."

I waited for him to roll his eyes and sigh in disgust. Why did I find so much perverse glee in making him uncomfortable? It was a rough world. We had to get our kicks where we could find them.

"I like that. Good one," he said without a hint of sarcasm.

That was new. No retort. "What's going on?"

"What?"

"I made a dumb joke, and you didn't hate it. Are you a robot wearing Everett's skin?"

"No. It was funny." His smile seemed robotic though, fixed and not entirely lifelike.

"But you don't find me funny."

"What? Me?"

"Yeah you. What's up, Everett? Do you need me to help you bury a dead body?"

His mouth gaped open as he tried to wrestle back control. "Raleigh, what are you talking about? And if I did have to cover up a dead body, why do you think you'd be the first person I turn to and not my friends?"

"Because I can easily lift the body." I bench pressed two hundred pounds. I could toss a corpse into a grave like I was throwing a javelin.

"If I ever found myself in that situation, I would call you. Because you're dependable. And you help people."

Perhaps Everett was under mind control or hypnosis. His

typical acerbic tone was missing. There was a hypnotist at the faculty Christmas party, but he couldn't hypnotize me. I was too mentally strong.

"How was rehearsal?" Everett asked.

"Practice?"

"Right. Are your guys prepared for the next game against St. Holy Cross?"

"We're getting there." I said my words slowly, a little fearfully. I couldn't handle nice Everett. "How did you know we're playing St. Holy Cross?"

"It's on the website, duh. You're on an impressive streak. You're really doing a good job coaching them. All those touchdowns and field goals and interceptions."

I was in a horror movie. Everett was possessed by an evil spirit who had skimmed the Wikipedia entry for football. He was going to pull the goalpost from the ground using telekinesis and spear it through my skull, wasn't he?

"Tom Brady is smiling down on you guys."

"Tom Brady is still alive."

"And he probably wishes you were coaching him."

"That's it!" I took three giant steps back until my calves hit the players' bench on the field. "What the hell is going on? Is an alien about to explode from your head? Because they just upgraded those bleachers."

"No. Wait, what? You got new bleachers? Half the seats in the auditorium are ripped." Everett shook his head. "Different conversation for a different time."

He bolted on another creepy smile, giving him a killer doll look.

"Stop." I pointed my finger at him. "Hearing you be nice is making my skin crawl. What is going on?"

"I don't want us to be enemies."

"Bullshit. What do you need?"

Everett broke, flopping onto the bleacher row. He dug his fingers into his hair, giving himself an Einstein-esque hairdo.

"Raleigh, I need a favor from you. It's a big one. And believe me, you are the last person I want to ask for a favor."

Hmmm...I was intrigued. Now that Everett showed signs of being his normal self, I felt comfortable to join him in the bleachers.

"Go on." I sat beside him and was able to catch details I usually overlooked, like the slight bushiness of his eyebrows and his determined chin.

"I have to go to a wedding in a few weeks, and there was a funny mix-up on social media." He let out a big, hearty, not-at-all-genuine laugh. "Now all of my friends think we're boyfriends, and they're expecting me to bring you. Surprise." He fluttered his fingers like a sad stripper popping out of a cake.

Neverett in a million years did I expect that to be the answer. Needing me to bury a corpse seemed more logical than this.

"You want me to go to this wedding? While pretending to be your boyfriend?"

"Yep." Everett maintained a game face I recognized from my players trying to stay positive after getting their ass kicked for three quarters. "We'd go there Friday night and come back Sunday afternoon. It would be less than forty-eight hours. Maybe forty-one hours total."

"Together. With you."

"Yes."

"And just to confirm, you're *not* planning to murder me."

"Correct."

Interestingly enough, I didn't dread the idea of spending forty-one hours with Everett.

"And we have to pretend that we like each other?"

He nodded yes.

Again, not something that sounded awful to me. For reasons I was trying to parse out, it sounded intriguing. But this was also the thick of football season. I couldn't skip a weekend for this ruse.

"When is it?"

"It's in three weeks. If you have a game, I totally understand. I shouldn't have asked because you're so busy with football. You need to focus on football. You only get four downs, so you better make 'em count. Forget that I bothered you." Everett stood up to go.

"We're clear."

He stopped mid-turn.

"We are?"

"The regular season ends the week before. Then there's a break before playoffs." And I prayed that we made it to the playoffs.

"The one weekend without football is the weekend of the wedding?"

"Yep. How's that for timing?"

Everett didn't seem relieved, only more nervous. "So you'll do it?"

"What would I have to do as your boyfriend?"

"Be your charming self. Be around my quirky theater friends. Dance, eat some cake."

"You called me charming."

"Cult leaders and serial killers are charming. I was stating a fact, not giving you a compliment."

I chuckled. I really liked that bitchy Everett was back. Nice Everett was weird.

"There may be some physical things...like holding hands."

"Would we need to kiss?"

"No!" He spat out a little too fast, red swirling up his cheeks. "We can keep it at holding hands. That's—we don't want to take attention away from the brides. And besides, this is already super homo for you, so I don't want to freak you out..."

"I'm cool with it."

"I know that the football world isn't exactly on board with gay stuff."

"I said I'm cool with it. I'm a holesexual."

"Excuse me? Gross."

"I mostly date women, but I've dated guys before. I'm attracted to the whole person."

"Oh. Whole w-h-o-l-e?"

"Yeah. Why is everyone so confused by that?" Hutch had the same reaction when I told him last year. Man, some people could be really narrow minded. *Sexuality is a spectrum, people!*

"Interesting. And your players are cool with it?"

"I assume so. It doesn't come up, but I've never heard any homophobic comments in the locker room. Two of my players have gay siblings. Nobody gives them any shit. They come to games, and everything is cool with them."

"Huh. I guess you and your players find the theater just a smidge too gay for your support then."

I had no idea what he was talking about. I was about to point out the stereotyping of calling the theater gay, but something told me it wasn't worth the fight.

"Will your theater friends be a *smidge* too snobby about you dating a dumb football jock?"

Could I make it through a whole weekend with Everett? A whole weekend of him and his friends making snide comments about sports and snickering at me for not knowing the lyrics to their favorite musical?

Maybe this was a pass.

"Why can't you take any of your friends as your plus one?"

"Because I don't need a plus one. I need a boyfriend. I can't face Noah with a plus one."

"Who's Noah?"

He opened and closed his mouth. "Oh, he's no one...he's just my ex-boyfriend. And he'll be there with his new boyfriend."

"So you want to make him jealous?"

"Kinda? I want him to want me back so that I can reject him like he did to me."

"You want him to see that you're thriving without him, and that not being with him was the best thing that ever could've happened to you."

I'd love to do that to Tori. I dreaded bumping into her and Coach Pale Cheeks. How dare they live a happy life and leave me to pick up the pieces? I couldn't get justice for myself, but I could help someone else get their justice.

That person would be Everett though, who loathed every word that came out of my mouth. He was a snob who thought he was saving lives by putting on a play. We couldn't be around each other for five minutes without bickering. And when he pretended to be nice to me, I assumed he was possessed by a demon.

"I'll go, if you can do something for me."

I could feel his body tense up. His ears flamed red. "What?"

"Follow me."

I led him onto the field. He marveled at its breadth. In the end zone was a net still up for throwing practice. I tossed Everett a football. It bobbled in his grip but didn't drop.

"Good catch," I said.

"What are we doing here with this?" He nodded at the ball in his hands.

"To be your fake boyfriend, I need one good throw."

"You want me to throw a football?"

I nodded yes. "One good throw, ideally in the center square of the net."

"This is ridiculous."

"Them's the rules, Ev."

"What will me throwing a football prove?"

"That you're serious about our fake relationship."

And I wanted him to see that playing football wasn't some easy sport that didn't require brain cells. It was harder than it looked.

"You want to lace your fingers over the white part of the–"

Everett reared his arm back with shockingly good form and sent the football in a clean spiral into the center of the net. Apparently, no instructions were needed.

What. The. Fuuuuuuuuuck.

"I'll be in touch with more wedding details later. Have a good night, fake boyfriend." He strode off the field, leaving me slack jawed and speechless.

7

EVERETT

I tried to catch Raleigh around school the following day, but he was nearly impossible to corner. Our free periods didn't line up. When I passed him in the halls, he was talking to a student or teacher. The man was popular, and the school was once again abuzz over the upcoming game.

I managed to catch him after fifth period in the faculty lounge; he was hunched over a notebook scribbled with X's and O's. He wore a navy Ralph Lauren polo with the horse logo prominently featured above his heart. The man was popular, good-looking, *and* rich? The world was truly unfair.

"Are you playing tic-tac-toe with yourself?"

He cracked a smile and laughed to himself. "Working on the playbook."

It wasn't that different from my notebooks when I blocked actors for the play. "Do you have a few minutes? I want to talk about–"

"Hey Raleigh!" Principal Aguilar swung by. "Excited about tonight's game!"

"It's going to be a barn burner." Raleigh and him bumped fists. "Working on some last minute magic." He tapped his notebook with his authoritative fingers.

Aguilar took a moment to wish him a good game. I could tell any uninterrupted time with Raleigh would be short.

"I wanted to quickly touch base about our arrangement," I said in hushed tones once Aguilar left. I kept my eye out for any other well-wishers. "I want us to get our stories straight."

"Ha!" Raleigh exclaimed.

"What's so funny?"

"Our stories straight. Because we're pretending to be a gay couple."

"Zing," I deadpanned.

"You're allowed to laugh, Ev. You don't always have to act like you're constantly constipated. Constantipated? Nah. Sounds too much like Constantinople."

I couldn't keep up with his tangents that had the humor-level of a second-rate '90s sitcom. But kudos to him for knowing what Constantinople was. Amos would be proud.

"Anyway, we need to get our stories *aligned* for the wedding, in case people ask. *When* people ask. My friends are excited to meet you."

Our social media post had unintentionally put the spotlight on me. My college friends were surprised that I had a boyfriend. Was it really such a shocker?

"Aren't we telling them that we met here?"

"Yes. But we need to flesh out our backstory."

"Cool. What's backstory?"

Oy. This was going to be Drama 101. I was like Annie in *The Miracle Worker* trying to teach Helen Keller how to read and write.

"Backstory is everything about our relationship. How we met, what we like and don't like, our backgrounds, memorable dates that we've been on. We need to be believable at the wedding. If we give different answers to the same question, then everyone will know this is a sham, and they'll know I was too scared to attend the wedding single, and I'll need to change my identity, and that's a whole thing. Going to court, petitioning to change my name, then updating all my credit cards...and I'm rambling. Anyway, that's backstory!"

Raleigh's eyebrows were headed to his hairline. "Sounds intense."

"Have I mentioned how much I appreciate you doing this for me?"

"You have." He cracked a smile that had this uncanny ability to instantly calm me down. "Did you know in college I once played a game with a sprained ankle, yet still managed to run seventy yards for a game-winning touchdown?"

I needed a map to find the point. "Great?"

"If I was able to play that game, then we can win this fake relationship game."

Despite the awkward analogy, which I was sure he only brought up as a humblebrag, I felt more confident that this crazy idea could work. Raleigh's aura was the definition of unfazed.

"I once performed in a production of *Death of a Salesman* with a 103 degree fever."

He wasn't the only one who could be a trooper.

"We got this, Ev."

"What are you doing?" My eyes traveled down to my arm, which he was petting with his calloused hand, his thumb gliding over my skin.

"Huh?"

"Your hand." I nodded at the scene in question.

"Just being nice. Is it bothering you?"

His touch was warm and soothing, and the only thing bothering me was how unbothered I was by the development.

"No. It's just surprising."

Had it really been so long without male contact that I literally could not compute?

"Ev, a little word of advice. If you want our fake relationship to be believable, you shouldn't freak out when your boyfriend touches you." He pulled his hand back, but the warmth lingered on my skin. "I need to work on some plays for the game tonight, but let's meet up on Sunday night to hash out our backstory."

"Sounds like a plan." I backed away slowly. I needed to get out of there before I did another stupid thing. "Good luck tonight."

"Are you coming?"

"To the game?" I'd gone to exactly one football game during my tenure at South Rock and it was just to sell concessions to raise money for the musical. It was freezing cold, people kept yelling like a pep rally on steroids, and the action on the field happened so fast I had no idea what was going on. "I can't. I have...a thing."

"Okay." Was I crazy or did he seem a little hurt that my answer was no? "Well, enjoy your thing."

———

RALEIGH ASKED that I meet him at his home on Sunday night. Considering his sharp clothes and general cool guy aura, I expected a different kind of house than what I pulled up to. It was an older, small ranch house with a cute little porch and freshly mowed lawn. Overall, I got an unassuming vibe, an adjective I'd never use for Raleigh.

I rang the doorbell and reminded myself that this charade was only temporary. I could swallow my dislike for him.

"Ev! Wassup!" Raleigh answered the door in nothing but a towel.

Water dripped off the thick ends of his lush, blond hair. Beads of water hung on his chest and trickled down his legit six-pack.

I knew Raleigh had a good body, but it was never naked in front of me.

"Hi. You're naked," I managed to utter, when what I really wanted to do was scream "howcha magoucha" and run my tongue over his chest like a paintbrush.

Why did annoying, obnoxious people have to exist inside hot bodies?

"I was taking a shower. Didn't want to leave you waiting out here. That wouldn't be very boyfriendy of me," he said, while still naked. His towel slung awfully low on his hips. The way my dick stirred reminded me that it'd been way too long since I'd been around a shirtless man.

"We're not boyfriends." My eyes drifted down that V that I thought only existed in underwear models to the bulge faintly outlined against the plush towel.

"Isn't that the goal?" He cleared his throat, a subtle way of telling me his eyes were up here.

He had no qualms about standing in front of me and his neighborhood in just a towel. How I wished I had that much confidence in my body.

"So, are you coming in or not?" He leaned against the door, with a cocky smirk that needled at my nervous reaction. He was enjoying this. "I don't want to give my neighbors a free show. This body is for my boyfriend only."

I would've thought that jerking off to oceans of pornography would have desensitized me to the sight of a naked, ripped man.

But there'd never been one this perfectly sculpted in front of me. In person. Close enough to...

I pushed past him. "Let's get to work."

Was he trying to make me uncomfortable? I always had a suspicion that he found a sick satisfaction in annoying me. I wouldn't break that easily.

"Put some clothes on," I said over my shoulder, refusing to give his statuesque body another glance.

Raleigh's living room reminded me of mine, which was to say, humbly furnished with mismatched furniture. A series of pictures from his old football days lined the fireplace mantel. His plush, burgundy couch was the standout, a piece that belonged in a grander room. It looked familiar to me, but I couldn't place it.

He darted into his bedroom, and I might have accidentally peeked at his firm ass bouncing under his towel as he walked.

"Be back in a second, boyfriend." He disappeared into his room.

"You really like saying boyfriend."

"I'm training myself since I've only dated girls lately," he yelled through the door.

Hmm. Smart move. I picked up the middle picture on the fireplace mantel. Raleigh had to have been in junior high, his body tiny under all that football gear.

"How old were you when you started playing football?"

"Nine, I think."

"Nine? That's so young! They're having little kids smash into each other at that age?"

"It was character building. Didn't you ever do any sports when you were a kid?"

The memories were still fresh, like sharp knives ready to attack. "I played Little League for a season. My parents made me. It was awful. It was three months of everyone realizing just how gay I was and giving me hell because of it." I did little pirouettes when I ran to a base, so it wasn't like I was hiding things. "By some miracle, I was a decent pitcher, but sadly that meant I couldn't ride the bench all season."

"So that explains how you were able to ace that football shot," he said from his bedroom.

"For some reason, Mother Nature decided that I should know how to pitch." Ironically, I was more of a catcher in other areas of life.

Raleigh reemerged wearing a pair of shorts, but no shirt. A towel slung around his broad shoulders.

"Where's your shirt?" I asked as heat crept up my neck. How dare my body betray me.

"I'm air-drying." He leaned against the threshold to the living room. Again with the leaning. Was he trying to be a teen heart-throb? "Am I making you uncomfortable?"

"I'm uncomfortable for your sake. Do you parade around half-naked whenever you have guests over?"

"As my boyfriend, I didn't think you'd find this a problem."

"Fake boyfriend." Even though he was wearing shorts and presumably underwear, the bulge remained. Oh, how it remained.

I wouldn't let him make me unravel. I took a step toward him and put on my toughest voice. "Are you trying to seduce me? Because unlike the IQ-deficient girls you hook up with, it's not going to work."

"Jesus, I'd hate to see what you're like at a public pool." He returned to his bedroom, and a few seconds later, reappeared wearing a South Rock High T-shirt that hugged his muscles. It wasn't much of an improvement from him being shirtless.

"Have a seat," he said. "Let's get started."

I studied his couch another moment before I sat down, finally remembering where I first saw it.

"Did you get this on Facebook Marketplace?"

"Yeah. It was brand new." Raleigh plunked down next to me so our knees were touching. I moved away, my body smushed against the arm. We weren't at knee-touching yet. "The husband brought it home–"

"And the wife hated it, but he couldn't find the receipt to return it." I wanted this couch; my couch was so beaten up, one might think it was being bullied by the other furniture in my apartment. This couch was even nicer in person. "Usually, I'm fast with Facebook Marketplace. I always wondered who snatched this up."

"You weren't fast enough. Everything in here is from Facebook, Craigslist, Nextdoor, or Goodwill."

"Huh," I uttered. None of this jived with the Raleigh I knew. "I didn't know you thrifted. I thought you were rich."

He burst out laughing and crossed his leg over his knee, taking up half the couch in a move that was textbook manspreading. Though, after seeing his bulge, maybe it was necessary.

"I wish."

"But I always see you with nice clothes. Your North Face fleece, Calvin Klein jeans, Ralph Lauren shirts."

"Have you been keeping an inventory on what I wear?"

Had I? A brief silence fell between us, and I worried that his question wasn't rhetorical.

"I shop at thrift stores in rich neighborhoods," he said, relieving me of answering. "Tori wanted me to 'dress for success,' which really meant 'dress to impress my friends.' I had to find a budget-friendly solution; it turns out rich people get rid of perfectly nice clothes all the time."

"That's how I got my pair of Gucci loafers. This wealthy kid in my dorm lost a bunch of weight, and decided that his skinny feet needed new shoes. I tried to tell him that feet don't lose weight, but he was already over them. I only wear them on special occasions."

"Will you be wearing them to the wedding?"

"Yes. I want to look my best for Bethany and Jordana." And if Noah happened to see me in designer footwear, then so be it.

Raleigh shrugged. "Maybe one day I'll be able to afford new things, but I don't know...it's against my nature."

"I don't think I could bring myself to pay full price at a store when I know there's good stuff I can get secondhand for a fraction of the price."

"Totally! Are you on the Sourwood Freecycle group email list?"

"Sourwood has a Freecycle group?" And how did Raleigh know about it, but I didn't?

"It started last year. I got a fancy desk chair that I put in my office at school. And this guy was giving away some cashmere sweaters last January that he got for Christmas. They were a little short on me, but I just wore an untucked shirt underneath. Nobody noticed."

Raleigh showed up at a faculty event wearing one of those cashmere sweaters. I assumed he'd gotten a bonus for coaching, or some football fan had bought it for him. Turned out he was just as frugal as me.

He typed on his phone. "I'm sending you the link to join the email list. I was thinking about joining Freecycling groups in other rich suburbs, see what other free stuff I could score. What's so funny?" he asked me, looking up from his phone.

"Nothing."

"You look like you were about to laugh."

My face flushed knowing it was being monitored so closely. "Looks like we actually have something in common."

"Well how 'bout that, boyfriend?"

I was starting to get used to him calling me "boyfriend." Attention was attention, even if it was all made up.

"I didn't take you for a thrifter either," he said. "With your love of theater and the arts, I thought you came from some blue blood and that the stick up your ass was genetic."

I should've been offended, but the comment made me laugh. "I don't think it's possible for you to be more wrong. With your powers of deduction, if the whole football thing doesn't work out, then you should consider a job as a detective.

"My parents were school teachers, and I have four older

siblings. We had to learn to make a dollar stretch. I lived in hand-me-downs. When I was a kid, I used to buy cases of bottled water, then walk up and down the Memorial Day parade route selling them for two bucks a piece. People never thought to bring water to these parades even though it was always hot out there. I made a killing."

"Are your siblings as frugal as you?"

I shook my head no. "My siblings all have big jobs making real money. Two are in software sales, one is in finance, and one is married to a cardiologist. They didn't get why I decided to become a teacher. They tried to talk me out of it. And yeah, they all make tons of money, but they all hate their jobs. They're stressed about hitting quotas or they're working all the time, and they're always worried about being laid off because they have no savings. I probably have more in the bank than they do. And my sister is forever competing with the uber wealthy moms at her kids' private school. They spend their big paychecks on stupid shit like new cars and big houses, but it doesn't make them any happier." Where the hell did all this word vomit come from? "Anyway, I'm rambling."

"I like hearing you ramble." Raleigh watched me with intent, his blue eyes flickering in the hazy light.

"Good." I cleared my throat and regained my footing. "Good, because I have a tendency to ramble, something you should know about your boyfriend. Speaking of, let's talk about the details of our relationship. I made a list of potential things people could ask us on my phone." I looked at my phone then put it down. "What about your family?"

"You can make up whatever you want." He waved it off, though I detected a slight edge. "I can be a Vanderbilt or something. I have the cashmere sweaters."

While I appreciated his desire to help me impress, I had an urge to use his real background. I wanted to know more about Raleigh. I obviously had gotten some things wrong.

"What about your actual family?" I nudged my chin at the photo on the mantel. "Looks like they had you playing football as soon as you could walk."

"I showed some aptitude. I played. Now I coach. They're good." He wiped his hands on his shorts. "I, uh, don't really keep in touch with them. So it's probably best that you make something up. Put that dramatic mind of yours to work."

He shot me a charismatic smile, but this time, it was like a shield blocking any further family questions.

"Where'd you grow up?" I asked.

"Allberg. Just up the river."

"I'm from Smithstown right next to you."

"Did you ever hang by the docks?"

I sputtered out a laugh. It'd been a good ten years since I'd heard someone mention the docks. They weren't anything special, merely some dilapidated, abandoned docks on the river. But as a teenager, they were the place to be.

"I wasn't cool enough to go." There were a few times when I walked by there with my friends and saw popular kids partying, but we didn't have the nerve to join them.

"I went to a few parties there. It was pretty lame."

"What'd they do there?"

"Drink and smoke. There was an old canoe, and kids would go behind there to hook up."

My shoulders sank at the utter lameness. That was it? I had built up the docks in my mind as this Xanadu of cool.

"Any brothers or sisters?" I bit my lip. We'd gotten so into the flow that I forgot to steer clear of family questions.

For the first time tonight, Raleigh's face hardened, his easy-breezy, laid back demeanor gone. He tried to remain pleasant, but as soon as I asked the question, I realized I'd struck a nerve too sensitive for words.

"I'll make something up. Say you were an only child."

"Perfect." He clapped his hands, as if to snap us out of that weird beat. "Did you want something to drink?"

"What do I like to drink?"

"I see what you did there. I don't have Sprite for your beloved vodka and Sprite."

A rush went through me that he remembered.

"What's your backup drink?"

"You tell me."

"You..." He studied me again. It was nerve-wracking to be under his microscope, yet also exhilarating to have someone try to figure me out. "You seem like a guy who enjoys fruity drinks. Something fun. Something warm because you hate the cold. I'm going to guess Tequila Sunrise."

"Mai Tai."

"I was close. Didn't go tropical enough." He snapped his fingers in an aw shucks moment that I found kind of endearing. "That's a fancy drink."

"It's new to my repertoire. Charlie ordered them for us at Remix once, and that night, I hooked up with a super hot guy. So I might as well keep drinking them."

Now, maybe I was pre-drunk. Or maybe the weird calmness of this night had frayed my sense of logic, but I could've sworn that Raleigh grimaced for a split-second, but it was gone as soon as it flared up.

"I don't need to hear about my boyfriend hooking up with other guys. I have beer, water, and maybe an old wine cooler of Tori's." Raleigh hopped up and jogged into the kitchen.

"I'll do the beer." I wasn't much of a beer drinker, and I only got excited about pumpkin beers for Oktoberfest season.

Raleigh returned with two pumpkin beers.

"You like pumpkin beer?" I asked as he flipped off the caps.

"It is Oktoberfest. Tis the literal season."

He handed me the beer. I was having trouble remembering why I couldn't stand him.

"To our fake relationship." He hoisted his beer in a toast.

"To our fake relationship," I repeated. Because this was fake. One night where Raleigh wasn't acting like a jerk didn't wash away the millions of previous hours where he was.

But it was a small start.

8

RALEIGH

One day later, Everett and I had our first test of our fake relationship. One of his friends from college was starring in a play; she had invited Everett and his "hot boyfriend" to a preview performance on Monday. (Her words, not mine.)

After football practice, I raced home to change into a debonair outfit. I landed on a button-down shirt with dark khaki chinos. Preppy but not nerdy. I'd worn something similar to meet Tori's friends, who I bowled over with my charm, as to be expected.

I picked up Everett. He said we could meet there, but it was the chivalrous boyfriendy thing to do.

On our way to the play, I brought up a very important topic we hadn't covered in our initial meeting.

"What's our name?"

"Our name? Oh, poor guy. Has the brain damage from your football days finally caught up to you? Me Everett." He pointed at himself. Then me. "You Raleigh."

I snorted a laugh. "I meant our couple name. If we're a real couple, we gotta have a couple name."

"You really have a thing for portmanteaus, don't you?"

"I don't know what those are, but what do you think about Ralverett?" The name came to me while I was refereeing a volley-ball game in gym class. I might've missed calculating a point here and there.

"Ralverett doesn't really roll off the tongue. Ralverett. Ralverett." The more Everett said it in different ways, the more the name lost its luster. "It's like I'm trying to say 'revolver' and 'over it' at the same time."

"Ralverett. It has a good ring to it." I said it a few times in my head.

"What about Everleigh?"

"You don't pronounce your name Ev-er-ett, though."

"So?"

"So then our name would be a boldfaced lie." Everleigh. Everleigh. I couldn't get into it. "Also, Everleigh sounds like a girl's name."

"And toxic masculinity rears its ugly head. Even though we're a gay couple, we can't be too girly."

"It's not that it's a girl's name, but Everleigh sounds like one of those rich girls who talk shit about people behind their back and whose dads buy them convertibles for their seventeenth birthday." I went to school with lots of Everleighs who rolled their eyes and snickered at my beat-up sneakers in that sharply cruel manner inherent in really rich people.

Everett took out his phone. "I'm hashtagging it in a picture of us."

Once he hashtagged Everleigh on social media, it was final. We would be Everleigh forever, or until we fake broke up next month. But a month being known as Everleigh was a month too long.

"Wait." I slapped my hand over his phone. "I have a fifty percent ownership stake in this relationship. I get veto power. And I veto Everleigh."

"But I get to be the tie-breaking vote."

"Why's that?"

"Because I came up with this relationship." He did this thing with his eyebrows jumping in smarmy know-it-allness that brought me a sense of joy.

"What about Reverett?" I threw out in a last-ditch effort.

Everett looked up and didn't kick my suggestion immediately out of the car. "Reverett," he repeated. "It's a little dorky, a little cute. Rolls off the tongue."

"Your name gets the majority of space, while my name kicks it off." Man, I wondered if brokering peace treaties was this intricate.

"Reverett. I like it." He tapped on his phone. "And hashtagged."

My phone buzzed with a notification in my pocket. We agreed on Everett posting about us three times a week. Pics or it didn't happen was a mantra for life today.

"You're taking this more seriously than I expected."

"I put one hundred percent into everything I do. I tell my players if you're going to half-ass something, then it's not worth doing."

"I say that to my actors, too."

"Great minds think alike."

Google Maps alerted me that our destination was on the right. We drove through a tightly-packed downtown strip with a few empty storefronts dotted among the businesses still hanging on. Parking meters dotted both sides of the street. Banners proclaiming we were in the town of Wheeler hung from lampposts.

"Google says it's right here, but I don't see any theaters." I squinted through my headlights.

"There's no marquee. It's there." Everett pointed to an empty storefront with blacked-out windows. A single light over the door illuminated a sandwich sign that read *Einstein in Retrograde 8pm $5.*

I had my pick of spots on the street. I parallel parked between two cars in front of a laundromat, mostly because I wanted to show off my parallel parking skills.

"Where's the marquee and the lights?"

"It's not that kind of theater."

I only knew about movie theaters and the performing arts auditorium in the MacArthur Community Center. What other kinds of theaters were there?

"It's a storefront theater. The theater group rented the space and converted it into a black box theater."

"Those things that record plane crashes?"

Everett smiled to himself. Yeah, I probably sounded like an idiot, but I didn't know what I didn't know. That was why God invented questions.

"A black box theater is a stripped-down theatrical experience. No sets except for a chair. No costumes. A black stage and black walls. It's up to us as the audience to fill in the rest."

Sounded like an awful lot of work for something that was supposed to entertain.

"If they charged more than five bucks a ticket, they'd have a bigger budget for scenery and costumes. IMHO." I shrugged. Somebody needed to say it.

"Have you ever seen a play, Raleigh?"

"I saw the ABBA musical *Mamma Mia!* on a school field trip." Something told me this play would be nothing like that. *Mamma Mia!* had sets. "Will there be songs, or will we have to fill those in with our imaginations, too?"

Everett rubbed his forehead. "I probably should've warned you about what we were going to see. This play isn't like *Mamma Mia!* It's edgy and avant-garde."

As the owner of the deli where I liked to grab a sandwich and matzo ball soup would say, Oy Gevalt. I could handle uncertainty on the field, but when it came to things I watched for amusement, I wanted to be unambiguously amused.

"How edgy are we talking here? Are they going to slaughter a goat onstage?"

"What? No."

"Is there going to be audience participation?"

"God no."

"Are people going to have sex onstage?"

"Uh, maybe." Everett seemed as perplexed by the question as I was by the answer.

"Will they be hot at least?"

Everett shook off the question. He turned to me, the light from the lamppost catching the wild green of his eyes. "*Einstein in Retrograde* is a nonlinear, experimental play about the nature of the universe and dismantling the patriarchy."

Oh, brother. Could I stack four cats in a trench coat to pretend to be me instead?

"Don't worry." Everett placed his hand over mine and gave it a light stroke with his thumb, sending a curious current of electricity down my arm. "I think you'll like it."

I'd rather watch goats getting slaughtered by people singing along to ABBA while having sex onstage.

"We can go home if you want," Everett said, likely reading my face. "I just wanted my friend to meet you, but I don't want to drag you to something you don't want to go to. I appreciate you offered to come at all."

I wasn't the guy to flake out on plans. If I could handle two-a-day practices in the hot August sun, then a weird play would be a cakewalk.

"I'm not going anywhere, except into this black box theater to see *Einstein in Utero*."

"*Einstein in Retrograde*. And thank you."

"By the way, you're touching me." I had him follow my eyes to his hands, petting my arm.

"Oh. Sorry." He yanked his hand back.

"Don't be." It felt nice. Natural. Something he would do without thinking had we been actual boyfriends.

A soft shade of blush spread on his cheeks.

"Ready to kick some fake boyfriend butt? Put your hand in. Reverett on three," I said.

"I'm not putting my hand in."

"Fine." I took his hand and placed it atop mine. That also felt nice. "One, two, three."

"Reverett!" we yelled. I caught a smile lurking on his lips.

Damn, I was the best fake boyfriend in the world for opting to see something called *Einstein in Retrograde*. I deserved all the fake sex. Maybe even fake breakfast in bed with fake homemade waffles.

9

RALEIGH

The play...didn't suck.

It was weird. Very weird. But in a cool way, like tasting a new food or the first time I felt my dick in someone else's mouth.

The play tracked Albert Einstein making big discoveries while also cheating on his first wife then leaving her and continuing to hook up with other women. The man was quite a player. Intermixed with the Einstein stuff was a plotline about a guy and girl dating in modern times. One actor and one actress played all the parts. The parallel seemed a bit obvious, but I'd keep that note to myself.

Scenes were performed in interesting ways. One was acted in reverse. Another had the guy and girl pretending they were atoms circling in space. And there was a musical number, too, with a surprisingly catchy song about misogynistic dating double standards that refused to leave my head.

Everett turned to me when the lights came up.

"What did you think?" His face tensed up as he likely expected the worst.

"Dude, the patriarchy is bullshit." I turned to Everett, my brain still processing what it had seen. "Being a woman does not seem fun. And who knew Einstein was such a player?"

"I guess women were into the hair." Everett raised a questioning eyebrow. "I'm double checking. You're not trolling me. You actually enjoyed it?"

"I don't know. It was interesting. But I did enjoy watching it. I interjoyed it." Most of the stuff I watched amused me then left my mind just as quickly. I had a feeling this play would linger for a while, like the scene in *Fast & Furious* where Letty died. She came back to life two movies later, but I didn't know that at the time. "How did the actor and actress memorize all that dialogue? They each had to play two characters."

Everett broke into a humoring smile, and it made me wonder if I asked a dumb question. He seemed like a guy who didn't believe in the "There are no dumb questions" mantra.

"I'm just kidding. Forget I said that."

"They're professionals. Just like how your players memorize all those football X and O plays. It takes dedication and hard work."

I breathed a quick sigh of relief that I didn't come off like an idiot. Again, not like I cared about what Everett thought. Okay, maybe I cared a little.

"This was cool. Something different."

"Something different is good!" Everett bumped my arm with his elbow.

I stretched my artistic comfort zone for a night and lived to tell the tale. Touchdown.

"What did you think of the play?" I asked Everett.

The guy went deep. He interjoyed the hell out of it.

Everett talked about the symbolism and the staging of the play, things I didn't consciously pick up on, like how Einstein was always standing at a distance from the female characters. Blocking, Ev called it. His face was aglow with passion for the subject, his body bouncing in his seat like he was made of rubber. Being in the presence of someone who cared was inspiring. It showed you what the human mind was capable of. I told my players that if they didn't truly care about football, then it didn't matter how much training they did.

I could watch Everett talk and talk, his face alive with animation.

"Like, how do you know if a play is well-directed?" I asked him. Again, I didn't know what I didn't know. "It's the actors doing what's in the script."

"The script is a blueprint. There are so many choices a director has to make to bring the script to life. They need to help the actors calibrate their performances so it's one cohesive unit. Imagine if the actor playing Einstein played him over-the-top. It would feel out of place with the heavy material."

"It's like making sure all my players are in sync with the playbook."

"Exactly."

I looked around and noticed we were the last ones in the theater. The black box lost its luster when the overhead fluorescents flickered on.

"Let's go outside to meet my friend."

I followed him into the makeshift lobby, where signs from past shows hung and a table was sprinkled with fun merchandise. I bought a bumper sticker branded with the theater group's logo.

The female cast member shot her arm in the air to wave us over. Everett slipped his hand in mine, sending another electric jolt down my arm. I wondered what he was doing for a second before remembering we were on.

I was not perfect. That I knew. But I'd cultivated boyfriend skills over the years of dating.

Fake Boyfriend Skill #1: Give good friend, i.e. charm the fuck out of my partner's friends.

Danita was the friend tonight, a spunky short woman with

creamy brown skin and a discerning gaze ready to suss out her friend's new boyfriend.

"You were awesome. Congratulations!" Everett gave her a hug, and she pulled him into a tight embrace.

"Everett! Ahhh! Thank you so much for coming."

They pulled away then immediately went back in for another mutual hug. Their friend energy was strong.

"Mesmerizing. I was mesmerized," he gushed with genuine excitement for his friend.

"Thank you," she said modestly, cupping her hands over her heart.

"I was thunderstruck. Am I using thunderstruck in the right context? I don't know, but the sentiment still stands. Thunder-fucking-struck."

I threw an arm over Everett's shoulders and launched into his tight theater circle. "What Ev means to say is you were incredible. Well done."

"Danita, this is Raleigh."

I reached out my free hand and gave her a gentle-yet-confident shake. "His boyfriend Raleigh. It's great to meet you."

"Likewise." She was sizing me up, her eyes no doubt having robot-like abilities to scan me and take in appropriate details. "I had no idea Everett was dating someone."

"Ev and I were taking things slow. Y'know, we were kinda friend-zoning each other for a while, and then things slowly slid into the boyfriend zone." I rubbed my hand across his back, and to my surprise, he leaned into my touch. The guy had really tense shoulders.

"That's so Everett." Danita chuckled to herself.

"How is that so Everett?" Everett asked, like a little kid whose parents were talking about him.

"It's just a saying, Ev." I gave his shoulder a squeeze and tried to loosen a knot while I was over there.

"I would like some context." He crossed his arms.

Danita and I shared a look. *That's so Everett.*

"Everett loves to keep guys in the friend zone. He doesn't believe in the boyfriend zone. Or he didn't..." Danita's smile held lots of secrets that I was curious to uncrack about my fake boyfriend.

Everett looked up at me with his big, green eyes. Two four-leaf clovers shining on me. "This is all blasphemy."

"To be blasphemous, that would mean you're a god," Danita pointed out.

"And your point..." Everett broke into a laugh.

"I totally hear you." I gave his shoulder a relaxing rub. He was skinny enough to fit in the palm of my hand, and so gosh darn squeezable like a plush toy. "Ev wanted us to be just friends for the longest time, but I finally wore him down."

"Ev. Adorable." Danita shot Everett a knowing look. "Everett used to be a stickler about nicknames. He hated them."

"I know. That's why I started using one with him. Driving Ev crazy is one of my favorite activities." I leveled a shit-eating grin at him. At least one part of this conversation didn't have to be a lie.

"It's true." Everett shrugged his shoulders. "Raleigh is the only person who's allowed to call me Ev." He leaned his head against my shoulder, sending an unexpected warm current through my chest, like there was no better place for a head to rest.

"I'd like to get that in writing." I hugged him tighter against me. Man, this guy was as huggable as he was squeezable. He nuzzled into my shoulder. Was he only getting in character?

Was *I* only getting in character?

Danita gave us a little eye roll. We were putting it on too thick. The game plan was to charm Everett's friend, not grope Everett in public, though that sounded really hot.

"Danita. You were seriously incredible tonight. Ev probably told you that I'm not the biggest theater guy, but the scene where you delivered that monologue to Einstein, confronting him over being a cheating bastard...that was some good shit."

Another part of the conversation that wasn't a lie. I got chills from her monologue.

"Thank you." She dipped her head. Why was everybody always weird with compliments?

"Seriously. The way you were able to go from the singing in a comedic scene then into that really heavy scene. I was like woah. It was like watching a running back make a break down the side of the field and into the end zone. You acted the shit out of your role."

Danita seemed taken aback, searching for words. She and Everett shared a look I couldn't decipher, like the refs reviewing tape before making a call.

"I like this one, Everett."

"Me, too." Everett threw his arms around my waist, and for a second, I couldn't tell if he was acting or not.

"How are you able to perform that monologue? Does your director give you a pep talk like I do for my players?"

"I summoned some experience with a former boyfriend."

"Primo dirtbag?" I asked.

"Yeah. A total jack ass. Kyle," she said to Everett, who nodded that he got it. "He was so in love with himself, I couldn't compete."

"So in love with himself to start dating his lookalike understudy?" I asked.

And yes, those were shots fired. Danita burst out laughing. The *dammmnnnn* was implied. I wasn't afraid to sling some mud about my boyfriend competitors.

"I like Noah, but that was savage." She didn't disagree with the statement, though. Point Raleigh. "Noah better watch out. You know he's going to be there at the wedding?"

"He RSVP'd yes? For sure?" Everett asked. He had a tinge of hope in his voice, which dampened my current savageness.

"Yep. He and Gavin will be there." Danita let out an awkward giggle. "Drama!"

She called it drama, but I called it competition. Like I told Everett, I loved to win.

"We're all adults." I pulled Everett closer against me and massaged his neck. "I'm looking forward to meeting more of Ev's friends."

I also wanted to meet this Noah shithead and see what a twerp he was.

We complimented Danita again on her performance before she had to leave. She had to be up early for her day job, a brutal slog I could empathize with as a former student who played football. She gave me a hug goodbye, told us we were a cute couple once more, and hurried to her car.

"I think we kicked ass," I said.

"Danita just texted me. She loved you." Everett smiled at the screen. "Thank you for tonight. I think we could actually pull this off."

I couldn't wait to wipe the floor with Noah. We'd be the cutest couple at this wedding—well, aside from the two brides.

I held Everett's hand as we walked to my car. "Is this cool, me holding your hand?"

"Yeah. It's good practice to keep me from flinching."

My car was the only one left on the street. Wheeler, New York was fast asleep.

Everett stopped before getting into the car. "I'm wired. Are you wired?"

"I have energy."

"This crazy idea is actually working. I'll bet Danita is spreading the word to our friend group as we speak. And she's giving our fake relationship high marks." Everett sucked in a chest full of crisp fall air. His cheeks were getting red from the cold. "You were right, Raleigh. You do give good boyfriend."

I gave him a salute. "At your service."

"I could use a drink." Everett looked at me, a glint of hope in his eye. "If you have to get home and prep for tomorrow, I totally understand."

"I'm up for a drink. I don't think we'll find any place open in this town."

Everett tapped his chin. "Since you enjoyed the play's musical number, I have an idea."

10

EVERETT

Six days a week, Stone's Throw Tavern was a sleepy local haunt. But on Monday nights, the gays came out for Musical Mondays. Instead of sportsball games showing on all the TVs, they played old clips from musicals. We strolled in as "Summer Nights" from *Grease* blasted on screen.

It was a song about friend groups learning about their member's secret hookup. Soon, my phone was likely going to blow up with friends singing "tell me more, tell me more" about Raleigh.

Speaking of, my fake boyfriend gazed around, mouth agape at the explosion of gay occurring in our town's popular watering hole.

"I come here to watch football. I didn't know…"

"Stone's Throw could be this fabulous?" Charlie had come up with the idea for Musical Mondays. He claimed he was straight when he thought of the idea. I claimed bullshit.

I ordered us two Cell Block Tangs from the special menu.

Patrons crowded around the bar or found spaces to treat as

their personal karaoke and dance floor. There was only one place to be on Monday nights, and it was here.

Raleigh and I found a space to stand by the large windows in the back which overlooked the Hudson River. We cheers'd to our successful night. Spending tonight with Raleigh wasn't a horrible experience. He could be fun and even a tad sweet when he wasn't trying to act like king shit at school.

A few strands of hair fell into his eyes, and I resisted every urge in my body to smooth it back.

"You were great tonight. I'm glad you didn't hate the play."

"Me, too. That would've been awkward."

"Here's the real question: Was it better or worse than *Mamma Mia!*?"

"Worse," he said without hesitation.

"Wrong answer, Raleigh."

"What do you have against *Mamma Mia!*? What did she ever do to you?"

I could tell my work was far from done. My dream of turning Raleigh into a theater aficionado after one show would not be happening.

"It's not a real musical. It's a bunch of ABBA songs, which are infectious and wonderful, with a plot shoved in between." I also couldn't process how a play about a woman so promiscuous she didn't know who fathered her child could be a family-friendly, universally beloved hit. "A real musical is about the story and songs working in simpatico."

As if the musical gods could hear my pleas, "Summer Nights" ended and "Prologue: Into the Woods," the sprawling opening number from the 1987 Broadway production of *Into the Woods, came* on screen.

"Like this." I pointed at the screen as if we'd uncovered buried treasure. "Sondheim, the greatest lyricist of all time. This is a twelve-minute song that introduces all of the characters in the show, all of their wants and fears."

"Twelve minutes?" Raleigh said, but I couldn't hear him. I got lost in the Sondheim, in the peppy speed of the music and intricate rhymes of the lyrics. I was transported. Writing a great song was hard. Writing several great songs that weaved together a compelling story was nigh impossible. Only the best musicals could do this, and that was why they were retold again and again.

I sang along, putting my full, unabashed theater kid heart into each lyric. It was uncontrollable, really. I cut my eyes to Raleigh, waiting for him to walk away pretending not to know me. Yet that did not happen. He watched as if he were entertained by my weird antics, the corners of his lips moving into a begrudging smile.

"I was eleven, and my mom took me into Manhattan to see a free production of *Into the Woods* in Central Park. I was...mesmerized. Have you ever been somewhere, and instantly known that this was where you were meant to be?"

"That's how I felt the first time I played football."

Playing football was nothing like watching a musical. Musicals were an artform. Football was a modern-day gladiatorial battle.

"You need to be less obvious when you roll your eyes," he said.

"What? I didn't roll my eyes."

"I get it. You don't like football. But you know what I think the issue is, Ev?"

He still insisted on calling me Ev, even though there was no one around to impress. "What?"

"You've never watched a football game."

"No thank you. If I want to see two teams go to battle, I'll watch *West Side Story*."

"Football and theater have a lot in common."

"They don't," I said flatly, not wanting to ruin what had been a successful evening so far. Raleigh and I proved we could be in the same room and not want to kill each other.

"Check out a Huskies football game this season."

"I'd rather fall into a septic tank." I softened my tone, as it seemed like he was dinged by my comment. "I don't think that's my scene, Raleigh."

"A gay bar playing showtunes isn't my scene either, but here I am."

"I'm not going to watch a football game."

"You'll like it. There's lots of drama involved."

He was actually being serious. "What's the big storyline? Who gets knocked down first?"

"Uh, yeah." The way his face lit up in excitement was cute, but also everything wrong with our society. "It's fun!"

"No, Raleigh."

"Y'know, I don't get why you hate football so much. Like, I'd get if it just wasn't your jam, but you actively hate it. Your face gets that mega deep red whenever it comes up, not your regular red. It's like you fell face-first into a tub of strawberry jelly."

"My face doesn't get that red," I said.

"It does," he replied with an unnerving matter-of-factness. "Even your ear lobes. I didn't know ear lobes could get red, except when they're pierced, but yours do. And they're not even pierced."

I instinctively felt my ear lobes. They were warm and not pierced. Who the hell noticed someone's ear lobes?

"But don't knock something until you've tried it. Football is a great sport. It builds character."

"Raleigh, let's get something straight. I will never like football. It signifies the demise of culture. It is built on stupidity and cruelty. How do you get a bunch of guys to work up the nerve to hit each other week after week? What halfway intelligent person would sign up for that? What kind of characters are you building? You cultivate hatred and meanness in them. I've experienced it firsthand. It's a miracle I stepped foot back in a high school ever again. Fuck, I might lose my job because of this great American pastime. So the whole school may worship you and your team, but to me, football players are just a bunch of dipshit bullies with brain damage."

As soon as I stopped and played back what I'd just said, I realized I'd crossed a line. I'd had speeches like these rolling around in my head for years, but when finally said aloud, they didn't hold the weight I thought they would. They just sounded mean.

Raleigh's face had a blank non-reaction, as if he switched onto human autopilot.

"Okay, then," he said, deflated. He took one final swig of his Cell Block Tang. "I didn't want to go to the play. But I'm glad I did. Maybe it's for the best that you find a new boyfriend."

He put down his glass in a soft, resigned motion. He wasn't angry like I was. He seemed...hurt.

And then he was gone.

And I was alone. Instantly feeling like shit.

And of course, "Dancing Queen" from *Mamma Mia!* came on the TV the second he left, sticking its Swedish, peppy finger into my wound. The crowd went wild, people holding up their drinks and singing along. I couldn't join in the festivities.

I ran out of the bar and sprinted down the empty street, my lungs and body not used to the physical activity. As I turned the corner to where we'd parked, Raleigh was getting into his car. The engine revved.

I knocked on the driver's window, barely catching my breath. He didn't roll it down, didn't even look at me. I knocked again with no luck.

As a lifelong theater lover, I knew how to be dramatic. So as he pulled out of his parking space, I leapt in front of his car like a completely normal person.

He bumper tapped me, but it was enough to send me to the ground, a reminder of how skinny and unmuscular I was.

"Shit! Everett, what the hell are you doing?" Raleigh hopped out of his car and extended his hand to me. Panic crossed his face.

"I was trying to get your attention." I rubbed my side where I'd landed, which hurt slightly more than the side of me that made contact with his car. "Next time, when somebody knocks on your window, do them a favor and roll it down."

"I'm sorry. Here." In one seamless motion, he pulled me up, like I was a pillow that'd fallen on the floor in the middle of the night. He must've miscalculated how light I was, because he pulled hard enough to have me smack into him. My thin body made contact with his hard, muscular chest.

It was dark out, but it looked like his cheeks blushed.

"How are you feeling?"

"A little sore."

"No shit."

"What are you doing?" I yelped.

His hands found their way up my shirt and skimmed my very sensitive sides.

"Checking for bruises and cuts." He was all business, probably worried about getting sued for vehicular almost manslaughter.

His calloused fingertips slid to the soft spot under my rib cage. They knew exactly what they were doing. I also realized that "weak in the knees" wasn't just an expression; our knees could literally go weak. I rested a hand on his broad shoulder to stay up.

"Does this hurt?" His thumb massaged me at the point of contact, rubbing deep circles into my skin.

"No." I bit back a moan. Jesus. Even in my random hookups from dating apps, I'd never been touched like this. Slowly, softly, with care. My interactions with guys were a race to naked, then a race to climax.

"Good." He lifted my shirt to get a better look, and a part of me thought he was going to whip it right off. And that made another part of me stiffen. "I don't see any bruises or signs of internal bleeding."

Raleigh worked with confidence and precision. His hands were warm, sending waves of heat into the affected area.

"How can you tell?"

"My players get hit all the time. I know what to look for. I will say, you took the hit well. Some guys can't take a tackle and they wind up really injured."

"That doesn't mean I'll be auditioning for the football team anytime soon."

"Trying out." Raleigh smiled as he removed his hands from my body. "Athletes don't audition. They try out."

My shirt fell down. I could feel the warmth of his hands linger on my skin.

"I'm sorry," he said. The street got very quiet.

"It's my fault. I jumped in front of a moving car." I prayed that he didn't think I was certifiable.

A sharp pain hit my side, an aftershock of the incident. I doubled forward.

"Maybe I do have internal bleeding? Can ribs get a concussion?" I leaned against Raleigh for support.

"Let's sit you down for a moment." He led me to a bench that had an ad for Roy's Car Barn. Their radio ads with a distinctive voice actor played ad nauseum.

Raleigh attempted to lift my shirt and rub my side again, but I politely pushed his hand away. I would do it myself, lest I have another potentially erotic reaction to his hands on me.

He jogged to his car and retrieved a South Rock Football water bottle from his backseat. It was warm, but it hit the spot. His kindness was making me feel worse.

"Raleigh, I'm really sorry for what I said in the bar. Do you ever have arguments saved up in your head that you think are brilliant, but then you say them out loud, and they sound kinda dumb?"

He didn't give me any reaction, even though I called myself dumb. His jaw tightened.

"My players aren't dipshits. They're in the same classes as your theater kids."

I nodded, feeling like a lousy teacher for talking shit about my students.

"I know you don't want to believe it, but they work hard. It's not easy going through a full day of classes, then getting the shit kicked out of you for practice. It's not easy doing two-a-day practices in late summer when the hundred-degree sun is beating down on you in full gear. And it's not easy being a teenager balancing school and a social life and family and the regular hormonal, angsty shit all the while staying focused on Friday nights when you know the whole school, the whole town, is watching you, depending on you, ready to cheer you on when things are good but just as quickly tear you down if you lose. Is all of that more difficult than acting in a school play? That's not for me to say. But I know these guys. I work closely with them. They're good kids, Ev. And I won't let you dismiss them as stupid and cruel."

It was a side of Raleigh I'd never experienced: the protective papa bear. Instead of feeling hurt, I found myself in awe of how deeply he cared about his players. It was the same protective urge I felt toward my beloved nerds.

"If you want to hit me with your car for real this time, I understand."

He cracked a smile, his gleaming teeth peeking through his full lips. I hadn't completely ruined the date. If this were a date...

"What did you mean in the bar when you said you experienced football's cruelty firsthand?" he asked.

I heaved out a breath as the pain dulled at my side and an old hurt opened back up.

"I was bullied by football players in high school. Theater kids were always an easy target. Surprise, surprise. Extra points if they were skinny and closeted. They made my life hell. Shoving me into my locker, stealing my script from my backpack, going to see the school play only to heckle us onstage. But they never got in trouble because they were the kings of our school."

It was years ago, but the feelings come back just as strong, as if no time had passed. Even now, a decade removed from graduating high school, my stomach twisted in knots like it did every morning when my alarm went off. The twists were faint compared to back then, but they lingered like a phantom waiting to attack.

"That's awful. I'm sorry that happened to you."

"Is that what you did in high school?"

He shook his head no. "I knew plenty of guys who loved to be assholes. It starts at the top. The team captain when I was a freshman was a total prick. He was so insecure about his game, he took it out on the weaker kids at school, and that gave other guys on the team permission to be pricks. His family was also loaded, so he loved going after poorer kids." Raleigh bristled at the memory like he had his own visceral reaction to high school. That his teenage experience wasn't anything but ideal was a surprise. "When I became captain my junior year, I put the kibosh on all that. I had a no-asshole policy, and I led by example. I started volunteering as a peer leader at school to be a resource for other students, and my teammates followed suit."

Huh. I gave Raleigh another look, literally and figuratively. He could've been an asshole. He fit the profile. I never would've pegged him as a nice guy who did things like lead by example. Maybe there was more to him than his objectively hot bod and killer smile.

"The rot always starts at the head."

"Are you feeding me a line, or are you being for real right now?" There was that part of me that had learned not to trust jocks, instilled from years of experience. What if this was all a prank?

"Damn. They really did a number on you, Ev." Concern ringed his eyes.

"Your players are treated like gods at South Rock. They get away with everything."

"Like what?"

"Like making all of us partake in those repetitive pep rallies, cutting our teaching time short. Like barely paying attention in class, but then being told we're not quote-unquote 'being team players' if we give them detention. You remember what happened to Amos last year. He caught an athlete cheating. When Amos rightly failed him, the athletic director tried to pressure him into changing the grade. The student's parents tried to get Amos fired."

On the surface, I played the part of tough-talking friend, pumping up Amos during this scandal. But inside, I was terrified they were going to get away with it, and that they wouldn't break a sweat while doing so. Amos's career would be ruined so some kid could play soccer.

"That was really shitty. It was, Ev." His eyes were deep wells of empathy, wearing down my cynical side. "That's not how I run my football team. All of my guys keep their grades up, and they treat the kids and teachers at South Rock with respect. Have you heard rumors of South Rock football players bullying kids?"

I opened my mouth, ready to list off a hundred different examples...only I couldn't think of any. Memories from my high school experience came to mind, but no stories from South Rock.

Except one.

"Your players vandalized my signup sheet."

"They did what now?"

"They wrote in fake names on the sheet."

"How do you know it was them?" He stared me down, waiting for proof.

"How do you know it wasn't?"

"That's not how our justice system works. If my guys did that, which..." He cracked a smile he was failing at suppressing. "is *not* funny. But if they vandalized your sheet, I'd reprimand them. I just need proof."

"Ask them. If they're such upstanding young men, they won't lie to you, Coach." This was ridiculous, and yet Raleigh had planted a seed of doubt in my head. I didn't know for sure it was the football team, but they were the most obvious subjects.

"And it's common knowledge that football players are strongly discouraged from participating in the school play." I straightened my back, emboldened with having right on my side. "They make fun of it, and as a result, none of the other students want to partake. The drama department may be discontinued next year." I stood up, ready to find a new way home. "You and your dumb jock brigade have scared off kids from getting involved with theater. You probably think it's just some singing and dancing, but it's a needed outlet for these kids. It's a way they can express themselves and come out of their shell. Not just with acting. They can paint sets, design lighting, and learn to lead. But if they're afraid of getting teased for joining the drama club, then they'll never have that chance."

"I've never heard of that rule about players not auditioning."

"Seriously?"

He nodded yes. He wouldn't risk lying to me at this critical point, especially with my foot kicking distance to his balls, which left me confused.

"It's been around for years. The old football coach told the players they couldn't audition or else they'd get shit for doing something so queer. 'Strongly discouraged' is what I heard."

Raleigh flared his nostrils as he exhaled a thinking breath.

"That sounds like something Coach Perkins would've said. He hated his players doing any activity that wasn't football. I heard he once yelled at a player for daring to go on a missionary trip with his church. That is not me. If that rule was still in place, I had no idea. I don't have any problem with my guys doing other activities outside the football season."

"Outside the football season," I repeated. "The musical is in December. Eight weeks away."

Raleigh bit his lip. He was trying to keep on his relaxed bro face, but it was obvious that was not cool with him. "That's during our playoff run."

"What does it matter? Your players think the play is stupid, and because of that, nobody wants to audition. I was so hopeful when I saw the sign-up sheet had been filled out. Maybe there was this secret contingent of artsy kids who could find connection and purpose through the play. But it was all a prank." My heart sank like a stone when I saw those fake names on the sheet. I couched it in righteous anger, but in truth, I was devastated.

I kept on rambling. Raleigh made it easy to do.

"I lied to the drama club. Told them we were doing *Into the Woods*. They were so excited. But there's no fucking way I can make *Into the Woods* happen with a tiny budget and only five committed actors. I'm dreading the inevitable conversation where I tell these bright, weird, wonderful kids that *Into the Woods* won't be happening. I wouldn't be surprised if the school canceled the theater program entirely by the end of this year."

It was a truth stirring inside me that I didn't want to admit. But there it was. This was probably the end of the theater program, the end of the chance for certain kids to find their outlet, not to mention the end of my employment once they found out I lied to the drama club. I slumped onto the bench, my heart sliding down my back onto the dirty sidewalk.

"I really fucked up. I'm still holding out for a miracle." Perhaps

Sondheim could take a break from chilling in heaven to put in a word with God. I could use a deux ex machina for the shitstorm I created. "And you know what sucks? I would've directed the shit out of that play."

I dared glance at Raleigh, who was quiet but having an introspective moment himself. The wheels turned behind his beautiful face. "Now I get why you hate sports so much."

"Sports started it."

"I guess going to all those pep rallies can really suck."

"Especially when the football coach decides to shout you out just to be an asshole." In retrospect, knowing how silly Raleigh can be, it was a little funny. When I wasn't watching my life's passion get funneled down the drain, I was able to take some ribbing.

"I won't do that again. You looked down on athletics and me from the first day we met. So I decided to give you a hard time back. It became fun." He smirked, a flicker of a flame alighting within me. Traitor. "And you may think we have it easy, but when the whole town is looking to you to win, that pressure is not fun."

"At least this town looks at you."

"Truce." He held out his hand, and I shook it like the gentleman that I am. "I'll miss giving you a hard time. I enjoyed those moments of looking out in the crowd during pep rallies and seeing your pissed off strawberry jelly face."

"My face does not get that red."

"When you're mad, it does. It's different from the normal swirls of red on your cheeks when you're embarrassed or when you're laughing. This is the red that goes up to your forehead and makes your eyes extra green. Or, uh, something like that. Approximately."

I had that many shades of red? I must've really stuck out in the pep rally crowd for Raleigh to notice, though it seemed like he was noticing me all the time.

What was Raleigh noticing this time? Because he was staring

at me like...almost like he wanted to kiss me. But that couldn't be right.

"Should we get going?" I asked to break the awkwardness.

"Uh, sure. We barely had time at Musical Mondays if you want to stay for a few more tunes."

"You know, right after you left, they played a song from *Mamma Mia!*" A small wave of guilt hit me over that. The members of ABBA were scowling at me from their Scandinavian castle.

"Maybe they'll play another one?"

I was willing to take a chance. Crap, now I had "Take a Chance on Me" playing in my head.

As we walked inside, I found myself not dreading spending time with Raleigh.

Weird.

11

RALEIGH

Musical Mondays slapped hard. The entire bar got into singing along to songs that they all magically knew the words to. It reminded me of how rowdy sports bars could get during a football game, everyone yelling at the screen. Instead of yelling, guys were singing.

I did my best to sing along to one song after the other. I made up the words when I didn't know them, or I'd try to guess what the next lyric would be. My rendition of "Michael in the Bathroom" from *Be More Chill* was a bunch of garbled gibberish. It drove Everett crazy as a lyrical purist. So naturally, I kept doing it.

Even though we'd made some kind of peace, I couldn't stop myself from giving him a hard time. It was just so much fun watching his face get red. I felt like a boy pulling a girl's pigtails on the playground.

This night was exactly what I needed. The pressure was on for the season. We barely made it to the playoffs. *You win some, you lose some.* Well, the administration and people in town didn't appreciate that concept. They only wanted wins.

Exhibit A: An older gentleman with a bushy beard and a tight

T-shirt approached me at the urinal. First, I thought it was for, well...that.

"You're Coach Marshall, right?"

I checked myself, and yep. My dick was out. I craned my neck and gave him an uneasy smile. I wasn't up to speed with gay bar protocol.

"That is correct."

"Go Huskies." He clapped my back hard. "We're not off to the best start, are we? You gotta bench your quarterback. He needs to learn to throw better."

Except for the urinal part, this conversation was normal. People came up to me all the time wishing me well while offering unsolicited coaching advice. We were Sourwood's team, and as a result, everyone had an opinion.

"Thanks for your support," I said diplomatically. I struggled to maintain a friendly face.

"He needs to be doing better. Coach Perkins would've whipped him into shape."

Ah, my drill sergeant predecessor. I loved hearing people compare me to him as much as I loved having random guys come up to me at urinals.

"You gotta turn things around, Coach."

"I'll keep that in mind."

"Good." The guy overtly checked out my dick, then flashed me a smile of approval and left.

Sad to say, that wasn't the most awkward interaction I've had with a Huskies fan.

I left the bathroom a little shaken, but when I saw Everett through the crowd, my spirits immediately lifted. There was something about him that filled me with good vibes.

He was actively engaged in conversation with our fellow teachers Julian and Seamus from the foreign language department. Seamus Shablanski also moonlighted as our baseball coach.

He had a dark mane of hair, a thick Staten Island accent, and didn't take shit from anyone. We bumped fists, athletes in arms.

"Greetings, earthlings," I said for some reason. Also for some reason, I snaked my arm around Everett's slim waist. I told myself we were practicing for the wedding and not because he was so damn huggable. There was something about his waist that fit my arm, or the other way around.

I gave Julian a fist bump, too. He flashed me a sweet smile. Unlike Everett, he was always warm to me.

Speaking of Everett, he was smiling awkwardly.

I knew this shade of red on him. Different from Red Hulk. The pink clouds flooding his cheeks meant my fake boyfriend was embarrassed.

To be seen with me? Nonsense.

"What are you guys doing here?" Everett asked.

"We had a department meeting, and we wanted to blow off some steam," said Seamus. He was a Spanish teacher who was half-Irish, a quarter Italian, and a quarter Russian. A true man of the world. "Jules suggested this place."

"I forgot it was Musical Monday."

"Sure, *Jules*," Everett said. He grinned at Seamus. "I hope you don't mind being around all these gays."

"It's all good." He thumped his chest. "Straight, not narrow."

Everett shot a weighted look at Julian, engaging in friend telepathy.

"What are you guys doing here...together?" Julian asked.

"Yeah, didn't you say he was a full-of-himself artsy snob?" Seamus asked me, forgetting that what gets said in the locker room stays in the locker room.

To my relief, Everett laughed it off.

"We went on a date to see this really serious play, then decided we needed a palate cleanser. And some Cell Block Tang." I held up my glass, the amber liquid glowing in the dark lighting.

"A date?" Julian asked with a pleased smile. "How nice."

"It was a fake date to strengthen our fake relationship," Everett said, not realizing how ridiculous that sounded to people who weren't us.

"Fake relationship? I'm confused," Seamus said.

"I have to attend a wedding where my ex-boyfriend will be with his new boyfriend."

Seamus held up his hand. "Say no more. I got it. I had an ex-girlfriend who went on to date a senator. I had a cousin pretend to be my wedding date."

"Did it work?" I asked.

"Yeah, up until she put her hands on my butt during a slow dance. Then it got weird."

I might have that same problem because Everett's backside was very distracting.

"He was a congressman, not a senator," Julian clarified. "At least he was when you first told me this story."

"What's the difference?" Seamus shrugged.

"A senator reps a whole state and has a longer term. Congressmen only cover a district. They're less prestigious."

"Let's split the difference and say that he worked in public service. That work for you, Jules?" Seamus smiled into his drink.

"I don't think your ex could bag a senator," Julian said.

"Cheers to that." Seamus and Julian clinked glasses.

"Anyway, this facade is a strategic ploy to not embarrass myself in front of Noah and all of my friends from college. That's all." Everett gave a firm head nod.

That was that. Whatever was going on in my head over Everett and his huggableness had to stay strictly in my head.

———

AFTER SHOOTING the shit with Julian and Seamus, we left a little while later.

The clouds that had lingered in the night sky earlier had swept themselves away, revealing a breadth of stars. It was a romantic setting for our non-romantic non-date. When we got into the car, I broke the awkward silence with some tunes.

"You listen to country music?" Everett asked in the same tone someone might use to wonder why I was licking a toilet seat. I did not lick toilet seats, for the record.

"Sometimes. It's good stuff." I turned it up, banjos strumming through the speakers.

"I've never met anyone who actually listens to country music."

"Not refined enough for you?"

"I thought it was a Southern thing." Everett acted disinterested, though his fingers tapping on his knee said otherwise.

"I spent some time in Tennessee growing up."

"With your mysterious family?"

No comment.

"Sorry. That was the Cell Block Tang talking. Would you look at that? She's asking to be decapitated." Everett nodded to the car in front of us, where a familiar woman hung her head half out the passenger window, a twister of brunette hair dancing in the wind.

The car had a North Point High bumper sticker.

"Shit," I muttered.

"You know them?"

"That's my ex and her new boyfriend."

"When was the last time you saw them?"

"In my bed, his ugly pale ass thrusting into her."

"Seriously? Damn, I thought shit like that only happened to Colin Firth in *Love, Actually.*"

I had to make a left at the upcoming light, and they were going straight. If we caught the red, things could get awkward.

"Shit," I muttered again as the light turned red. I slumped down in my seat.

"What are you doing?" Everett asked.

"Uh, hiding."

"Don't you think they'll recognize your car?"

As we got closer, I could see them smiling and laughing through their window, making me feel car sick.

"I have an idea," Everett said as he rolled down his window.

Before I could ask what the idea was, Everett bent down and put his head in my crotch as the car came to a stop next to Donovan's.

Everett's head was dangerously close to my junk. And I was dangerously close to poking his eye out.

"Raleigh? What's up, man?" Donovan called from his car. Fortunately, hearing that asshat's voice was an instant boner crusher. Tori gave a half-hearted wave from the passenger seat.

"Hey," I said like a total chump. I stared at the light and willed it to change.

Just as the moment was getting painfully uncomfortable, Everett popped up from my lap. He wiped his lips.

"Fuck, Raleigh. Your cock is so big. My jaw hurts." Everett turned and waved at Donovan and Tori. "Oh, hello. Lovely night, isn't it?"

He applied a coat of lip balm and returned to my crotch.

The light turned green, and I left my ex and her boyfriend in the dust.

I sped through town, getting as far away from them as I could while laughing my ass off.

"Thanks," I said when I caught my breath. The gob smacked looks on their faces was priceless.

"You got that bent out of shape over an ex-girlfriend? I thought you had so many of them, they were like toenail clippings."

"Nice visual."

"You're a player. In the time I've worked at South Rock, you've had well over twenty girlfriends."

Was he keeping count?

"What's so special about that one?"

"She was my fiancée. She broke my heart."

That was the first time I'd ever said that aloud. I'd told myself that we rushed into marriage, that things weren't that serious. But they were. I was in love. It was like being on the field with no protective gear.

"So that's why you stick with these barely there relationships?"

"Yeah. I'm not making that same mistake again."

Everett turned his head to me, and I could tell he was going to dig into that. But I didn't want to ruin the evening, so I made like I was getting rushed by the offense and pivoted. "What's the deal with you and that Noah guy? Why do we hate him so much?"

"I'd probably duck if I saw him in a car with his boyfriend. I can't duck at the wedding."

The side streets led us through a neighborhood of historic old houses. I missed the peacefulness of driving with no real destination in mind.

"Did he cheat on you with this lookalike guy?" I asked.

"No cheating. He was the star of our drama program. And he decided he wanted to date me. Little, insignificant Everett. I thought being with someone like him would make me feel cool and wanted, but for some reason, I only felt small. He dumped me at graduation."

"At literal graduation?"

"I cried into my mortarboard. It was something he'd been laying the groundwork for, I found out later. Making arrangements to move to Manhattan, getting an agent. He pulled the rug out from under me. I should've seen what was happening. I don't want to show up at this wedding and feel small."

"Don't let him–"

He put his hand on mine to stop me.

"I know that Eleanor Roosevelt quote. 'Nobody can make you feel inferior without your consent.' I know that, Raleigh, but I can't stop it from happening. He has achieved everything he set out to. Our friends still revere him. And next to that, I feel like my life is a boring mess. Not even a fun, hot mess."

Comparison was the killer of joy, but that couldn't stop us from doing it. I told my players to focus on improving themselves, not watching what their teammates are doing. But they still did. I didn't have any wise words for Everett.

"I think you have a nice life." I gave his hand a squeeze. It wasn't much, but I meant it.

I pulled up to Everett's apartment building, a squat structure that blended into the ones just like it. It was in the older part of town, like my house. My heart dipped knowing that our fake date was really over.

Why was my heart racing? This wasn't like a normal date where it would end with a kiss, even if it kinda had goodnight kiss vibes hanging in the silence.

"Thanks for tonight, Raleigh." Everett turned to me, his lips red against his creamy skin. "You're...interesting."

"What does that mean?"

"You're not what I was expecting. You can still be an ass, don't get me wrong, but you're...pretty cool."

"Likewise." This was one of the more enjoyable dates I'd been on. There was no vapid chit chat over an overpriced bottle of wine.

"Here's the part where if this were a real date, we would kiss goodnight," Everett said, breaking the tension. Or trying to.

"Would it be a date if we were already boyfriends? Dates are how you lure them in."

"Nice analogy."

"Better than calling my exes toenail clippings."

"If we were actual boyfriends and we'd gone on an actual date, then I'd invite you up to spend the night." Everett let out a nervous laugh, his voice practically squeaking. It was charming in an odd way. "Which I'm not doing."

"This is a business relationship. No sex. Although, if you were my boyfriend and this were a real date and you did invite me up to spend the night, then I would likely blow your mind. With my sex."

"You do have a big head, Raleigh."

"I've been told it helps with stimulation."

Everett flushed a remarkable shade of red that would rival the fall foliage. "Nice, Raleigh."

The pupils in his eyes blocked out all color. I couldn't hear anything except the sound of my heart pounding in my skull.

"But it's all a moot point. Because none of this is real," he said.

"Correct. It was all a strategic mission, to use your words."

A heavy silence hung between us in his car. If this were a real date, we'd already be making out. My dick was having trouble telling the difference.

"Good night, Raleigh." And in seconds, Everett was shutting the door and walking into his apartment building, giving me and my dick a definitive answer.

I waited until I saw the light in his apartment flick on before driving off. It's something I would've done if this were a real date.

12

EVERETT

Julian: Hey Everett, how was your DATE WITH RALEIGH??
  Amos: What's this?
  Chase: Date?
Amos: With Raleigh?
Julian: Yes. It happened. I spotted them at Musical Mondays.
Chase: How did Raleigh fare at a gay bar?
Amos: Tell us everything!
Julian: They looked very cute together. Very couplesque.
Chase: There is a strange paucity of Everett on this chain.
Julian: He's hiding.
Amos: He's doing the walk of shame from Raleigh's house.
Amos: If he's able to walk at all.
Julian: Zing!
Chase: I don't get it. How would vigorous lovemaking inhibit someone's ability to walk?
Chase: I just got it.
Everett: I would like off this text chain please.
Amos: Why? Are you still riding the Raleigh train?
Julian: Zing again!

Chase: I would hope not. Otherwise you'd be late for school.

Everett: [picture of giving the middle finger]

Everett: This is what I think about this conversation.

Julian: Me-ow.

Everett: And zing, J? Are you eighty?

Everett: There was no date. It was a strategic move against Noah. Raleigh graciously agreed to accompany me to Bethany and Jordana's wedding. We attended a play that my college friend Danita starred in, so she could meet Raleigh and provide social proof that we were a real-life couple. And then we had to further practice being around each other without fighting, which we accomplished at Stone's Throw Tavern, where I had a non-repulsive time. Everything was legal, above board, and by the book.

Amos: Yawn.

Julian: You guys looked nice together. You seemed *very* non-repulsed.

Everett: I thought the same thing watching you and your "friend" Seamus.

Amos: Seamus went to Musical Monday with you, J?

Everett: What was his nickname for you? Jules, was it?

Julian: We went to grab a drink after our department meeting. Stop avoiding the subject, Everett.

Everett: I am doing no such thing.

Chase: I'm shocked you two can hang out without fighting.

Everett: Oh, we definitely fought. There was yelling. He tried to run me over. But no tears. Like I said, a win. This fake relationship may not be the worst idea in the history of human existence.

Chase: I would argue that the worst idea in human existence was developing a nuclear bomb. But to each his own.

———

I HAPPILY AVOIDED everyone I knew at school the next day. I didn't need my friends giving me shit, or worse, giving off giddy looks as if they watched Raleigh and me kiss during spin the bottle.

I also avoided swinging by the gym to see Raleigh. Why would I need to do that? Why was I wanting to do that? There was nothing to discuss since last night.

Yes, I had a not-horrible time hanging out with him. I might've sized him up wrong for all these years. (Though judging by his large hands, and my proximity to The Bulge, there was one part of him I knew I was sizing up right.) He was still a total bro, but he was also a good listener and thoughtful guy.

No matter what, he was agreeing to be my fake boyfriend— emphasis on the fake—as a favor. Not because of any other reason that I might be concocting in my head. So even though there was a moment in the car when I was considering kissing him, when my body was about to propel me forward into his manly chest, I reminded myself that none of this was real.

It'd just been *so long* since I'd gone on a date that good. I wish all my dates were as delightfully unexpected as last night. We zigzagged between teasing each other to baring our souls, and it felt totally natural. We cut through the usual bullshit with ease.

For the love of Sondheim, I needed to get a grip.

A week ago, Raleigh Marshall was the bane of my existence.

All we had to do was pretend we liked each other for one weekend.

To keep myself focused, I posted pics from last night on social media. Raleigh took a great selfie of me, him, and Danita post-show. His big goofy smile took up a chunk of the frame. The picture Julian took of us at Musical Monday was cute, too. Up they went.

Hashtag Reverett.

In my morning public speaking classes, I worked hard to focus on the students and their awkward speeches. No letting my thoughts drift to last night. The students had to give an introduction speech. Many chose family members, and others chose famous people like Lebron James and Zendaya.

I gave extra notes, helping each student with their delivery and writing their speech. Public speaking was something none of us could avoid. It was essentially theater for non-theater people.

During a speech introducing Kylie Jenner, I caught a student nodding off in the corner of the classroom. Jackson was on the football team, and while normally I would've rolled my eyes at him for not paying attention, Raleigh's defense of his athletes played in my head. Between school, homework, practice, and a town full of people expecting victories out of him, I could potentially see how he'd be exhausted.

"Hey." I wrapped softly on Jackson's desk. "Do you need to go to the water fountain, get something to drink?"

"Sorry, Mr. Calloway. No, I'm good."

Did I just voluntarily go easy on a football player? What the fuck was Raleigh doing to me?

———

JULIAN and I worked the cafeteria for lunch that day. We were lunch monitors—every teacher had to do it—making sure students didn't goof off or start a food fight.

Though I was very close to throwing today's lunch special into my fellow monitor's lap.

"Hello, *person.*"

"I'm sorry," he said to me. "We were just giving you a hard time on the group chat."

"It's fine, J." It was hard to stay mad at that sweet face. "It was news. Group chat worthy." I took a seat at our table in the corner of the cafeteria. "I was going to tell everyone about the fake relationship."

"How long has it been happening?"

"Uh, five days."

Had it only been five days since Raleigh and I were on speaking terms? It seemed way longer. I felt like I knew him better than most people in my life.

"For the record, you looked like the real deal."

After what Raleigh had told me about my propensity for redness, how transparent was my reaction right now? "That's good. That's what we want. For people to believe us."

Especially Noah.

Noah was going to be floored when he saw me walk in with a hot jock boyfriend.

"So you didn't hate your time with Raleigh then?"

"He was mildly annoying, but overall spending time with him no longer makes me want to crawl out of my own skin."

Raleigh strolled through the hall with other coaches, laughing up a storm, recounting some funny story. I watched him through the windows of the cafeteria, my heart doing that funny thing it did in the car last night. I had to constantly remind myself that this was all fake. He was mostly straight and mostly used to going through girls like tissues. He had no real interest in a skinny theater nerd.

Raleigh found me through the window, gave me a quick nod and half-smile. It sent a fuzzy feeling down my spine.

Perhaps that just meant I needed to see a chiropractor.

"What about you?" I turned back to Julian, hoping he didn't witness that exchange. "I didn't know you were on a date with Seamus."

"We stopped there after a–"

"Department meeting. On Musical Monday. The one night where it's gay, gay, gay."

"I forgot it was Musical Monday."

"Did you think it was Musical Wednesday? It's a good thing

Seamus is such an 'ally.'"

Now Julian was the one squirming and turning red. His crush on his friend and fellow teacher became more obvious with each passing year.

"There's plenty of homosexual fish in the sea. Might be worth looking elsewhere. Maybe it's time to join Milkman."

Julian rarely discussed his dating life, which as part of our friend group, was a bit odd. Amos and I were oversharers, and Chase never left out a detail from one of his occasional hookups. But Julian wasn't on any apps, and for how close the four of us were, his sex life was a mystery.

Though, I was currently fake dating a guy who unironically refers to himself as a wholesexual, so I was in no position to judge.

After lunch, I moseyed by the auditorium to check on the signup sheet. I had extended tryouts to see if there were any late-comers willing to give it a shot. My heart tightened at the sight of a new name, but when I got closer, the letters came into focus.

They weren't letters at all.

Someone had drawn a dick squirting out drops of what I hope was semen in one of the lines. Did Raleigh actually believe a foot-ball player wasn't behind something this immature?

I got through my afternoon classes focusing on the work. I might've been extra critical of my students' speeches as an outlet for my frustration, but all of my criticism was warranted. When the final bell rang, I hustled to my car to get home for alone time.

I checked my phone, and my eyes lit up when I opened the social media app. My pics with Raleigh had tons of likes. Well, tons for me. I wasn't at influencer level. I dutifully checked all the people who'd liked the picture. Several friends from college who I knew would be at the wedding liked it.

Including Noah.

Cute couple, he commented.

I did a spin dance in the parking lot. This was more communication than Noah and I had had since we were together. He followed me on social media, but he never engaged with a picture before, and definitely never commented. I assumed I was one of many people he followed but didn't care about.

I darted back into the school and practically ran through the halls. It was a good thing teachers couldn't get detention.

Rounding the first floor corner of the art wing, I sling-shotted past the cafeteria and main office and into uncharted territory: the athletics department. I made my way to the end of the hall, where the football team's pristine locker room was.

I pushed open the back door. The bright sun shined in the blue sky over the football field, where the Huskies were rehearsing. Er, practicing. Running drills, it looked like.

Some ran a loop around the field. Others were doing sprinting drills. It was warm out for October, yet there they were in heavy gear. Helmets and pads under the beating sun. They smashed into each other in brutal ways, then set up for the next play. They hit practice blockers, big pads meant for running into. Over and over.

I stood by the bleachers and watched for a few moments, feeling exhausted for them. I was tired from a full day of classes. I didn't have to do grueling exercise and practice. My body winced at their bodies clashing and colliding, the clacking of gears echoing when they hit each other. Sweat and pain wafted off them, but they kept going.

Weaving through the practice setups was Raleigh with a watchful eye. Gone was the fun, dense jock. He gave advice to one player who was hunched over, then went over plays with another. He had the most energy of them all, giving and giving. His stern eyes watched over the team. He was everywhere. Giving feedback, demonstrating how to block.

Raleigh followed the gaze of a football player who found me watching them. He immediately lit up, back to that fun Raleigh that I remembered from our date.

Fake date.

"Hey." He jogged over, a sliver of sweat trickling down the center of his chest. Sweat glistened on his face, making his eyes an impossible shade of blue. "Did you get lost?"

"No. School just ended. Practice already started?"

"I don't like to waste any time. Time is of the essence. The sooner we start, the sooner my guys can get home."

And start homework and eat and try to live a normal teenage life until they crash in bed.

Raleigh gripped a bleacher seat above him and leaned forward, inches from my face. His thick arms popped from his polo sleeve. "This is technically a closed practice. No spectators."

"Wow. Fancy stuff. You don't want people stealing play secrets?"

"That's a better reason than the real one. I don't want parents watching and second-guessing every coaching decision I make. Which does happen."

Fortunately, I didn't have to deal with parents like that in theater, probably because they didn't care that their kids were in plays. But I could only imagine how intense sports parents could be. Images of parents yelling at their four-year-old from the soccer sidelines during the one season of my life when I tried sports flashed in my mind.

Raleigh let out a weak laugh, the hell of stage parents (or whatever they were called in sports) all too real.

"Some parents can get really into it. I don't need my players to have that pressure."

I looked over his large shoulder. "You're working them hard."

"I have to. I gotta teach these boys to hit because life hits back."

"I'll go. I don't want to break the closed practice rules."

"That's okay. There's an exception for the coach's boyfriend."

"Fake boyfriend." Judging by the way Raleigh's gaze seemed to change, the blush had flourished on my cheeks. Fake boyfriend, I reminded myself. "And it's only for the wedding. We don't need to confuse people in school."

"Good call."

Was he really going to tell people that we were dating?

"Also, I asked my guys if anyone defaced your signup sheet. They all said no." Raleigh raised his eyebrows in a blatant "I told you so" bit of body language.

"They could be lying."

He shook his head no. "I have a very strong bullshit detector."

"Maybe you want to believe them."

"Ev, it's not as easy to lie to someone's face as you think. If my guys weren't telling the truth, I'd know. It wasn't them." He looked out on practice, and for a moment, the way the guys excitedly chatted with each other between drills reminded me of my drama students.

Raleigh shot me a refrain of his "I told you so" eyebrow raise, but there was something sincere underneath.

"Okay. Then the search for the real culprit continues." Before I could run through a new list of suspects, something on the field caught my attention.

"What is that?" I asked, pointing at the pads the players were willingly running into.

"That's a blocking sled."

"A blocking sled?"

"Yep. Santa isn't the only dude with a sled. Four pads are connected by a rail on the ground, and the sled can only move backward if all four players make a coordinated attack."

It looked like it cost more than my entire musical budget.

"You want to try something fun?" Raleigh asked, a tempting grin on his lips.

"What?"

"You want to ride the sled?"

"That's not a euphemism for anything, correct?" I had to be sure since my mind was frequently going places it should not.

He took my hand and led me onto the field, where the boys awkwardly nodded at me. Raleigh stepped onto the small platform on the back of the sled, then pulled me up to join him.

It was like being on a stage about to be rushed.

"What are we doing?" A bunch of jocks with devious smiles were prepared to run at me. My nerd senses tingled.

"Do you trust me?" Raleigh asked.

I squeezed his hand. Hard.

Raleigh gave the call, and his players charged at the pads, a line of young men with carnage in their eyes.

We flew back across the field, wind surging through my hair, the laws of time and physics pausing just for us. This was like a steroid-infused version of that "I'm flying, Jack!" scene in *Titanic*. It was only scary for a second, then it became an absolute rush, like horizontal bungee jumping. I leaned into Raleigh's shoulder for support, screaming and laughing with complete abandon.

"Nice job, men!" Raleigh blew his whistle, and the players went back to being chill teenagers, as if their rage could be turned on and off like a faucet.

"You okay?" Raleigh asked as I dug my fingernails from his palm.

"Yeah. That was...your players have a lot of spunk."

Raleigh took me by the hips and helped me dismount, something I could've done by myself, but I didn't mind his firm touch. I let myself gaze into his eyes, the rush of quasi-flying lingering in my lungs.

"So what was it you wanted to tell me?" he asked.

It took me a moment to recall why I came here in the first place.

"Our plan is working." I showed him the posts on my phone. "Look at all those likes. People like us."

"Nice."

"One person in particular." I scrolled to Noah's comment.

"Cute couple," he read flatly, like he was rattling off letters on an eye chart.

"Noah has never commented on one of my posts. Even when we were dating, he didn't. He claimed he wasn't active on social media."

"Seems active now. Damn, he and his boyfriend really are twins." Raleigh rolled his eyes as he scanned through their videos. "They went thrifting for Halloween costumes? I hate those videos. Some people have to shop at thrift stores for their clothes."

I remembered those days of going with my parents to the thrift shop for clothes. Noah grew up in the bougie suburbs of Westchester; it wasn't his fault for not knowing.

"We're getting away from the point. He thinks we're a cute couple! That means we're on his radar."

"Yippee," he said with none of the enthusiasm the word entails.

"We're going to look so good at this wedding. He's going to regret breaking up with me."

"Is that what you're hoping for? Getting back with him?"

It was something that had flitted in the back of my mind, and Raleigh brought it to the forefront. What was the goal here? To show Noah that I was better off without him, or that we'd be better off together? What did I want?

"I don't know. Anything's possible." I kept it vague since I didn't have an answer, just like I didn't have a good answer for why I needed to travel to the football field to tell Raleigh about the Instagram post rather than texting him.

The light on Raleigh's face dimmed as he craned his neck back to his team. "I gotta get back to practice."

"Yeah. I totally get that. Didn't mean to interrupt."

"And of course we're a cute couple. I'm half of it," he said with a sarcastic grin.

Vomit. Did his ego know no bounds? And did I have to find him so freaking charming?

"What are you doing Sunday?" He walked backward back to the field.

"Grocery shopping."

"Nope. You're coming with me to watch the Sunday NFL game at a sports bar."

"What? Pass."

"No passing allowed unless you're the QB. I'm half of this fake relationship, and I deserve to have a say in what we do."

"Raleigh..."

"What if your friends ask us what we do as a couple? Is it only going to plays and talking about theater?"

That was the dream. "You know I don't like football."

"Then why are you dating a football coach?"

Ugh, I hated his sound logic.

"Fine. One game. But if I'm about to die of boredom, I get to leave at intermission."

"Halftime."

"Whatever."

13

EVERETT

Hell was a sports bar.

I knew there were gay guys out there who would be unbelievably turned on in this setting. Packed to the brim with testosterone. Men all around, yelling and aggressive, and in their wildest dreams, ready to gangbang the lone gay guy in the bathroom before going home to their wives. It was like a Roman bathhouse but with wall-to-wall TVs.

It was a hard pass from me.

Sure, I was a tolerant person and put up with straight guys in society. It wasn't their fault they were hetero. They were born that way, and we should value people no matter who they chose to love. But I didn't want to spend an afternoon with them.

The game didn't start for forty-five minutes, but already the place was packed.

Raleigh pushed through the crowd and secured us a high-top table. I stared up at the wall of TV's mounted above the bar.

"I didn't know Stone's Throw Tavern used those TV's for sports. I thought it was just for airing musical clips."

Stone's Throw Tavern had a much different atmosphere today

than on Musical Mondays. I'd never been here on a Sunday, and I understood why. The crowd was like the upside down version of the people who showed up for LGBTQ+ night. Instead of tight pants, there was a sea of baggy jeans. Instead of fitted T's and polos, there were boxy T-shirts and sweatshirts with the NFL team logo.

At least there was one familiar face. Charlie gave me a cock-eyed look from his and Mitch's office in the loft space above the bar. He pointed me out to Mitch, his hulking bear of a husband, who was just as confused by my presence.

I made a finger gun, pressed it under my chin, and pulled the imaginary trigger. Raleigh looked back at me, and I pretended I was scratching my peach fuzz.

"You doing okay, Ev?"

"I'm happier than a pig in shit. Speaking of, have straight guys not heard of deodorant?" I was grateful for the stench of stale beer to cover up the other stench.

"You don't know if all of them are straight. Weren't they at Musical Mondays the other night?" He nodded at a quartet of bearish guys huddled around a neighboring high-top, who only a week ago were singing songs from *Dreamgirls* into their beer bottles. "There are lots of football fans from all across the queer spectrum."

So maybe Raleigh was right, or at least, not completely wrong. Didn't change the fact I was stuck here for who knew how long.

"Don't be so close-minded," he said with a teasing smile, though in this case, maybe he was right.

"Hey guys!" Charlie came over with Mitch behind him. He clapped me on the back, getting lots of enjoyment out of seeing me here. "Everett, this is truly a surprise."

"I love sports," I deadpanned.

"You once called sports theater for people missing brain cells."

The bears at the next table over glanced our way.

"I was drunk when I said that," I explained to the bears and to Charlie. "I'm here to support my friend Raleigh."

"Another thing I never thought I'd hear you say." Charlie was supposed to be sweet. He was having a helluva time at my expense.

Raleigh got between us, did the arm wrestle clasp to back pat thing with Charlie that bro-y guys had an instinct for. He then shook Mitch's hand the normal way, because Mitch was older and didn't put up with shit like that.

"I wanted to show Ev that football is an exciting, entertaining game. Open his mind like he did by taking me to see a play."

Raleigh sounded genuine, taking me by surprise. I had wondered why he wanted me to watch a football game. Was it revenge for the play? Another way to get under my skin? But maybe it was more genuine than that.

I would be a good sport, no pun intended.

"I'm ready for it. I can take watching sports for an hour."

"An hour? You're leaving early?" Charlie asked.

"The game's only an hour. I looked it up online. There are four quarters of game time, fifteen minutes apiece."

Silence befell our small circle. Looks were exchanged between Raleigh and Charlie, and Charlie and Mitch. I was the monkey in the middle.

"I looked it up. That's what the internet said." I turned to Raleigh, almost frantic. "Did I look up the wrong sport?"

"There's an hour of pure game play, but the clock stops whenever the ball goes out of bounds. Or there's a time out." Raleigh spoke hesitantly, like he was stepping through a minefield.

"How often does that happen?"

"A lot," Mitch said, never one to mince words. "Games last about three to four hours."

"What? How is that possible? That literally defies the physics of time."

"Nice! Here come the cheerleaders," said a guy in a backwards cap behind us. On screen, a dozen grown women in scantily-clad outfits and sparkly pom-poms danced and writhed for the home team. Someone in the back of the bar catcalled them.

I was officially in hell. Put here by Raleigh, who brought me along to...what exactly?

"We're gonna continue to mingle. Relax, Everett!" Charlie patted me on the back.

"Pray there's no overtime," Mitch whispered to me then followed his husband.

"Overtime? You mean there could be more game?"

Sensing my tension, Raleigh pressed a firm hand on my shoulder. "It's going to be okay. I promise. I think you'll have fun. Even if I'm not a fan of either team, I always have a good time watching a game." The sparkle in his eye made the heterosexual prison around us disappear for a moment, letting me believe him.

Lots of people enjoyed watching sports. Perhaps they were onto something.

And if not, at least there were food and drinks here.

I pressed my hand around Raleigh's thick upper arm. His muscles tightened under my touch. Was he flexing? "Okay. Let's give it a whirl."

"You won't be sorry. I'll get us some drinks. Your usual?"

Vodka and sprite. He remembered. I nodded yes.

"I'll order us some apps, too. What apps do you like?" he asked.

"I love bruschetta."

"I don't think they have it on the menu."

"They do." I'd been here enough times to have the menu practically memorized. I pointed to it under the pretzel with beer cheese option.

"Cool. What about chips and guac?"

"I love guac!"

"Hell yeah. I love guac, too. We won't get the salsa, though, since it has cilantro."

"You don't eat cilantro either?" I asked. I was one of the unfortunate people who thought it tasted like soap.

"I do, but I know how much you hate it. At the faculty pot luck last spring, you couldn't eat the tacos because Barb Healy sprinkled cilantro over the meat."

"She knew that I hated cilantro. I considered it an act of violence." Rather than make a scene, I played the good sport and stuck to Chase's lentil chili.

"I'm jealous. I thought I was the only one you were feuding with."

"Sadly, no." Barb couldn't banter like Raleigh. Nor was she hot enough to put up with. "Wait, how did you know that I hated cilantro? Did one of my friends tell you?"

Raleigh shrugged and focused on the menu. "I just remember you saying something."

His listening skills were uncanny. CIA-worthy. I felt bad that I didn't have that type of memory when it came to him. My listening skills needed to be better tuned.

We poured over the menu that lived under the spill-proof plastic liner covering the table.

"What about that pretzel and beer cheese?" he asked. "I love a soft pretzel. Whenever I go into Manhattan, I still get one from Central Park, even though they're totally a rip-off."

"Yes. I am in love with soft pretzels, but I'm not a fan of beer cheese."

"It also comes with a honey mustard dip."

"Honey mustard rules." My stomach was doing backflips at the food coming our way. "Are we getting too much?"

"Nah. We'll be here a while."

"Oh. Right." Three to four hours. Or more if there was overtime. Four hours with Raleigh didn't sound like hell, though.

"When we're at the wedding, I'll know what you like and don't like."

And something told me Raleigh would remember. I watched him fade into the crush of bodies at the bar.

I made a note in my phone. *Raleigh: likes nachos, soft pretzels, beer cheese.*

What beer did he drink? I was slipping as a fake boyfriend.

My phone screen was taken over by incoming texts from the group chat.

Amos: How's the football game? Charlie said he saw you there.

Everett: Did you know they can be up to four hours long?

Julian: Hopefully there's no overtime.

Everett: Barf. That's what Mitch said.

Everett: I'm here with Raleigh. On a fake date.

Chase: You two go on a lot of fake dates.

Amos: [gif of guy pointing up and saying THIS]

I grumbled at my phone. Damn my friends for being so observant. To the outsider, things looked blurry. But I knew where we stood. This was all preparation for the wedding. Raleigh wasn't into me like that, and I wasn't either. Neither of us wanted real boyfriends.

Please, if we were actual boyfriends, I'd have to attend these football games on a regular basis.

"One vodka and Sprite." He slid my drink onto the table, then pressed that hand into my lower back as he hopped onto his stool. Was that a move? It had the suave coordination of a move. His cool hand sent a fluttery chill up my spine.

"So tell me again why you wanted me to watch a football game with you?"

As in, I just want to confirm that this isn't a date, and that what I'm thinking in my head has no connection to reality.

"It'll help with the charade. Since we're fake dating, we should each know a little about what the other person's into. Otherwise, this is a one-sided fake relationship."

"Makes sense." Unlike the rules of football.

On the wall of screens was the pomp and circumstance before the game. Bulky guys who looked constrained by their sport jackets waxed poetic on the players' stats.

Natasha, the other assistant manager of Stone's Throw who always had an opinion, came over with our apps. "We've got bruschetta, chips and guac, and a pretzel with beer cheese and mustard."

She raised her eyebrows at me as if to say *get it*. I shook my head no. Her eyebrows then said *really?*

"So fill me in. What's going on? Are these men gossiping about the players?" I waved my hand at the talking head on screen.

"They're former football players who give commentary, not gossip."

"What's the difference?"

"Less sass." Raleigh gave me the rundown on each commentator, information that went in one ear and promptly scooted out the other. "They're setting the stakes for today's game. The Wolves, that's our team, is lower ranked, and they're facing the Leopards, the top team in the division."

"Are all football teams named after vicious animal predators?"

"Most. The Leopards have the best offense, but the Wolves' defense can't be discounted."

"Who's that?" A headshot of a guy with an overgrown beard and stern scowl flashed on screen next to a jumble of numbers. He made Mitch look polished and clean cut by comparison.

"Matt Rivers. He used to be the Wolves' quarterback."

The camera cut to a shot of him warming up with his teammates, who all had matching overgrown beards.

"Why do all the cast members—"

"...Players..."

"—have mountain man beards? Are they going for a Viking aesthetic?"

"It's superstition. They don't shave until the season's over."

"When's that?"

"If they go all the way, early February."

Ick. I was not into the bearded look. I preferred my men clean shaven, like Raleigh.

Just as an example.

"Beards are a no for me."

"Too bad. I was planning on growing a handlebar mustache. Or not," he said off my grossed-out reaction.

"Unless you're secretly a 1970's porn star, I'd refrain from the handlebar."

Though it might be fun to ride on that handlebar.

Or not.

Or not!

"You'd look good with one." Raleigh said. His eyes on me made me gulp back a lump.

"I didn't shave during a grueling rehearsal for a play in college. My facial hair comes in all rusty."

Raleigh's eyebrows jumped, intrigued. "That'd be hot."

My unrusted cheeks burned red. Raleigh stared at me for a good, long moment. Picturing what exactly? The burning didn't stop.

He cleared his throat, pulling his gaze back to the TV. "Uh, anyway. Rivers was at the bottom of the draft when the Wolves signed him. At the time, it was seen as a dumb move, but it paid off. They saw the potential in him. But once the rest of the league saw it, the Leopards offered him more money."

"He stabbed us in the back."

"Big time."

"So really, this is a story about underdogs and revenge." My flair for drama went to work. "We're the underdogs, and our trusted leader left us. This is our chance to show him and the whole world that we won't go down without a fight. Am I on the right track?"

"Actually...yeah."

"I take it there are no soliloquies that give us better insight into Rivers' internal monologue?"

"I don't know what those are, but I'm going to say no. The cameras get real good close-ups of his face, though."

"SoliloQBs," I said. "Soliloquies for quarterbacks."

Did I just create a corny portmanteau? Raleigh had officially infected my brain.

"Nice." He smiled at me, very pleased and looking as cool as a beach sunset.

The game started with a coin toss, a very undramatic opening scene. Soon, the ball was kicked. Then it was thrown and sometimes caught, sometimes not. I tried to stay invested, but the drama wasn't there.

I couldn't tell what was happening on screen. I didn't know if a good thing happened for the Wolves until everyone in the bar cheered or booed. They were vocal, though. When I went to sip my drink or bite into an app, I'd be startled by the noise of the patrons. Why were people yelling so much? Nobody could hear them on the field. And unlike in a play, the players didn't stop what they were doing to pause for the applause.

I pretended to be engaged, but my eyes fought to stay open. I thought about other things I could be doing. I scrolled down social media. Noah and Gavin had posted a video pumpkin picking and carving. They carved the same things into their pumpkins. Did Noah choose and make Gavin go along? I had a memory of how stringent Noah took Halloween, forcing us to get matching costumes, even though it was way out of my budget. He let out a passive-aggressive sigh when I told him that I could have a fancy costume or lunch for the week. According to him, I was being melodramatic.

Raleigh nudged me in the side. "What do you think? It's a good game."

"Oh. Yeah. Right. I'm riveted." I tried to sound genuine.

"If you're still bored by halftime, we can go."

"No, that's okay. I am here with you. You went to see a play. I can sit through one football game. But just out of curiosity, how much longer until halftime?"

"There's eight minutes left in the second quarter so...forty-five minutes?"

I bit back a groan. I would swallow my dislike for one afternoon. Raleigh had put in a lot of effort for this fake boyfriend gambit—a lot more than I expected from him. This was the absolute least I could do.

And the apps were good.

And I could order more to drink.

So I went up to the bar and did. "One vodka and Sprite," I said to Mitch, who was taking his turn behind the bar. His flannel shirt matched the colors of the home team.

"You're the only person I know who drinks this. And I've served a lot of customers."

"I like what I like. How's grandpa life?" I asked him. Mitch's daughter Ellie was good friends with Amos, and she had an adorable baby boy last year. Kids were not in my future. Pass on that. But I was happy for everyone else to have their germ-infested rugrats.

"He's keeping us busy. I go over there Sunday mornings. He started crawling." Mitch maintained his stoic expression, but the light in his eyes was undeniable.

"The best part of grandkids is if they ever get to be too much, you can hand them back to their parents." My parents loved doing this with my siblings' kids. As did I. I was fun Uncle Everett only up to a point.

"Charlie's great with him." A wistful tone took over Mitch's voice. "He'd be a great dad."

I wondered if that ship had sailed. Mitch was only in his early forties.

Mitch garnished my drink with mint. It was made with care. "Does your boyfriend want another beer?"

"Yeah. Might as well." My brain snapped to attention. "He's not my boyfriend. We're colleagues. Friends-ish."

"I smell bullshit." Natasha came up next to me to put in an order. All of her meals came with a free, unwanted opinion.

"What you smell is beer, greasy food, and sweaty patrons."

"I know what I saw." Natasha smiled to herself.

Jesus, was the whole freaking world intent on giving Raleigh and I shit for our fake relationship today?

"I serve a lot of people. Couples. People on first dates. People on second dates. People who've been together for years. People who are on the verge of breaking up."

"And your point?"

"If you and him are faking it, then you're doing a fucking A-plus job." She examined me closer. "Or maybe the fucking hasn't happened yet."

"Goodbye, Natasha." I took my drink and Raleigh's beer and scurried to the high-top as fast as I could maneuver through the rowdy crowd.

Raleigh's eyes were fixated on screen. The crowd got to their feet, yelling and cheering at the screen.

"What happened?" I asked.

"We intercepted a pass and ran it back for a touchdown. We've tied the game."

"Did Rivers throw the pass?"

"Yep. It was intercepted by Dwight Lincoln, who started on the team the same year as him."

"His former friend using his weaknesses against him."

"Exactly. This was supposed to be an easy victory for the Leopards. Rivers is panicking. You can see it on his face and in his sloppy passes."

He was right. The camera cut to a close up of him coming out of a huddle, and any actor could tell the noticeable signs of fear. He called the next play, and while I was no football expert, I could see the hesitation before passing. He looked left, then right. His pass was way off where his scene partner could catch it.

"That was a sloppy pass! It looked like he was trying to change his mind at the last minute."

"You're spot on, Ev."

I was spot on. My insides did a little end zone dance.

Raleigh slid a hand across my lower back as he reached for his beer.

"Practicing for the wedding," he said at my eyes following his hand.

"Good call." We had to get down these little touches so we seemed like a real couple. Still, my breath hitched at his firm touch.

There were ten seconds left in the second quarter. Time was remarkably fleeting in football.

Raleigh leaned in, his hand still at my side. "The Leopards need to decide if they're going to have Rivers go for a touchdown, or if they're going to bring in a kicker to get the field goal for three points."

"If the coach chooses the kicker, it'll be a blow to Rivers."

Raleigh nodded. "See? You're catching on." He winked at me. How dare my body have any positive reaction to that.

"Oh crap!" I exclaimed as the coach called in the kicker. Rivers tried to stay stoic, but as someone who'd been cut from productions, I knew the look of frustration as he put on a brave face.

Stone's Throw went wild.

"Rivers could be the tragic figure of today's game. He was at the top of his game, but he couldn't escape the guilt of leaving his former team. They were back not for revenge, but to show him and the world that they could survive and thrive on their own. The world might've cast them aside, but they weren't going down without a fight. Damn, I really wish there were soliloQBs because Rivers could go off."

Raleigh laughed and kept looking at me, that kind of looking that soaks a person in. His hand ran up my back and gave my shoulder a squeeze. "Do you still hate football?"

I pressed my forehead against his. It took two people to fake tango. "We still have halftime and two quarters left. Ask me when it's over."

———

ONE HALFTIME and almost two quarters later, I was...a fan of a compelling drama.

"Come on! We can hold 'em!" I shouted at the TV. Not that I expected them to hear me, but maybe if enough people yelled at their TVs, the players could. My heart raced and every synapse in my body fired on full focus.

"We can do this, right?" I turned to Raleigh. The Wolves were up by three points. The Leopards were four yards away from a touchdown, which would give them the lead and victory. We could hold them back at the four-yard line, couldn't we?

"The Wolves have got this." He nodded intently, his confident chin jutting out. I used to find it cocky, but today it was reassuring.

"Do they? This is the do-or-die moment for Rivers. Will he

succeed and live up to his destiny, or will he succumb to hubris? Will the underdogs triumph?"

"Are you sure you've never been a sports fan? Because you sure do love the underdog." He ran his thick hand through my hair, playfully messing it up, something he'd been doing throughout the game. It was all part of building our ruse. Hair tussles and shoulder squeezes and lingering looks. Judging by the occasional stiffness in my pants, I didn't mind it.

I shushed him before he could make another remark about my sudden interest in this compelling drama which just so happened to take place on a football field. It was time for the first down.

The bar went silent, but you could tell they were poised to explode with noise. It was the moment a pin pushed into a balloon right before it popped.

The player positioned for doggie style hiked the ball to Rivers. He searched for an opening. I couldn't see his eyes, but I knew what they were communicating. The pressure. The stakes.

Drama!

He found a player open in the left corner pocket of the end zone. He tossed a line drive that zoomed over the players' heads. The receiving player jumped up to catch it. The ball danced on his fingertips before landing on the ground.

The bar shook with noise. I made...I don't know what sound I made. Some kind of primal yell. Mostly to expel tension.

I looked back at Raleigh. I wanted his reaction.

"That was close," he said.

My heart was beating like crazy. If the player had jumped up another half inch, he would've caught it and game over. Fate had other plans.

Raleigh got behind me and massaged my shoulders hard, his strong palms grinding in my soft tissue. "This is what I do to stay relaxed."

"Yeah, that's cool." The excitement of the game mixed with the caress of his hands made me both anxious and euphoric.

He draped his hands over my shoulders and rested his chin on my hair. Our heads were like a totem pole. He smelled fucking amazing, musky cologne and fruity shampoo with a hidden layer of fresh soap.

But first: second down.

Doggie style guy snapped the ball to Rivers. He searched and searched amid the crush of bodies. How were quarterbacks able to decipher what was going on in the field? They only had a few seconds to suss out a path in the chaos. I was officially impressed.

Rivers took too long to find a pocket. He tried to run through the mash, but was tackled at the two-yard line.

The crowd had a muted reaction, unsure what to make of the development. The Leopards moved forward, but they weren't at the end zone yet.

"Shit," I said. "They're at the two yard line. Rivers could power into the end zone on sheer will."

"Not if our guys stop 'em."

My heart couldn't take it. There were twelve seconds left in the game. An eternity! Everything was riding on these twelve seconds. Team fortunes. Narratives. Careers.

"He's got one more down. Then the coach is going to bring in the kicker to tie the game and take us into overtime."

"Is that what you would do?" I asked him.

"Yeah. Rivers wants the fourth down to himself for the glory, but he knows what's up."

"How did you stay focused and make these snap decisions one after the other? I would shit my pants."

"How do you memorize all those lines yet say them so convincingly as an actor? I would shit my pants." The vibrations of his laughter rolled down my spine.

"He can try and win in overtime."

The notion of overtime didn't sound like a bummer anymore. It was higher stakes drama.

"Go back to massaging my shoulders," I ordered my fake boyfriend.

"You got it."

I rolled my neck to iron out the tension. Raleigh had the magic touch. The back of my head brushed against his solid chest, taut with muscle. I was already one kind of excited. I didn't need the other.

"Here we go," he said.

I sat up straight and watched the teams get in formation. Each word out of Rivers' mouth dragged, but eventually the ball was hiked.

He searched for an opening. Thick knots of players crowded his vision. His hand was locked, ready to pass to someone. Anyone. The clock was ticking. My throat went dry, as each second crawled.

Rivers wasted too much time. Our tackle pushed back the wall of players surrounding Rivers and sacked him. The quarterback tumbled to the ground.

Every person in Stone's Throw leapt to their feet and cheered until the walls shook.

Raleigh squeezed my shoulders and shook me. The bar erupted into pandemonium.

"Take that, Rivers!" I yelled at the screens.

"Fuck yeah!" The bear next to us gave me a hi-five so hard my fingers nearly snapped off.

Rivers left the field, head down. The kicker ran out to the field. The tension in the bar eased up. The kicker would get the three-point field goal and bring us into overtime where there was potentially an extra ten minutes of gametime.

I kicked back the rest of my vodka and Sprite. Raleigh dipped the final piece of pretzel into the beer cheese then his mouth.

"Did you want to leave after this?" he asked.

"Not before the game is over. I'm too emotionally invested!"

The teams lined up. The ball was snapped to the kicker, lined up perfectly. His leg swooshed in the air like a Rockette.

The football sailed through the blue sky and...

HIT THE GOALPOST.

It tapped the metal and flung to the side.

My heart literally stopped beating.

It took the whole bar a second to process what had happened and then...earthquake.

Stone's Throw rattled with ear-splitting screams. Absolute screams of relief and shock and victory.

"Holy fucking shit." I clapped a hand over my mouth.

"We won!!" Raleigh yelled. "We won!"

"Holy fucking shit. We won!"

I spun around on my stool to join in Raleigh's shocked excitement. I thought we'd go for hi-fives. I didn't expect him to kiss me.

My mouth flooded with heat and the lingering taste of beer cheese as he pulled me close. His lips were assured and just as confident as him.

I had *never* been kissed like that. I thought kisses like that only happened on the cover of my mom's romance novels.

Raleigh's eyes bugged open, a pair of pale blue dots eclipsed by blown pupils, likely matching my reaction. We stared at each other in stunned silence, the crowd roaring around us.

Holy fucking shit.

14

RALEIGH

I wasn't sure what was going through Everett's mind, but all I could think was "Holy fucking shit."

That was one thousand percent unplanned.

But holy fucking shit.

Being a proud wholesexual, I'd kissed men, women, and non-binary folks. Yet none of those past lip-locks could hold a candle to the heat of Everett's mouth. His lips were a little bit salty and a little bit chapped. Probably from his nonstop talking.

In the Fast & Furious movies, characters will hit the NOS (nitrous oxide) button to give their cars a surge of power and pretty much make them fly.

Everett's mouth was my NOS button.

Unfortunately, the moment had passed because he blinked at me like a queer deer in the headlights. His cheeks were a deep crimson shade I'd never seen before, and his pupils were ablaze. I couldn't tell if he was horrified or hungry for more.

"That was a good game," I said. "We won."

I pointed at the row of TVs, where the Wolves congregated on the field, and Lincoln was being interviewed by a reporter. He seemed uncomfortable having to speak in complete sentences, when it was so obvious he wanted to go wild and celebrate.

Same, pal. Hard same.

The energy in the bar calmed down. People closed their tabs and drained the last of their beers.

"What happens after the game is over? Is there an afterparty?" Everett looked at me for a second before turning his attention to the TV.

I watched the TV too. Eye contact felt...weird.

"No afterparty. People usually go home. At certain bars, after a victory, it becomes an all-out party."

"I'm not really feeling an all-out party." Everett rubbed his neck. "It's a school night."

"Yeah. I should get you home." My breath hitched in my throat. I did not mean for that to be loaded with sexual innuendo.

Everett's neck was a bright red usually reserved for the most severe sunburns.

———

IN THE CAR, there was dead silence.

I kept my eyes on the road and tried not thinking about Everett and that kiss and other things I wanted to do to build on the foundation of that kiss.

Being around him made me wired in a good way. I loved getting a rise out of him, yet this was a whole new reaction. He was nervous and subdued. Did I break Everett?

I pulled the car up to his apartment building and faced him. It'd be weird if we didn't look at each other at all. And selfishly, I really wanted to look at him.

"So, we're still on for Operation: Wedding this weekend?" I snaked a hand around the back of his headrest.

"Yep. We can leave straight from school. It's a bit of a drive, but I'll, um, I'll download a podcast or an audiobook or something."

"That's cool. Whatever."

"Cool. It's going to be great." Everett licked his bottom lip, sending a hot shiver up my back. "And you know, it was good that this happened. It's a crucial element of a fake relationship. I mean, how strange would it be if you kissed me at the wedding, and I freaked out?"

"For the record, are you freaking out here?"

"No. No, it was good. I'm loath to feed your ego, but...it was good. And, you know, it was unplanned."

"Very unplanned," I said.

"If it was any more unplanned, it'd be a teen pregnancy."

I snorted. Even in the middle of an awkward situation, Everett could make me laugh.

"So now we know what it's like to kiss each other." Everett smiled through his blushing. "And I hate how red my face is probably getting. You're loving this."

"I think you're a good kisser, too."

"You surprised me, so I didn't have time to prepare and get into the right headspace for a kiss."

"Well, you did a good job. A really good job."

All this awkward talking around things was making me oddly horny. It was like verbal foreplay. Could he see me getting hard? I'd have one epic jerk off session when I got home.

"I should go. Into my apartment." He pointed to his building, just in case I'd forgotten that we were outside of it.

I found myself leaning closer to him. He did the same.

"Cool. I'll see you tomorrow," I said.

"You, too."

I didn't know who leaned in for the kiss first, but it didn't fucking matter. We were making out. Hardcore making out. If we made out like this at Stone's Throw, we'd get kicked out.

I couldn't catch my breath. My fingers slid through his hair and pulled him close. The more I had of him, the more I wanted. Everett made the sexiest moan against my lips.

He climbed over the console. His ass bashed against my car horn, which honked extra loud.

"Shit!" He fell back into his seat. "Sorry."

"That wasn't me. That was the steering wheel. Come back here," I growled.

I moved my seat back so Everett could straddle me. I slapped my hands on his thighs and squeezed. I pulled him down by the shirt with one hand, and slinked my other hand up his back, palm pressing against hot flesh. He had no objections. He writhed against my crotch, knowing exactly what he was doing.

"Is this also part of our practice?" I asked, my kink for giving him shit still alive and kicking. "Just in case we find ourselves making out in front of your ex-boyfriend, we should know what we're doing."

"Oh, Raleigh. I have no idea what the fuck I'm doing." His red, swollen lips hovered over mine. Rust-colored hair fell in his eyes.

"There's only so much we can accomplish in a two-door car."

"If I invite you up..." Everett kissed along my jawline, making me hiss with barely contained lust. "Then we need to be clear about one thing: this is hate sex. Because I'm still not sure if I like you."

Fuck. I was here for hate sex. Where was the sign-up sheet?

"Total hate sex," I said.

"No feelings."

"Except hate." To be clear, hate had no place in the world– except in this car.

"Let's get inside," Everett said through hungry breaths. "Because I really want to hate fuck you and hate swallow your come."

Unnhhhh. A dirty mouth on an uptight nerd was hotter than

the best porno. I wasn't going to make it to his apartment. I'd devour his stuck-up self on the stairwell.

I slid my hand from under his shirt and down the crack of his ass. He kissed me hard and bit my bottom lip.

"Ev, prepared to get hate fucked."

15

RALEIGH

Because I was a gentleman, I waited until we were inside Everett's apartment before I tore all his clothes off.

I politely nodded at the young couple living underneath him who we passed on the stairs. I hoped their ceiling was reinforced and soundproofed.

Once Everett shut the front door behind us, I was on him like the defense was on Rivers. He wrapped his legs around my waist as my tongue dipped into his mouth.

I needed him, needed his air inside my lungs, needed his skin on mine, needed my cock enveloped in his mouth.

I pulled him off me and drank in the sight of him. I couldn't wait to fold his body like a pretzel. He was long and lean, his creamy skin glowing with heat, and his eyes...fuck. They were a forest fire, sizzling and unrelenting. Smokey the Bear was shook.

Everett began unbuttoning his shirt, but I stopped him.

"I want to undress you," I said.

"I know how to take off my own clothes."

"It's something I like to do. It turns me on." My voice trembled.

It was nerve-wracking sharing my turn-ons, even scarier than doing it.

A curious smile cracked his lips. "What turns you on about it?"

"It's like unwrapping a gift. I get to discover the mystery of what's underneath one piece of clothing at a time." I snaked a finger down his chest. "I get to be the one who strips you, button by button, until you're all mine. Is that weird?"

"It's the weirdest thing about you. I like it."

He took my hand and brought it to his shirt's top button.

His bottom lip trembled. There was no snarky answer to be found, just a head nod tight with want.

I unbuttoned his plaid shirt, fighting between the urge to get him naked ASAP and taking my time to savor this moment. We only had one chance to see someone naked for the first time.

My fingertips danced in his open shirt, sliding over his smooth skin, as I continued my way down to his waist. Everett rolled his head back, letting out soothing moans.

I pushed his shirt off, watching it slide off his arms, revealing his beautiful chest. He was naturally thin, with God's intended definition. The dips and curves of someone who had been scrawny but began to fill out as an adult. Not one of these jacked guys (like me) with severe ridges of abs and pecs.

I kissed each pink nipple. His fresh scent of cologne, detergent, and the lingering smell of the bar flitted up my nose and put a big smile on my face.

"Raleigh," he cried out.

"What is it?"

"Sorry. Keep going. I still hate you, but keep going."

I planted a soft kiss on his lips. This wasn't the animalistic hate sex he probably had in mind, but that would come in a little bit.

I flicked open the button of his jeans and slid down the zipper. I pushed the denim to his ankles, savoring his pale white thighs, his legs dusted with a fine coating of rust-colored hair, which got darker on the shins. I kissed the tender light skin of his inner thighs.

Everett had on a pair of white boxer briefs, which thanks to his obvious excitement, left nothing to the imagination. I lifted each foot to remove the jeans, then each sock. Everett let out a tiny gasp as I dragged down his underwear, his hard cock flopping in the air, surrounded by a surprisingly neat patch of hair.

"You trim," I said.

"I like to be prepared."

I took a step back, drinking in the sight of this absolutely stunning man. Everett was vulnerable and sweet in this moment, his normal acidic shield gone with the rest of his clothes. A shy, hopeful grin creased his face that openly wondered if I liked what I saw.

Hell yes. And he was all mine. At least for the rest of the night.

"You're hot," I told him. "Really hot."

I wanted to tell him he was the most beautiful man I'd ever seen, but that didn't seem hate sex appropriate.

I fondled his dick and balls in my hand, pre-come slicking my fingers. I got on my knees and took him in my mouth.

His voice cracked with need. He grabbed onto the kitchen table behind him while I went to work. Damn, he tasted good, his salty musk mixing with bitter pre-come. I became insatiable, wanting him in the worst way. I deep-throated him, taking him in voracious gulps, fire and energy consuming me.

"Wait, wait." He pulled out.

"What is it?" I worried about this. I'd been with mostly women. Even though I was a guy, what if I sucked at giving head?

"Since we're sharing turn-ons, maybe I could share mine."

"Yeah." *Yes, yes, God yes, that would be amazing.*

"I like rubbing my dick on a guy's stubble or beard, or even if they're clean-shaven."

"What do you like about it?"

"I love the way it feels. Even with a guy who shaved, you can still feel the tiny pricks of his facial hair. And it's...manly. Swarthy. It reminds me that I'm hooking up with a guy, something I dreamed about doing all the years I was in the closet." He smacked a hand over his face. "I can't believe I'm telling you this. I've never told anyone this. And I'm stark naked while telling you."

"Well, you won't be the only one naked in a few seconds. And it's another weird thing about you. I like it." I liked every weird thing about Everett. I needed more weird in my life.

Blush crept across his cheeks. The best kind of red.

"Speaking of naked, you're still clothed. You're the one with the Thor-like body. Let's see it." Everett signaled with two fingers for me to get up and get in my birthday suit.

Yes, sir.

I wasn't one of those guys who was full of themselves, but I knew I had a good physique. I worked at it, hitting the gym regularly. How could I train my football players to get into shape, or preach physical education to South Rock students, if I didn't practice it myself?

Everett seemed to approve of what he saw. His cock twitched.

"I was never into muscled guys," he said. "But I'll have to make an exception here." He smoothed a hand over my pecs. I made them jump in response.

"They like you," I said.

"Of course you think your pecs are sentient." He rolled his eyes, which made my dick twitch with pleasure.

I hissed with lust as Everett's hand drifted over my abs, down my happy trail, and grabbed my throbbing cock.

"I really hate feeding your ego, but...damn, Raleigh."

"While I'm always a fan of compliments, I have a job to do." I got back on my knees and stroked Everett's rock-hard dick. I rubbed it on my cheeks, going back and forth as he requested, sliding it over my lips as it dragged across my stubble.

It drove Everett wild. He vibrated under my touch. He dug his fingers into my hair for balance, short breaths coming from above.

"Yes. God, yes," he panted.

His cock pulsed with desire. Its heaviness heated up my cheeks. I sunk it back into my mouth for a beat before returning it to my face. Everett grunted and shook.

"You're gonna make me come. Oh my God."

"Not yet." I stood up, every fiber of my body consumed with lust. Everett's grunts and groans and shaking combined with the taste of him made my head want to explode. Both heads. "There's still some hate sex to be had."

Everett's eyes were drunk and glassy. His mouth pouted with a vulnerability that hit my heart.

"Please tell me you have lube and condoms," I said.

"Bedroom."

I picked him up and carried him to said bedroom, a small room dominated by a bed, walls covered with framed posters of what I assumed were Broadway productions.

"You go to a lot of theater," I commented. I reached into his nightstand for supplies without putting him down. I didn't want to go a second without feeling the heat of his skin.

"These are all posters from shows I directed."

"You directed all of these?" I took in the sheer number of posters on the wall.

"I'll try not to direct our sex scene, but since this is hate sex," he said between kissing me. "I expect it to be rough."

We fell onto the bed and made out, our kisses quickly escalating into full-on sucking face. Our cocks grinded against each other. I wanted to be inside him so badly. I slapped his ass and let my finger drift down to his hole. Everett groaned against my lips. He lifted his leg to give me better access.

I played with his hole as much as I could with a dry finger. He hummed with delight. I loved all of his noises.

"Get on all fours."

His eyes blew wide open at the demand. He got into position on the bed, giving me a sweet view of that round, white ass. A faint trail of freckles dotted his skin. I gave his hole a warm-up lick before I slathered it with lube, spreading him with my thick fingers.

His ass lined up perfectly with my crotch, which didn't always happen with doggie style. It was meant to be. I got myself sheathed and slick.

"Ready?" I asked.

"Yeah. Give it to me."

"Because there's no going back. I'm about to ruin every other guy for you."

"God, you're one cocky shit." He turned around and shot me a glare that was both withering and hungry for more.

"Well, you can't spell cocky without—" I plunged inside his tightness, his warmth enveloping me and sending me straight to heaven. Imaginary confetti rained down on this fucking amazing feeling.

Everett cried out.

"You okay?"

"Yeah. Just a shock. Not that you need any more compliments but you're one of the bigger guys I've been with."

"Not the biggest?"

"Technically, no. I once hooked up with a guy who was huge, really huge, and we couldn't even have sex. It was too big. I felt bad for him. Tough life."

"I'm glad I passed your Goldilocks test." I slid back inside him, savoring the feel of him tightening around me, of his hot skin under my grip.

"I swear I'm not a size queen. But it was sheer physics. It wouldn't work."

"How are you still this chatty with a dick in your ass?"

"Natural born talent."

I laughed into his back. How was I laughing during sex? Sex with Tori was always deadly serious. It was like church. No talking and no taking the lord's name in vein. Even when we were trying to be rough and dirty, Everett turned this into a fuckload of fun.

I thrust my cock deep inside him, making his spine arch. That shut him up.

His voice cracked with a lusty moan, instantly turning the mood from fun to needy.

"You like that?" I grabbed his hair and spanked his ass.

"Uh huh."

I spanked him again as I delivered another wanton thrust. Fuck, I loved watching myself disappear inside his opening.

"Fuck me like you mean it, Raleigh."

I didn't need to be asked twice. I slammed my cock into his ass over and over. My hunger devoured me from the inside out. Everett was a craving I could never satisfy. There was no more chit chat, just the sounds of our bodies coming into contact and his bed trying to withstand the heat.

I fisted his hair – not easy with a guy – and pounded into him. His hole clenched around my cock, sending waves of ecstasy and heat coursing through my veins.

Everett sunk to the bed like a tired doggy, his body contorting into a triangle, ass up in the air. I slapped both cheeks hard, leaving red handprints on his creamy skin.

"Fuck, Raleigh. Give it to me. Give it to me," he murmured into the bed.

And I was. I was giving him all I got, tearing into him with pure fire. I cradled his balls. Pre-come dribbled onto my fist.

"I'm gonna come." The vice-like grip his hole had on my dick confirmed this.

I barreled to my climax. Usually, I could last longer, but the second I sunk inside Everett, I knew my stamina wasn't long for this world. I was on borrowed time.

Despite how freaking hot this position was, I wanted to see Everett's face when he came. I wanted to stare into his fiery eyes and watch him lose control.

I flipped Everett onto his back without leaving him. His chest was red and sweaty, his cheeks flushed. His wide pupils blazed with need, begging me to finish the job.

I gripped his cock with one hand, and one stroke later, he creamed across his chest and stomach. He seemed as shocked as I did that he blew so quickly.

I pulled out, ripped off my condom, and pretty much rained come on him. I hit everywhere from his neck to his trimmed bush. I'd been so busy with football, I realized I hadn't jerked off in a week. My swimmers were backlogged.

"Do you have a towel anywhere nearby?" I asked. I had an urge to cuddle with him, but we definitely needed to clean up first.

Everett flung his hand at the hallway. He couldn't string two words together. I took that as a compliment.

I found the bathroom and pulled two towels from the rack. I tossed one to him, and used the other to wipe myself off. Sex wasn't always pretty. It was more like a nature documentary than we wanted to admit. But there was a certain kind of intimacy and vulnerability in the cleanup.

Everett cleared his throat, and I knew a rationalization was coming.

"Well, we had to get that out of our system. People would be able to tell if a couple hadn't had sex."

"We need full authenticity." I wiped a streak of spooge that had landed below his armpit. "You missed a spot."

"Am I good?"

I examined his body for any other stray seed. I wiped a last bit off his shoulder.

"Wow. You really drenched me. I should've worn the poncho I got at Niagara Falls."

I dipped my head, feeling the heat on my cheeks. "Sorry about that."

"Don't be. I used to say guys like you were young, dumb, and full of come. At least one of those was true."

"You bring it out of me. Literally."

Were we talking this much about my ejaculation? Despite the awkward topic, I felt completely at ease. I couldn't remember being this comfortable with anyone after sex. With most of my past lovers, as soon as we came, we'd grab our phones and scroll through social media.

Everett gazed at me, fiddling a finger through the waves of my hair. I brought it to my mouth for a light kiss. The weird cloud that usually hung over sex drifted into our atmosphere.

"You're still a stupid jock."

"And you're still a theater snob."

We drifted into a hazy post-sex sleep. I woke up a little while later, just before midnight, with Everett nestled in the crook of my arm.

If I stayed in bed and fell back asleep, I wouldn't wake until morning. That would mean we spent the night together. Waking up next to Everett sounded like a dream, but it was a bridge too far for me. I didn't trust myself to spend the night with him and then go back to normal in the morning. There were some things I couldn't fake.

I got up, got dressed, tucked a blanket over him, and crept out without making a sound.

Before getting in my car, I stared up at his window, already nostalgic for tonight.

We were ready for this weekend. We would ace being a fake couple. All I needed to do was keep my real feelings out of it.

16

EVERETT

J ulian: It's wedding weekend!

Chase: Time to party with your fake boyfriend.

Amos: And shove it in your ex-boyfriend's bloated face!

Everett: Did you coordinate that?

Amos: We're just wishing you a good time. Nervous?

Everett: Honestly? Yeah.

Everett: What if this whole thing blows up in my face?

Chase: In theory, there's little to be nervous about. The possible scenarios we can extrapolate from this setup don't point to any kind of social ruin. At worst, Noah and your friends won't care about your new relationship, and things will continue status quo.

Amos: Using extrapolate in a group chat is grounds for excommunication.

Chase: How is extrapolate worse than excommunication?

Amos: No SAT words allowed, unless it's "banal" since it has anal in it.

Amos: Speaking of anal, excited to spend the weekend with Raleigh?

Everett: It'll be fine. We've practiced. We're ready to go on.

Everett: He's driving at the moment, but he just gave a thumbs up.

Julian: Have you two gone on any more dates? Excuse me. I mean non-dates?

Everett: As a matter of fact, no. We've been super busy this week. Have you and Seamus gone out for post-department meeting drinks again?

Julian: I didn't know it was Musical Monday!

Chase: Then again, if someone discovers that you and Raleigh are faking your relationship, then the embarrassment of that development could destroy your standing with your friends and lead to social ruin. So I guess you're right to be nervous.

Everett: Chase, I love you dearly, but don't make me shove a beaker down your throat.

Julian: That won't happen. You and Raleigh make a very believable couple. You have fake chemistry.

Amos: Very good fake chemistry.

Everett: We'll see what everyone thinks this weekend. I hope I haven't made a big mistake.

Julian: A mistake with the lie or with choosing Raleigh?

Chase: I'm not pointing out that fake chemistry isn't a thing. But I'm also not not pointing it out.

———

"IS EVERYTHING OKAY?" Raleigh asked from the driver's seat.

"Yeah." I slipped my phone into the center console cup holder.

"I've never seen anyone text so fast. Do your thumbs hurt?"

"No, grandpa." I did some quick hand stretches to stave off any potential cramping.

"Here, let me help." He took my hand without taking his eyes off the road and massaged small circles in the center of my palm. "How's that?"

I just discovered that my fucking hand is an erogenous zone.

"Good." I gently took it back and folded it in my lap. I could've had Raleigh massage my hand to orgasm, but I had to hold back. The wedding weekend hadn't even begun. I had to keep myself in check.

Raleigh insisted that he drive us to the wedding, which was taking place a few hours upstate near the gorges of Ithaca. He said he wanted to contribute, and that it would look more believable if he drove. My guess was that he just wanted to be in the driver's seat. He was a top through and through.

And what a very fine top he was.

My phone buzzed and rattled in the cupholder.

"Amos, Chase, and Julian are wishing us a fun, successful weekend." I turned my phone on silent. I didn't need my friends in my head, talking about Raleigh and fake chemistry.

If they knew that Raleigh and I had fucked, the phone would never stop buzzing.

Usually I was the guy who told everyone about my sexual exploits right after it happened. It made good group chat fodder. But even though I'd been thinking nonstop about Raleigh and our amazing adventures in hate sex all week, I couldn't bring myself to talk or text about it aloud.

Not to my friends.

Not to Raleigh.

Not to myself.

Because it was just combustive sex, spurred on by tension between two consenting adults. It was physical, chemical, animal. It wasn't emotional. Hell, Raleigh didn't even stay the night. He hit it and then subsequently quit it. It was fucking-with-a-capital-F, and I was totally cool with that.

Mostly totally cool.

It wasn't the kind of sex you were supposed to think about with a wistful feeling in your heart. I was supposed to dream about the hardcore fucking of it all, not in the way Raleigh made me laugh, or in the way he set my body on fire as he undressed me.

And so I wouldn't be talking about it. Though, unfortunately, that led to a car ride full of awkward silence.

"Did you want to listen to a podcast or something?" Raleigh asked. It was a sunny fall day, the colorful leaves crisp against the blue sky. He wore a tight white T-shirt with a quilted vest over it and aviator sunglasses that added a whole extra layer of hotness to him.

"It was a one-time thing," I blurted out.

An eyebrow quirked from the top of his sunglasses. And yet another layer of hotness was born.

"Is that the name of a podcast?" The corner of his lips perked into a cheeky smile. *Ugh, stop being sexy!*

"Should we talk about it?" I had to remember that Raleigh hadn't been involved in the ongoing conversation in my head.

"Did you want to talk about it?"

"I..." Damn him and his good questions. "Is it something that needs to be talked about? How are you feeling?"

I put it back on him. Let Raleigh navigate through this.

"I feel good."

What the fuck was I supposed to do with that? That answered *a* question, but not *the* question.

"It was a one-time thing," I reiterated. "A really great one-time thing, but a one-time thing. Shakespeare didn't write any sequels of his plays. He believed in one-and-done."

"What about *Richard III* and *Henry V*?"

"Those aren't sequels."

"Then why do they have numbers in their titles?"

"How are you name-dropping Shakespearean plays right now?"

"I skimmed Shakespeare's Wikipedia page in preparation for this weekend, to get better on your wavelength."

He did research for this weekend? He toed the line between genius and doofus better than anyone.

I pinched my arm to stop myself from going googly-eyed at him. This was a fake arrangement, and I couldn't distract myself from the goal of this weekend.

"One and done," I repeated. "Just so we're on the same page."

"Cool." And that was that.

Raleigh drove one-handed, letting his right arm drop to his lap, which drew my eyes to his crotch.

One. And. Done.

This wasn't Shakespeare in Lust, *Everett.*

"Can we pull over at this rest stop?" I pointed to the highway sign notifying drivers of a rest stop in one mile.

"You got it, Ev."

Had I mentioned that my heart did a little kiddie roller coaster loop when he called me Ev?

Like all public rest stops, this one was squat, kinda dirty, and hadn't been updated in a good forty years. It was as if the government had scored a deal on the most depressing shade of brown and tan. The dusty, creaky front door led to a small lobby with a vending machine that only took coins, a vestibule with brochures for local attractions, and entrances to the men's and women's restrooms.

"Are you following me?" I asked Raleigh en route to the bathroom.

"I gotta go, too."

"Fair enough."

I picked a urinal as far away from him as possible. It was the children's urinal, so I had to squat down to go. Pilates and pissing. It was not my most graceful moment.

We used the bathroom in silence. We washed our hands in

sinks as far apart from each other as possible. My sink had no hot water and the soap dispenser was crusted over with a decade's worth of film.

I used a hot air dispenser at the opposite end of the sinks. It was weak, like it was coughing on me. But at least the sounds of the hot air drowned out the silence. I wiped my hands on my pants.

We exited the bathroom like total strangers, Raleigh walking in front of me.

Everything was going fine. That was, until Raleigh spun around and pushed me against the vending machine. His mouth collided on mine, a rush of heat and intensity that threatened to melt all the expired candy bars behind me.

His big hands locked me in place, digging into my flesh like hooks.

"Just so you know, hearing you talk about how you don't want to talk about shit is a major fucking turn on." His pupils exploded wide in a surge of dark blue.

"And just so you know, watching you drive in your fucking yacht club wannabe sunglasses is equally a turn on. Where did you get your wardrobe? Eighties Movie Villains R' Us?" My fingers curled into his thick waves of blond hair. I couldn't catch my breath. My breath couldn't catch me.

"Since we're technically a couple this weekend, can we make an exception to our one-and-done rule?" He grinded against me, his cock hard and poking through his jeans.

"That's probably for the best. We need it to be believable. It'd be like method acting."

"What's that?"

"Doesn't matter. Just kiss me, Raleigh."

He did. Holy Fosse, did he kiss me. He thrust against my body, making the vending machine shake. I was two seconds from turning around and letting him take me doggie style while I stared at a row of Hershey bars.

"Ev, remember on Sunday night when you said you wanted to hate swallow my come?"

"Uh huh."

"That's been living in my head all week." His rough, lust-strained voice lived in mine.

"Like generations of gay men before us, I'm going to suck you dry in a rest stop bathroom stall."

———

THIRTY SECONDS LATER, and after almost tripping over the brochure stand, we made it to the bathroom stall at the far end, tucked away in the corner. I could kiss Raleigh forever. The man's lips were two sticks of dynamite. But we had business to attend to and a hotel room to check into.

Like Sir Walter Raleigh himself, this Raleigh laid down his quilted vest on the floor for my knees. His dick was on the verge of busting through his jeans.

Once I freed it, a smile overtook my lips. It was just as I remembered. Thick, cut, and ready for its closeup.

Raleigh let out an unabashedly loud moan when I took him in my mouth.

"Dude, we're in a public restroom," I whisper-yelled.

"It's empty."

"For now."

"Better get to work then." His lips curled into a devious smile.

So damn smarmy. But he had a point.

There was a growing list of things that I liked about Raleigh. The newest one was that he was an active participant in blow jobs. He was a coach off the field, showering me with compliments and approving grunts. Even in the tight confines of a stall, and under pressure of being caught, he continued to be effusive in my abilities. As someone in the arts, I never got tired of plaudits.

It was a glaring contrast to Noah, who went silent when we used to be intimate. A few times, I caught him looking at himself in a mirror, as if critiquing his performance in real time.

"Fuck, you're amazing. This feels so good," Raleigh mumbled in his deep register. He arched his hips to meet my lips, letting me take all of him at once.

"Shit. You're incredible, Ev."

Were my mouth not full, I would've thanked him. I loved reducing this big jock to mumbly compliments.

He threaded his fingers in the back of my hair and pushed me down.

"Is this cool?" he asked, a total gentleman.

I gave him a thumbs up, then returned my hand to stroke him. Bitter pre-come hit my throat.

I grazed a greedy hand up his shirt to caress his abs. I was hooking up with a guy who had abs! I didn't bring the same thirst trap energy to this relationship. What turned him on about my pale, skinny body was beyond me. Yet I would never, in my whole life, get over how he looked at me when we had sex. To think that most people on planet earth would never get looked at that way was heartbreaking.

It was very convincing hate sex.

"I'm coming. I'm coming," he croaked out.

I gave him another thumbs up, which had to be the dorkiest thing to do mid-blow job, but it fit with us. Sex brought out Raleigh's quirky side. In another world, one without sports, he could've fit in with us nerds.

I stroked him harder, faster, my tongue working overtime to slide over his thick rod. With both hands, he pushed me into his crotch as he released another epic load, which I swallowed like a champ.

"Fuck. That was so hot." Raleigh massaged his thumb over my bottom lip. I gave it a teasing bite. "So was that."

We got ourselves situated and left the restroom right as a scouting troop barreled into the lobby.

"What the heck happened here?" asked one of the leaders, a tall, uptight man. He examined the knocked-over brochures.

The other scout leader, a chubby guy with a lush beard, strolled over. "Papers fell. I assume gravity was the culprit."

"Do people have no respect for public property?"

Raleigh and I traded a red-faced look. It was an accident. A casualty in a sex tornado.

"Russ, please don't go into one of your speeches again. This is supposed to be a short bathroom break." The bear-like scout leader's voice sounded familiar, but I couldn't place it. "We're already running ten minutes behind schedule."

"Because you wouldn't let us leave until you found the right playlist to put on, Cal." Russ smirked as he said it, giving me the sense that these two were lovingly bickering more than fighting. "Did you see who did this?"

Russ put his spotlight on us.

"Nope. It was like that when we came in," Raleigh said in quick cover.

"It looks like they also shook the vending machine," said one of the scouts.

"They did? Free candy!" Cal beelined to the vending machine.

"Falcons, before we use the restroom, let's help clean up this mess. There are some selfish, rude people in this world. We won't be one of them." Russ clapped his hands, signaling the band of pre-teens to get to work. In his defense, he got down there with them.

"Why would someone do this?" asked one of the kids.

"Vandals," said the scout leader.

Or two people who had an uncontrollable urge to consummate a fake relationship. Again.

Raleigh and I got on our knees to join them. He was faster to the floor. My knees were a little sore, natch.

"Thanks for helping," Russ said to us.

"I'm sorry. Uh, for the companies behind these brochures." I dipped my head and focused on corralling brochures for a zip line place.

"Sad news. Despite some snacks being loose, we weren't able to get any vending machine freebies." Cal sulked. "Capitalism strikes again."

He offered us a bag of Frito's, then handed out a few snacks to the scouts. I smiled to myself. If the Falcons had a sassy leader like him when I was young, maybe I would've signed up.

Cal joined us on the floor. I didn't realize just how many brochures we toppled over. New York tourism would suffer because of us.

"Where are you guys headed?" Cal asked.

"A wedding," I said. "Friends from college."

"It's a lovely weekend for it," said Russ. "We're going camping."

"Nice," I said, trying to mask my disdain for the outdoors.

"I used to feel that same way. Why would someone choose to sleep outside? But the woods are a magical place." Cal flashed a split-second wink at Russ, telling me all I needed to know about these two. "It's a good idea if you two ever need ideas for a romantic getaway."

"Oh, we're not—"

"Thanks for the tip," Raleigh butted in. "I've been trying to get this one to go hiking with me for the longest time. He prefers his stationary bike." He nudged his finger in my cheek in a cute, obnoxious, we're-one-of-*those*-couples way.

"What's the point of hiking? You walk and you walk, and then you turn around." I shrugged.

"Sounds familiar," said Russ.

"I've come around," said Cal. *"Cal Hogan used to never leave his house. But after a chance encounter with the Falcons, he's...Nature Man."* He said this in a deep voice like the guy from movie trailers.

And that's when it clicked.

"I know your voice. I've heard you do ads on the radio for Roy's Car Barn! Your voice has been stuck in my head."

"That's the greatest compliment a voice-over artist could hear," Cal said.

"And you recorded the audio tour for the Sourwood Historical Society's museum," I said. Amos dragged me to that sucker twice. It was basically a tour of an old rich person's house. I could've saved my time and watched an old episode of *MTV Cribs*.

"Wow. I'm honored that you recognize my voice."

"Everett's in the arts, too. He's a theater director, and a great one at that."

I blushed at Raleigh's praise. He'd never seen one of my plays, but he sounded confident in my talent nonetheless.

"I dabble with acting," Cal said.

"He runs the theater program at South Rock, and he directs the school plays." Raleigh beamed with pride. He was literally describing the base responsibilities of my job. He made it sound like I was curing cancer.

"What are you doing this season?" Cal asked.

"Still TBD," I said.

"He's putting on *Into the Woods* by Steven Snodgrass."

"Sondheim," I corrected.

Raleigh didn't have to put on this show for a bunch of strangers, nor did his supportive partner act have to sound so convincing.

"That'll be quite a production! If you need someone to play the Narrator, I can narrate the heck out of it."

"Cal, sweetie, I think he wants the cast to be all students." Russ stood up and wiped dust off his knees.

"Oh. Right. That makes sense." Cal deflated, and it made me want to make an exception to the casting rule. If nobody auditioned, Cal might get his wish.

The Falcons finished arranging the brochures to their regular position. It was time to get back on the road. I hoped I saw Cal again. Another actor in Sourwood!

"Have fun at your wedding," Russ said, as we all walked to our vehicles. The Falcons had a large van packed to the gills.

Raleigh insisted on holding my hand. Probably for the best. Practice and all that.

"Don't upstage the brides," Cal said.

"What do you mean?" I asked.

"You two." He pointed between Raleigh and me.

"Cal," said Russ, in a tone that he probably used often.

"You know I'm right. You guys will probably be a cuter, more lovey-dovey couple than the one actually getting married. You're adorable!" Cal got into the passenger side.

Raleigh and I watched them drive away, stunned and still holding hands.

17

EVERETT

When Jordana and Bethany decided to get married, they already had a plan for what they wanted their wedding to look like. They'd gather all their friends and family at the rustic outdoor amphitheater where they'd done summer stock. They'd get married on the same stage where they'd once performed, then have everyone camp under the stars as they danced and drank until dawn.

Their parents, who were footing the bill for this shindig, had other plans. Their friends and family, who drove luxury cars and employed cleaning ladies, wouldn't be camping under no stars. After much negotiating, both sides compromised. The ceremony would take place in the amphitheater, and then the reception and guest accommodations would be held at a nearby four-star hotel with comfortable beds and running water.

The brides had kept us updated on the push-and-pull, and I was secretly on their parents' side. I was too pretty for camping. The only rustic thing I appreciated was minestrone soup. I breathed a sigh of relief as we pulled into the hotel parking lot. It had the sheen of a newly-built hotel, which meant it had all the newest amenities.

We grabbed our stuff from the trunk, then looked at each other before entering the hotel.

"This is it. You ready?" I asked.

"Let's fucking do this. On the count of three." Raleigh put his hand in the middle. I reluctantly joined. "One. Two. Three!"

But instead of throwing our hands in the air, on the count of three, Raleigh took hold of mine and pulled me into a quick kiss.

Delicious.

My heart pounded in my chest as we approached the hotel. This wasn't real. I was playing a character.

Everett Calloway, late twenties, enters stage right hand-in-hand with his hunky athletic boyfriend.

"We need a selfie to feed the social media beast and announce our arrival," Raleigh said. He was really into this, to my ongoing surprise. He played to win.

He pulled me against his chest with his hook-like arm and raised his phone high above us for the optimal angle. I loved being in his embrace. It was becoming familiar, like a favorite blanket.

"That's what I'm talking about!" He showed me the photo. It was a little bit awkward, a little bit staged, and a little bit sweet. It was a classic selfie.

Danita ran over and gave both of us a hug.

"Hey guys! I was wondering when you'd get here. How was the drive up?" she asked.

Raleigh and I exchanged another loaded look. It was a rest stop to remember.

"Good. Uneventful." I shrugged. "Are we the last ones here?"

Was there a couple who could be confused for gay twins anywhere per chance?

"People are trickling in. It's so good that we can all be together like this," she said.

"That's what sucks about adulthood. The only time you can get together with friends are weddings and funerals," Raleigh said.

"Ugh, I know. I miss college and being able to walk to my friend's dorm. Don't you, Everett?" She turned to me.

"Yeah." I didn't miss it as much as I should have. College was a quintessential time in our lives. But I got to see my friends every day at South Rock High, and I didn't have to share my apartment with a gross roommate.

"Danita, how's the show going?" Raleigh asked.

"We had our final performance on Tuesday. It went well. *The Hudson Valley Gazette* gave us a nice write-up. Thanks for asking. How's football season?"

"We have playoffs on the horizon. My guys are resting up, but they know come Monday, we're gonna be practicing hard. They appreciated that Ev pulled me away this weekend." Raleigh kissed my hand. "I can't wait to meet all his friends and hear about his college days." He kissed my cheek. "This weekend is going to be joytacular."

"Joyous and spectacular," I clarified for Danita, who wasn't fluent in Raleigh.

He kissed me on the lips.

Two sticks of luscious dynamite.

Boom.

Raleigh was being very on top of the PDA and keeping up appearances. I was too distracted wondering when I'd bump into Noah and Gavin.

"I'm going to check us in," I said.

"I'll wait right here." He pointed at the floor, ensuring me he wouldn't move.

The front desk was being manned by a woman my age who wore an oversized blazer with a nametag. I'd cashed in all my credit card points to help cover the room. Raleigh had offered to split the room with me, but I didn't feel right bringing him into this ruse and making him pay.

The concierge went over the final total and reminded me that eating from the minibar and ordering porn were going to cost an arm and a leg. My eyebrows jumped at the bottom line. Going to weddings was expensive. It was like a vacation where you had to bring a gift. I used to have a touch of envy for the people I knew who had large groups of friends and went to tons of weddings. They must've been broke by this point.

"Do you need one key or two?" she asked.

"Two. I have a boyfriend."

She had no reaction as she continued typing on her computer. It was good practice for the weekend.

She slid over two keys in a neat envelope.

Raleigh was true to his word, staying in the same spot where I'd left him. But he wasn't alone.

He was surrounded by all of my old college friends. Holding court. Regaling them with stories of who-the-hell-knew-what. I hadn't fully prepped him to meet everyone. What was he saying? He didn't strike me as someone who could improv. I should've left him tied up on the sidewalk like a golden retriever.

Or maybe he could tie me up one night.

I gave my forehead a much-deserved smack for that thought, then joined the circle.

"...And so one day, I finally went up to Ev, and I said 'Ev.' And he said, 'I hate when you call me Ev.'"

My friends laughed. They hung on his every word, a rapt audience. Jordana and Bethany were front row.

"So I said, 'Everett, we've been doing this dance for months. Eyeing each other during pep rallies. Exchanging awkward hellos in the faculty lounge. Bumping into each other at parties.' Look, I know we work at a high school, but we're not *in* high school."

He paused for a laugh from the crowd. For someone inexperienced in theater, he sure knew how to deliver a monologue.

"So I put on my most confident, cockiest grin, and I say, 'Everett, you're the most interesting person I've met, and I haven't even gotten the chance to talk to you. I think at the very least, we should grab a cup of coffee.'"

"That was ballsy!" Jordana said.

"Ev can be intimidating. And even though I was playing it cool, I was shitting bricks inside. I remember I was tossing a football between my hands, and my palms were so sweaty, I thought I was going to drop it. Then I'd really look like an idiot. Here was this cool, unique, really intelligent guy who knew Shakespeare and shit, and I was just this jock."

I remembered this moment, only he didn't ask me out. Last year, Raleigh cornered me in the teacher's lounge while tossing a football in his hands and asked what I was up to over summer vacation. The football went back and forth in his hands like a metronome. I told him I had tickets for summer stock in the Poconos; he thought I was talking about livestock, and I quickly exited the conversation. Hearing him recount this altered version of events made me wonder what was really going on in his head back then.

"So what did he say when you asked him out?" Bethany did the hand spinning motion to push Raleigh to get on with it. *I'm right there with you, gurl.*

"He looked me dead in the eye, and said, 'One cup. And I get to pick the place.'"

"That's so Everett," Bethany said, and Jordana nodded along.

It was?

"I was going to suggest Starbucks, but he found this funky local coffee shop."

"And he showed up?" Jordana asked. "I thought Everett had sworn off dates."

"He showed up." Raleigh found me in the back of the crowd and gave me a sly head nod.

I sauntered up to him, and he swung an arm around me, which I was now classifying as a typical Raleigh move. I did not object.

Raleigh gazed down at me, making everyone disappear. "And we talked. A lot. Because Ev loves to talk. The man's got opinions."

"And shockingly, I didn't scare you off."

"Not yet." Raleigh winked at me. Was there a public bathroom I could drag him to?

The awws of my friends brought me back to earth. We turned back to our audience.

"That is so freaking sweet," Danita said. Like some of the others, her hands were nestled over her heart. "I knew when I saw you guys at my show that you had something special."

"You did?" Between her and the scout leaders at the rest stop, people were convinced that Raleigh and I were couple of the year.

"Raleigh, you are perfect for Everett," Bethany said. "You two balance each other well."

"I'm learning a lot about the theater from Ev."

"And I watched a football game with Raleigh. It's surprisingly dramatic. You can't help but get invested in the characters."

"Players," Raleigh said, to more sweet laughs. "I'm excited to see the show y'all are putting on tomorrow night instead of a service. What's it about?"

"It's a series of scenes charting the most important moments of our relationship." Jordana giddily scrunched her shoulders up to her ears, a typical Jordana move.

"A live clip show package. Sounds cool!" Raleigh said with enthusiasm. "I can't wait to watch."

"Hey! Wait!" Jordana got on her tiptoes, a classic sign of when inspiration hit her. "I have an idea. Raleigh, even though we just met, I am loving your energy. You have a good soul. I'd written a monologue for Everett, but what if I rewrote it to be a scene for you both to perform?"

"What?" My eyes wanted to jump out of my skull.

"I have zero acting experience," Raleigh said.

"This isn't a professional production. I think you'll be great. You have a natural *It* factor," Jordana said.

"I do?" Raleigh smiled to himself. Great, another thing for him to have a big head about.

"We'd love for you to take part in the celebration." Jordana turned to Bethany, who nodded in agreement.

"Sure. What the hell. Live life with no regrets, right?" Raleigh shrugged, and that was that. "Is that cool with you, Ev?"

"Yeah, of course."

Fake boyfriends I could handle.

But scene partners?

This was going to be rough.

18

RALEIGH

Was I an actor?

Sure, I'd delivered speeches at pep rallies, and I'd given kickass wedding toasts. But this was going to be a whole different beast. I flashed back to the only time I attempted acting: the second grade Christmas pageant.

I was chosen to play Santa Claus because of my natural star quality. When it came time to summon my reindeer, I choked. I got Comet and Cupid and Donner and Blitzen; I drew blanks on the remaining four. The audience went dead silent, gawking at me as panic rose in my throat and I started to cry.

It was ho, ho, horrible.

When Everett and I arrived at the amphitheater for our first rehearsal later that afternoon, those familiar symptoms of panic—the swollen tongue and drenched palms—stirred within me. Which was a shame, since the setting was gorgeous. The outdoor theater was in a park surrounded by mighty, lush trees all turning for fall. We were awash in reds, purples, and yellows popping against the gray, overcast sky. If we could have the same weather tomorrow, it would be a wedding to remember. So long as I didn't fuck up my part.

"Are you sure you're cool with this?" Everett gave my hand a squeeze, then rubbed the excess sweat on his pants.

"Yeah. I can't wait to read the playbook."

"Script," he corrected.

We walked down the center row to the stage, where Everett's friends stretched and paced around chanting odd things to themselves, like "unique New York" and "a cup of proper coffee in a copper coffee cup."

"How intense will this play be?" I asked.

"Jordana's plays lean into the dramatics, but she's good about adding in elements of comedy."

"So is that a yes or a no?"

"We'll find out." Everett's intense eyes softened for me. "Are you nervous?"

"No. Maybe. I never told you this, but I was in a play once, and I forgot my lines."

"What'd you do? Did you improvise your way through?"

"No. I cried."

"Don't worry. You are fake dating an experienced director."

Jordana waltzed to center stage and snapped her fingers in a rhythmic pattern until everyone joined her. Bethany stood behind her, holding a stack of freshly printed playbooks–er, scripts–in her hands.

"Are we ready to make some mischief?" Jordana asked.

Everyone around me screamed and whooped, reminding me of my players before they ran onto the field.

"The script is a one act, and after heated discussions with our parents, we guaranteed it wouldn't run longer than thirty minutes." She signaled for Bethany to distribute the scripts.

"What is the play and what is my part?" A loud, booming voice came from the back.

We all whipped our heads around, where a guy stood on the back row, chest puffed out, chin up, like he was a short, scrawny Superman coming to save us.

"Noah!" Jordana squealed.

Ah, so this was the ex. Noah strutted to the stage, with his doppelgänger following closely behind. I assumed that was Gavin. They wore the same thin sweater but in different colors. They were really going for the twinning look.

Everett's friend's faces lit up as Noah and Gavin approached. Their excitement could barely be contained. Calm down, people. He wasn't Dwayne Johnson.

"Sweetie, I was wondering when you'd be here." Bethany planted a big smooch on his cheek.

"I was held up at the stage door by selfie seekers. Sorry, it still feels weird to say that. I can't believe there are people who want a selfie with me." Noah brushed a calculated hand through his hair as he blushed with fake modesty that could be seen from the nosebleed seats. This guy was a professional actor? "Speaking of, shall we?"

He whipped out his phone and snapped a selfie with Jordana and Bethany, then went to work hashtagging and posting.

"Brilliant." He took center stage and addressed the rest of us. He blew us all a kiss. "It's so good to see everyone! A reunion of friends under the most wonderful of auspices. This weekend, we shall eat, drink, and be merry."

Was this guy for real? I leaned over to Everett, who was turning a swirly crimson, which meant he was very nervous.

"How did this guy get through high school without a permanent wedgie?" I whispered to him.

Everett cracked a smile, a sign that I hadn't totally lost him to the well of anxiety. "He attended a performing arts high school. The same one that Timothée Chalamet graduated from."

"Am I supposed to know who that is?"

"I want everyone to meet Gavin." Noah took Gavin's hand and brought it to his lips for a kiss. "I've been telling him about all of you for months."

Gavin seemed uncomfortable with the attention, like he was dying to pull his hand away.

"How's Broadway life?" asked one of Everett's friends, a guy with a magenta streak in his hair.

"Magical. Fabulous. A whirlwind. I've been so busy. Between the show and recording my new album and prepping for my first movie, I barely have time to sleep. At least Gavin and I get to see each other at the show."

"You're starring in a movie?" Jordana asked, eyes bugging open.

"They're adapting my musical into a movie. It's going to be announced in *Variety* on Monday."

Everyone buzzed with excitement. Except Everett. He was decidedly unbuzzy.

"We can heckle it when it opens," I whispered.

"But listen, this is not the Noah and Gavin weekend." Noah put an arm around each bride. "We are here to celebrate Jordana and Bethany. Their love, which has endured for almost ten years, is an inspiration. Let's send them into matrimony on the highest note possible!"

That got a big round of applause. I joined in, since it was the only thing he'd said so far that wasn't about him.

Jordana handed him a script. "Thank you so much for being a part of this. I know you're having to miss some shows."

"Nonsense." Noah held up his hand. "I wouldn't miss this. A few sold-out crowds can't compare to watching you two walk down the aisle." He pulled a pen from behind his ear. "Is it okay if I make some notes on the script?"

"Sure. This is a collaboration," Jordana said, stumbling for a second. "And for everyone, we're not expecting you to be off book. We'll be doing this as a staged reading."

"A staged reading is when the actors sit on stage and read the script all the way through, but don't physically act it out," Everett told me.

"Phew."

Bethany stepped forward and checked her watch. "My parents ordered lunch that should be here in a few minutes. Everyone, take a little time to read through the script, and we'll start practice in an hour." She gave us a thumbs up and waited for us to reciprocate.

A delivery team brought sandwich and salad platters, plus a tray of brownies. It was quite a spread. My stomach rumbled. All this driving and bathroom hooking up fueled my appetite.

We dispersed among the seats, balancing our food on our laps as people leafed through the script and others continued to catch up with each other. Noah and Gavin made the rounds among Everett's friends, charming each one as if they were the ones getting married. Every so often, Noah would look our way, his eyes fixed on Everett before slightly narrowing at me.

Dude, it is so on.

I flipped through until I found my name. There I was. With lines. Chunks of dialogue.

"Oh, you got a good part. Every actor goes through their script to see how much dialogue they have," Everett said.

"Great." More chances for me to make an ass of myself. "At least we're acting together."

"Don't worry." Everett rubbed a thumb over my hand. It wasn't PDA because I doubt anyone could see such a small, intimate move. And yet he still did it. "I never leave my scene partners hanging out to dry. Let's run lines."

"Is that like practicing?"

"Yes. You're catching on!"

When I signed up to be a fake boyfriend, I didn't know I'd have to act. I thought having a good meet-cute and holding hands would be enough. Now I risked making a fool of myself and embarrassing Everett.

Our scene didn't seem challenging, fortunately. My character was J, and Everett was B. Our characters discussed where to order dinner from. J wanted to order from their favorite Thai place, while B had a hankering for Mexican food. B tells J that they always order Thai on Fridays, and that actually, they think the Thai place's food isn't that good. J finally agrees to give Mexican a try. Groundbreaking stuff. Not really sure how this was a foundational moment in their relationship, but maybe the brides were really particular about food.

We ran lines, which consisted of talking through the scene. I was saying all the words on the page just fine, but everything that came out of my mouth sounded so flat.

Everett breathed life into his dialogue. Like, how was that possible? This was a scene about food. He got this script at the same time as me, but he was able to hit punchlines and find these little nuances in his lines that gave cool new meaning to the scene. It was as if he memorized the playbook his first time on the field. Conversely, I sounded as if I were learning how to read.

"Let's go from the top. May I?" Everett took my script and made notes. He bit the corner of his bottom lip in concentration that totally threw off mine. This guy had so many hot poses that he wasn't even aware of.

"You're really going to town on my script," I said while rubbing his knee because I had this compulsion that I had to have my hands on him. I blame the lip bite.

Everett didn't look up. He scribbled away, and the amount of writing was making me nervous.

"Are you rewriting the play?"

"Never. The playwright's words are golden. Here." He handed it back to me.

The margins were covered in Everett chicken scratch. Every line of mine had a note. Every sentence had a word underlined. I needed a Rosetta Stone to translate this.

"Whoa."

"Each line should tell a story that reflects your character. Since you're a rookie actor, we want to leverage your natural charisma, your *Raleigh sais quoi*, if you will."

"So you're saying I have natural charisma?"

"At times. Sporadically." He cleared his throat. "This will help you pinpoint the conflict in the scene. Conflict is drama. That's what audiences come to see. They don't want to see two people getting along. The struggle, the tension, the gap between two people, that's where the magic lies."

"But we're not fighting in this scene. There's no yelling. We're trying to figure out where to have dinner. Not exactly dramatic fireworks."

"The scene isn't about ordering food. There's a whole layer of tension underneath."

"There is?"

Everett closed his eyes and took a here goes nothing breath. "In the first *Fast & Furious*, there are scenes where Bryan and Dom are getting along and having mundane conversations about preparing for their drag race. The tension in those scenes comes from Bryan being an undercover cop. The more he connects with Dom as a friend, the more he risks if he gets found out. That layers everything in those scenes, even the fun ones where nobody is fighting."

"Hold up." My jaw was on the floor, and my heart was...somewhere. "Did you just deconstruct *The Fast and the Furious*? That means that you saw *The Fast and the Furious*."

"Guilty. I had to watch it at a sleepover that my parents forced me to go to."

My mind and my dick had something in common: they were both blown today.

"It's a masterpiece, right?"

"It's entertaining. Seeing Paul Walker was a gay awakening for me. RIP."

"Some people say I look like Paul Walker."

"I can see it." His blushy cheeks told me he could really see it. He buried his head back in my script. "But the point is, there are two layers of conflict. There's the surface discussion about where to eat. But then there's the deeper level. J always has Thai food on Fridays. That's been her thing. But now B wants to change that. J has been living her life on her terms. Now she has to make room for another person. Giving up her Friday night routine is like giving up a piece of her identity. And for B, she's put up with J's Thai habit for a while, even though she isn't a fan. This is her moment to stand up for herself. She's a part of this relationship, too. When we start dating someone, we stick to our usual ways. But there comes a point in a relationship where you realize that you have to start changing and compromising because you're becoming a we. Someone else has a say in your life now. B is ready, but J is still hesitant. Can she make that adjustment and take a step toward being a we? I just said a lot of words. I can get carried away. But does that make sense?"

Everett was able to pull all of that from a scene about ordering food? I thought about what to say back, but nothing would sound as eloquent as his analysis. I was in awe of his intelligence.

"Holy shit. That was good. I remember that moment with Tori. You know the bottomless shrimp promotion that Anchor's Away does every August? I loved going to it for my birthday. But Tori's allergic to shrimp, so that put an end to that. It was the end of an era, but it meant that things were getting serious with us. It was a we decision."

"Why couldn't you go with another friend?"

"Tori was worried about me coming home with shrimp breath and triggering her allergies."

"That's a thing?"

I shrugged my shoulders. I didn't look it up on WebMD.

"So you were never allowed to eat shrimp when you dated her, even if she wasn't present?"

"I guess so." It sounded bad when he said it. How scientific was shrimp breath? Was it just about control with Tori?

One of the major benefits of being single: no compromising.

"Let's try it again from the top," Everett said. "Remember the push-pull."

This time, when we ran through the scene, I could feel myself getting better; I could feel the push-pull in our dialogue. Each line Everett said back to me was like the opposing team giving me another hit. I could see the tension that belied our exchange, like I'd tapped into a secret code. I knew what my character wanted, and he was going to get it.

"You were a little aggressive at the end, but that was much better," he said. "Not Tony worthy, but we're getting there."

"Nice! Which one of your friends is Tony?"

Everett smiled at me like I said something cute.

"I decided that J is laser-focused on getting Thai food because it's been a source of comfort for her."

"Look at you. Thinking about your character and coming up with backstory. I think you just became an actor, Raleigh Marshall."

"It's because I have a great coach."

"Director."

"Right." I caressed his cheek, letting my thumb slip just under that sexy corner lip. His determined eyes softened as he gazed at me, with a look that I instantly felt between my legs.

What would a fake relationship be without some fake kissing for all to see?

Unfortunately, I didn't get my chance to find out because some asshat cleared their throat above us.

"Everett." Noah stared down at us.

"Noah." Everett broke away and stood up to greet him. "And Gavin."

"Hi." Gavin waved at us. Was it me or did he mimic the way Noah waved and spoke?

"It's so good to see you," Noah said. "It's been a long time."

"Yeah. Well, I wouldn't miss this wedding."

"I feel so out of the loop. It feels like this budding relationship you have sprung up out of nowhere."

"It hit us both like a lightning bolt." Speaking of things ready to strike, I hopped up. "I'm Raleigh. Norm, right?"

"Noah."

"Noah. Like the flood guy."

"Aren't you funny?" Noah said in that dry tone that meant the exact opposite.

"Nice to meet you, dude," I said. Noah struck me as a guy who hated being called dude. "Pretty sweet about the movie, dude."

I held out my hand, and when Noah shook it, I squeezed hard. He winced, and for a split second, I thought he was going to start crying.

"You've got quite a grip."

"Like my dad always said, shake like you got a pair down there."

"My dad used to say that, too," Gavin squeaked out behind his boyfriend.

"Nice to meet you, too, Gavin. Love your sweater." I was much more gentle when I shook his hand.

Fake Boyfriend Skill #2: be extra nice to the ex-boyfriend's new partner to show that you're a gentleman.

"Okay, then." Noah turned back to Everett. "So what've you been up to? Are you still a teacher?"

Maybe it was because I already hated this guy, but I thought I sensed a certain snide way he said "teacher."

"I am. I teach public speaking and theater. Mostly public speaking." Everett wasn't following his own script for putting up a strong facade.

"Oh. That's nice," Noah said and didn't mean that either.

"Our careers have taken interesting paths." Noah chuckled to himself. "Gav, wasn't there a time when you thought about teaching, when you were having trouble booking gigs?"

"Yeah, for sure." Gavin gave an identical chuckle.

"I like it. It's good work," Everett said.

"Everett's being modest," I said. "He's also the director of the school plays. He's got kids clamoring to be cast. I can't tell you how many of my players want to be in the school musical."

"Awesome. You're the Joe Mantello of the high school scene," Noah said.

I didn't know who that was. That better not have been an insult.

"He's better than Joe Mantello. He's putting on *Into the Woods.*" I threw my arm around Everett.

"Wow. *Into the Woods.* That's quite a production."

"Ev can handle it."

"I love *Into the Woods*," Gavin said.

"You're a slut for Sondheim, babe." Noah put his arm around his boyfriend, who froze for a second at his touch. Or maybe I was seeing things.

"I saw the Central Park production a few years ago," Gavin said. Noah pulled him closer.

"Me, too," said Everett.

"Well, you guys will have to come watch Ev's production. It's going to bring down the house. He's going to take the audience into the woods, and they're never gonna want to come out." I had no idea what *Into the Woods* was about, but I had to assume that there was a forest of some kind.

"I played Prince Charming in high school," said Noah. "I was the only actor who had the range to hit the low notes of 'Agony.' It's rare to find teenagers who can sing it well."

"Everett found them. He's a kick-ass director." I let my hand drop down to his ass. "If you want to see the performance this December, let him know sooner rather than later because it's probably going to sell out."

"That's sweet that your town goes to see the school musical. How adorable. How *Our Town.*" Noah spoke fluent dickhead. "Maybe one day, you can produce a version of my musical for your school."

"Meh, we'll see," I said, refusing to cede any ground to him.

"And Raleigh, you're a gym teacher, right?"

"Yeah," I said with absolute confidence. I loved being a gym teacher and gave zero fucks about people who looked down on us. "I also coach football."

"Lovely. Helping our young men get brain damage."

"Aren't you funny?" I chuckled extra loud and clapped him on the shoulder extra hard.

"Well, I'll let you two get back to practicing."

"In the theater, it's called rehearsal," I said. I raised my eyebrows at him, then at Everett to back me up. He'd been awfully quiet, an odd phenomenon for him. "Nice to meet you again, Gavin."

"Likewise."

"Everett, I hope I'll get to see you around this weekend so we can properly catch up," Noah said.

"Yeah. I'll be here," Everett said.

Noah clasped Gavin's hand, and they walked away to mingle elsewhere.

Everett exhaled.

"How do you think it went?" he asked.

"Noah hates me. I'd call that a smashing success."

19

RALEIGH

After our lunch break, we all threw ourselves into rehearsals. We were tired, antsy, excited. We were a mess of contradictions, and it added to the thrill of putting on a last minute show. I caught the buzz in the air.

Bethany and Jordana had each set of actors go through their scene on stage. They gave notes; the actors asked questions. For a fun wedding ceremony show, I respected how invested everyone was. I'd be the same. When my friend hosted a game of Thanksgiving day touch football, I got very into it. We all wanted to do our best work.

Bethany and Jordana's parents showed up to check on everyone and watch rehearsals for a bit. What would it be like to have parents who showed up for you? A twinge of jealousy needled at my neck.

While I wished that Noah was a sucky actor, he was actually decent. He knew how to hit a line, as Everett would say. Gavin was the real stand out. His character was fully formed, making us laugh and sympathize with him in the audience.

Yet after each run, Noah had as many notes for him as Bethany.

He passive-aggressively second guessed each of Bethany's directions, wondering if that was the right journey for the character, a character who he'd only met an hour ago. I'd dealt with players and parents like this, who believed they always knew better. Bethany and Jordana tried to keep things light, but toward the end, they were getting fed up.

"I forgot what it was like to direct you," Bethany said with an aggrieved laugh, like deep down she wanted to slap him.

Everett watched Noah perform, captivated. When Noah got out of his way and got into the zone, he was spellbinding. I could see how someone could fall for him.

I did relish the sniping between Noah and Gavin during their rehearsal. Noah kept giving Gavin notes, kept telling him to do it a certain way, even though the way he was doing it was good. Finally, at one point, Gavin threw down his script.

"Noah, shut up! Who's the director here?"

"Babe, I'm just trying to give a little feedback."

"A little? Stop. This is Bethany and Jordana's play."

I leaned into Everett, getting a glorious whiff of his citrus body wash, which I remembered spying in his bathroom post-hate fuck. "Reminds me of a showboaty player. Was Noah like this in college?"

"Yep," Everett said, three letters loaded like a baked potato. "He's a raging perfectionist."

"Is perfectionist a theatrical term for asshole?"

"Actually...yeah." Everett sighed through his nose as we watched Noah pinpoint a line in the script that he found emotionally confusing. "But it worked. He's more successful than any of us here."

"Success has many definitions. And if success means having to be around this guy day in and day out, I'd happily choose failure."

"I wished success only happened to nice people."

"Who says you aren't successful?"

Everett rolled his eyes and gave me a humoring smile that simultaneously spread across my chest and irked me.

"What?" I asked. "I think you're a success."

"You really don't have to do this, Raleigh. You don't have to get carried away with the fake boyfriend schtick. Noah is performing to sold-out crowds on Broadway, and I'm leading a high school drama program that's on the verge of being eliminated."

"Everett and Raleigh." Bethany nodded for us to get onstage.

Gavin stormed off stage with Noah right behind him breezily descending the stairs.

"You can call us Reverett," I said.

"I love that!" Bethany signaled for us to sit at the two seats in the center. A music stand was set up in front of each seat for our scripts. My heart leapt in my chest. It was just a rehearsal, but we were still on stage, performing, in front of people. I really hoped I didn't forget how to read.

"Comet, Cupid, Donner, Blitzen, Dasher, Dancer, Prancer, Vixen," I mumbled to myself.

"What are you saying?" Everett asked.

"Uh, nothing. Just psyching myself up."

"You got this." Everett gave me a sly wink. We hadn't even performed, and a part of me was already giving us a standing ovation.

I crossed my legs.

Bethany approached with a stool and sat in front of us, leaning forward so much I thought she'd fall over. "All right, so this is a tricky scene."

"I love it," Everett said. "I'm here for a challenge."

"This scene chronicles the moment when Jordana and I realized that things were serious. We weren't just dating, we weren't just a pair of college sweethearts. We were in love. It's that part in a relationship when you realize this is it. 'Til death do you part' isn't just a saying."

I remembered that feeling with my ex-fiancée. Apparently, this feeling could be one-sided.

"I responded to the tension between our characters, that push and pull about how we liked each other, but there was something more we were afraid to admit. We were dancing around it," Everett said.

"Like Bryan and Dom in the first *Fast & Furious* movie," I interjected, proud to show off our analysis. Though maybe this wasn't the right crowd for that reference.

"Michelle Rodriguez in those movies. Damn." Bethany bit her lip. Or maybe it was! "She's one of the celebrities that either of us are allowed to cheat with."

Since they were lesbians, why couldn't they just have a threesome? It was probably best to leave that question unanswered. And ultimately, it was Michelle's call who she wanted to get into bed with.

"Raleigh, you're going to be great. I love your fun energy, and for this scene, I want you to keep pushing for that fun Raleigh. You're scared about where this relationship is headed, so you want to keep things light and fun. Status quo. Everett will be pushing back, trying to break through that wall. He's me in this situation."

"Jordana didn't want to take the next step?" I asked.

"Oh, she did. Deep down she did. But she freaked out. She's always been gun-shy about relationships."

"You want to jump in, but you know how easy things can unravel," I said, a familiar pain hitting my heart.

"Yep. Nobody said love was easy. But who wants easy?" Bethany shrugged. "All right, let's take it from the top."

When I coached my players, I told them to visualize themselves scoring the touchdown, making the pass, catching the ball. If they can imagine themselves doing it, then they can make it happen. I visualized moments of my past relationships. The fear bubbled back to the surface. It gave me passion and strength that I poured into my dialogue.

Everett seemed taken aback, but he gave as good as he got. I was pushing, and he was pushing. Two characters who wanted something, but the other person stood in their way.

Conflict.

Drama.

I shook out my hands when the scene ended, energy still crackling under my skin. I found myself on a high, as if I just ran for a touchdown.

"How was that?" Everett asked.

"That was awesome!" I exclaimed before realizing he was asking Bethany.

"You guys were good, but I feel like it's missing something." She turned to Jordana sitting in the front row with the script in her lap. "What do you think?"

"Yeah, it needs something else. The scene just ends." Jordana stared intently at Everett and me trying to figure out the answer.

"B doesn't get a chance to express how she feels. She needs to show J that she wants this, that what they have is worth the leap," Bethany said.

"I have an idea. Give me a few minutes." Jordana began writing feverishly on the back of a script page.

"She's rewriting just like that?" I asked.

"This happens all the time in theater. A script is constantly changing through rehearsal. The playwright can see how a scene is playing and make changes to get it right," Everett said.

"Like trying a new play on the field?"

"Exactly."

Bethany pushed her chair closer to us. "Everett, one note. You seemed reserved."

"Reserved?" Everett reacted as if she called him a dirty word.

"We need to open you up, get the chemistry flowing."

"You don't think I have chemistry with my boyfriend, Bethany?"

I thought Everett would take constructive criticism well since he was a director, but Bethany struck a nerve. She treaded lightly.

"Let's try an exercise," she said, clapping her hands together. "Tell me what attracted you to Raleigh. What made you fall for him?"

"What? I've never heard of this kind of acting exercise." Everett let out a nervous laugh, and the longer he took to answer, the bigger the weird feeling in my stomach got. His eyes flicked to me, then to the ground. "I, uh, well, Raleigh's hot. Obviously. And he's...he's a good person."

Being called a good person had never felt like such a back-handed compliment. It seemed there was one question that we hadn't practiced in the run up to the wedding. Everett wasn't the improviser he claimed to be.

Before Everett could stumble more, Jordana ran back to us waving a script page over her head. She slapped it into Everett's lap.

"New ending to the scene. Everett, your character desperately needed a monologue to properly express her feelings."

I was grateful I didn't have to recite that whole chunk of dialogue, but Everett seemed to relish it.

"Everett, you're good with a cold reading, right?" Bethany asked. Everett responded with a thumbs up. "Cool. Let's take it from the top."

We ran through the scene again. I gave it my all, leaving nothing on the proverbial field. I tried to make as much eye contact with Everett as I could while reading. These words on a page were coming alive. We were Raleigh and Everett and J and B and anyone and everyone who'd ever been in love. I was mother-fucking acting!

We came to the last page. The spotlight turned to Everett. Bethany and Jordana leaned forward to watch. Everett took a breath and launched into his monologue.

Holy. Lombardi.

Everett stared at me with such intense focus as he acted his heart out, infusing each line of his monologue with meaning and passion. B wanted this relationship. She wanted them to get serious. Was it Everett saying these words or B? At some point, I lost track.

What was once a block of text on a page turned into a freaking sermon. He took everyone to church. Every line and every beat pounded into my soul. His passion and intensity transformed every single word of his monologue into thunderbolts of emotion. I got to watch someone in their element. The stars aligned.

Everett wasn't just the sarcastic teacher. He was full of life and vibrancy, and it was all pointed at me.

Fear and hope.

Love and anger.

Hunger.

I was a fucking goner for him.

Bring in the doctor. Call it. Time of death: 5:52 p.m.

Bethany clapped her hands wildly. If she had roses, they would've been thrown at us.

But fuck the roses. And fuck the outside world. I had an *experience.*

Who the fuck knew that a play could evoke this out of me, mash me up and chop me up and spit me out?

"That was...wow." Bethany had no other reaction but to laugh.

I kept looking at Everett, praying to every acting and football god that we didn't break this moment, that it wasn't just in my head.

This fake relationship had never felt so real.

———————

EVERETT and I walked to the car, then drove to the hotel in complete silence. What was he thinking? His blush was frustratingly under control right at the moment when I needed it to give me some hints.

"What are you up to now?" I asked when we strolled into the lobby.

"I don't know. I'm tired. Probably watch some cable TV in the room."

"I'm gonna hit the gym."

We waited for the elevator. My heart beat in my chest waiting for each floor to ding closer. I had to get my gym shoes and burn off this energy. The elevator doors dinged open.

Everett stepped inside.

"You know what? I think I'm going to use the stairs." I stepped back.

"Really? It's four flights." Everett shoved his hand out to stop the elevator door from closing.

"I need the exercise. I've been doing a lot of sitting and driving today."

"You're going to the gym to exercise. Isn't taking the stairs redundant?"

I needed to be alone with my thoughts right now. I needed to calm myself down from this confusing high before I did something really stupid, like tell Everett that I was into him. No faking around.

"Gotta get my steps in! I'll meet you up there." I jogged backwards and waved at him as I headed for the stairs.

Why were all stairwells so depressing to be in? It was like all the prettiness of a building had to stop as soon as one hit the stairs.

"Get it together, man," I said to myself. My idea was that

jogging up these steps would reverse the blood flow that was happening in my groin. Yet my brain kept cutting to images of Everett, staring at me, reciting those lines about love and wanting me (er, J).

I was the one having an emotional crisis, and he was cool as a cucumber. Jesus, emotional crisis? That was such an Everett thing to say.

"Get out of my head!" I said to imaginary Everett as I reached the fourth floor. I marched down the floor and hoped he was already asleep.

I flicked my key card at the reader. When it turned green, I pushed open the door to find Everett leaning against the hotel room wall wearing only his boxers.

"Still want to go to the gym?"

20

EVERETT

I wasn't one of those people who liked being naked. Naked was a means to either showering or sex. It was a layover to better things. I was skinny and pale. I didn't even sit around in my underwear. People like me were why they invited clothes.

But Raleigh, for some unknown reason, liked me naked. He ogled me like I was a stripper. I could feel his eyes rake over my skin, making a list in his head of things he wanted to do to me.

Without saying a word, he closed the gap between us and enveloped me in a hungry kiss.

"Just so you know, this is still a one-time thing," I said.

"But we've done it twice." He kissed along my neck.

"It's an umbrella policy."

"Why is there an umbrella?" His hand dipped down my chest, skimming over my stomach, activating a mountain range of goosebumps.

Raleigh wasn't a wordsmith. That's what the muscles were for.

"This doesn't count," I said in between kisses. "This is still animal hate sex." And more kisses. "We're getting into character."

Raleigh palmed my crotch, making me moan into his mouth.

"You were saying?" His lips curled into a classic smarmy grin over mine.

I was out of excuses. My energy was better spent undressing this drop dead gorgeous stud.

I quickly undid his vest, then whipped off his shirt. Fuck. This chest. I didn't have the willpower or motivation to give my body a chest like this, but I was more than happy to admire Raleigh's. My fingers grazed over each ab, with The Bulge waiting below. I smiled at it pushing against his jeans.

"Hey. My eyes are up here."

"Yeah, but your dick is down there."

And so was I. I got on my knees and freed The Bulge from its confinement. It was down my throat in seconds. Raleigh nearly collapsed against the wall, filling our room with guttural groans.

"I thought we were going to make out more."

"We can do that after," I said while catching my breath. I lapped up his musky taste, loved the feeling of him taking over my mouth.

When I looked up, Raleigh was gazing down at me with this oddly sweet smile that made things feel more intimate.

It was that same look he gave while we were rehearsing. Raleigh was getting really into the scene, the conflict adding yet another layer of sexual tension between us. But it was the way he gazed at me while I delivered my monologue that I'd never forget. It was different. His face was filled with this mix of lust and admiration in a way that nobody had ever looked at me before. It caused a hot chill to slide across my chest.

Despite us sitting on a stage being watched, I'd never felt that kind of intimacy with another person, where we could create our own world just like that.

By the end of rehearsal, I had to have Raleigh, the way the human body selfishly needed to inhale oxygen every few seconds. I craved more time with him.

I was fucked up.

And now he was gazing down at me, caressing my cheek. I was blowing him, not reciting a sonnet!

This is supposed to be hate sex! We're supposed to be animals!

"Get up," he commanded, his voice hoarse.

Getting up would mean I'd have to look at him again and feel more of these weird intimate feelings. I chose fellatio.

"Shit." Raleigh collapsed back against the wall. He grabbed my hair and jammed his cock completely inside me. "You like that?"

"Mm hmm," I managed.

"Fuck. If I do that again, I'm going to come." He pulled out and shimmed out of his jeans. Then, before I could protest, he lifted me up and carried me to one of the beds.

"You got a room with two beds?" he asked.

"This was before we started sexing."

It was wild that there was a before, and it wasn't too long ago. I felt like I'd known Raleigh for years.

"One bed for sleeping, one bed for dirty fucking," he smartly suggested. Sex got messy. A good messy, but still...messy.

I spread out on the sex bed, a snow angel against the white comforter. Raleigh put his thumb in my mouth. I gave it a nibble. His fingers tumbled down my flesh, past my belly button, and dipped inside my underwear. The cotton didn't stand a chance. He rolled my boxers down my legs and threw them over his shoulder.

He took me in his mouth, sending waves of heat coursing through my body. I stared up at the ceiling, blissed out of my mind until I felt a prickling against my dick.

Raleigh rubbed my dick over his cheeks, his faint, manly stubble flooding me with lust.

"You remembered," I said.

"Of course." Raleigh went back to sucking. He remembered everything.

Sensing that I was on the verge of blowing my load, Raleigh

climbed on top of me, our faces dreamily close. It was another intimate moment. One that made the idea of lazy Sundays in bed with him come to mind. Lazy Sundays had no place in hotel room hate fucking.

"Do you know what blocking is?" I sat up.

"When the offense is rushing at your QB?"

"No. In theater, blocking is determining where actors should be positioned in a scene."

"That's cool. Can we talk about blocking later because it's kinda cockblocking right now...?"

"I still have my director hat on," I said. "Lay down. I want to get on top of you."

He was correct in a way. I was giving his dick stage directions. I was cockblocking.

Raleigh gave me a captain's salute that was both corny and fucking sexy. He lay flat on the bed, his cock sticking straight up. I mounted him for a sixty-nine. His breath danced against my opening.

"Shit," he grunted as I sucked him. Meanwhile, thanks to his expert rimming, every inch of me was covered in the good kind of pins and needles.

I really hoped this hotel had thick walls because I moaned for all to hear. I went completely non-verbal. Raleigh's tongue had the dexterity of an Olympic gymnast. Tens all across the fucking board. I deep-throated him mostly to shut myself up.

He gave my ass a hard slap. I bet it was all red from his touch.

"Ev, please tell me you brought lube and condoms. I'm begging you."

"Of course. It's like ID. I never go anywhere without them."

Fuck. At this point, I'd wrap a shower cap around his dick if I had to.

I rolled off him and rifled through my suitcase. A sharp pain hit me.

"Did you just bite my ass?"

He cocked an unashamed eyebrow. "Guilty."

"That stung."

"You love it."

I tossed him the supplies.

"Now get over here." Raleigh patted the empty side of the bed.

He pulled me on top of him for a deep, luscious kiss, rubbing his hands over my shoulders and down my back. We were like teenagers making out. The sounds of our lips smacking together was music to my ears; the feeling of his rough hands threading through my hair sent tingles down my spine.

"Is making out allowed in hate fucking?" Raleigh asked.

"I'll allow it. You're a good kisser."

"A compliment from Everett? I'm in shock."

"Here's another one. I used to wish that you were one of those guys that talked a big game to make up for having a small dick, but..." I glanced south at his blessing from Mother Nature. "That's very untrue."

"Would it be pushing it if I said I'd been told that before."

"Yes."

"Fair enough." He laughed against my lips. Laughing! During kissing! While naked! Who knew sex could be this wonderfully weird?

I got on all fours, ready to be pummeled like he'd done last time.

"Actually, get on your back."

I was caught off guard by the request, but went with it.

Moments later, Raleigh leaned over me, hair falling in his eyes. He entered my hole with his thick rod and my whole body reacted, back curling up and moans escaping from my mouth. I shook with quenched lust as he sunk deeper inside me.

The tender expression on his face hovered inches from me. I

let myself return the expression, no barrier, no armor of witty banter or sarcastic comments or hate fuckery.

He tucked a lock of my hair behind my ear.

Our lips met each time he thrust inside me. Heat built in my core. I couldn't look away, and I was soon overcome by the moment. I dug my nails into his back pulling him close, his sweaty chest heaving against mine, my dick smearing pre-come on his stomach.

"Ev," he said, as a whisper, as a prayer.

"Raleigh." I caressed the sides of his face, breathing in his salty sweat, his hungry grunts. Our bodies collided in heat and thunder.

And then we were mobile. He picked me up in one swooping move. Raleigh got on his knees, keeping me on his lap, his dick not leaving me while we switched positions.

"Impressive," I said.

He wrapped his muscled arms around my thin frame pulling me close, locking us together, two souls truly intertwined.

I rested my forehead against his, my pants and his choked grunts filling the meager space between us. The bravado and unshakable confidence that he wore every day of his life was stripped away, leaving a vulnerable, raw man looking for connection. That was the scary thing about dating and sex and everything that came with it: we all just wanted somebody to see us.

I saw Raleigh. I knew instinctively that I was seeing a part of him nobody had seen before. Just me.

I dug my nails into his back as I reached climax.

"Ev, come for me."

And that did it. I collapsed onto his chest as sticky warmth hit his stomach. He held me tight as I came down, kissed the side of my head in an intimate gesture that felt like something we could've done for years and years.

There was nothing hate sex about it.

Raleigh grunted out an untethering release before filling his condom to the brim.

Neither of us said anything as we caught our breaths. He smoothed his fingers through my matted, sweaty hair, breathing in our spent scent. I kissed the side of his head, my body craving an intimacy I once thought I could live the rest of my life without.

After another minute or so, the afterglow faded. Raleigh grabbed washcloths from the bathroom, and we wiped off the mess.

"Thank God for the sex bed," he said. "I wouldn't want to sleep on these sheets."

We were gentlemen and did our best not to get jizz on the comforter, but they were still covered in hot, glorious sweat.

We fell back onto the bed. He spooned me like it was the most natural thing in the world. His chin fit perfectly on the dip of my shoulder.

"So that happened. Again." Raleigh let out a gravely chuckle. "You love doing surprise sex attacks."

"They're just as much a surprise for me."

"I'm not complaining."

"You bring it out of me. Are you hungry?" My stomach rumbled. A hookup who was an aspiring fitness influencer once shared that sex burned over three hundred calories per hour.

"Would it be crazy if we got room service?" Raleigh quirked a curious eyebrow. The sight of his face used to make me nauseous; now it was more effective than Viagra.

"I've never gotten room service before."

"Neither have I. It's stupid expensive."

"They tack on a ridiculous surcharge. It's cheaper to go downstairs and get it to go."

"Did you want to do that?" he asked.

I looked down at my naked self, covered in the fruits of same-sex sex. "No. Did you?"

"No. We can make a one-time exception and get room service."

"This is the weekend of one-time exceptions."

"Room service is covered by the umbrella policy, right?"

The thought of dinner made my stomach rumble.

"Did your stomach just growl?" he asked.

Shit. He heard that? Body noises weren't sexy. Yet instead of running away, Raleigh laughed into my shoulder.

"Wait. Stop that," I said. My body began to tighten and convulse.

"Stop what?"

"When you laugh against my neck. It's ticklish." I bit my fist to hold back an uncontrollable, tickle-induced laugh.

"So you're saying I should do it again?"

"No!" I tried to shuffle away, but Raleigh held me in place.

He laughed again.

I burst into a wild thrash of giddy, possessed laughter. "Are you seriously tickling me? What are we? Seven years old?"

"Six and a half." His tickled me with his fingers. A chihuahua-esque yelp escaped my lips.

"You have to be ticklish, too." I whipped around and began searching for his tickle zone. I found it on his side.

Mr. Football Jock Man unleashed a high-pitched squeal. "Careful!"

"I'm always careful."

We broke into a full-fledged tickle war, laughing until our eyes watered.

21

EVERETT

I rested my head against the upholstered headboard and tried to make sense of things. "I can't believe we did this. I never do this."

"We did it. And it was fucking fabulous. Now take your burger." Raleigh, clad only in boxers, handed over the plate of burger and fries – that we got from room service!

"And your brownie." He handed me a smaller plate with a big, dark, perfectly square brownie – that we also got from room service!

"I can't believe we ordered room service. Never in my life have I ordered room service."

"It's worth it." Raleigh dug into his mozzarella sticks, letting out an *mmmm* in approval.

"We probably could've saved money ordering from a restaurant who could deliver. Though are there any restaurants around here? We're in the woods."

Raleigh waved off my line of thinking. "Forget it. We're allowed to indulge once in a while. A toast." Raleigh held up a mozzarella stick. I held up a French fry. "To a successful wedding weekend so far."

"Cheers." I bit into my crispy, parmesan garlic fry.

Raleigh snuggled next to me with his mozzarella sticks and chicken tenders. We deemed this bed the mess bed, for eating and other activities. The other bed was untouched. We'd be sleeping there. Together.

Unless Raleigh decided to bolt again.

We both got under the blankets, turned up the volume on the TV, and dug into our room service dinner. Despite being hungry and eating, the second Raleigh's leg brushed against mine, I got hard again.

We had no commitments for the rest of the night. There was a small rehearsal dinner for out of town guests, most of which were family. I texted Bethany and Jordana and said we were wiped, and they were cool with us skipping.

I kinda wanted to skip the whole wedding thing and not leave this hotel room for another twenty-four hours. We proved our fake relationship bonafides. We could find understudies to take our role in the wedding play, right?

"How's your burger?" he asked in between bites.

"Good?" I wasn't confused on the burger. It was delicious, but I was still processing this whole scene. If someone had told me at the start of the school year that Raleigh and I would wind up eating room service (!) in bed together (!!) after having mind-blowing sex (!!!), then I would've joked about pigs flying.

But the pig had flown.

Oh boy, had it ever.

Raleigh was fucking hot, even eating mozzarella sticks. His golden chest and tousled hair were cast in the waning sunlight peeking through the blinds. He was a beautiful man, yet it wasn't his looks that were making it hard for me to enjoy my burger.

Raleigh was a good guy. Unexpectedly. I wasn't used to being around good guys. I thought of dating as a kill or be killed proposition. Not like we were dating for real, though.

"How are your chicken tenders?" I asked, changing the subject in my head.

"Delicious. They mastered the breading to chicken ratio."

Raleigh threw an arm around me. He'd been doing that a lot today, and I didn't mind. Something about his touch was both highly stimulating and utterly calming.

"I can't believe I'm eating in bed with someone I just had sex with." I laughed at the scene.

"What do you usually do?"

"Kick them out. Or they sneak out."

Raleigh got quiet for a moment. I could kick myself for potentially squashing this vibe we had going. "That wasn't my finest moment."

"I was kidding. I totally get it," I said, trying really hard to play it cool.

"There's a difference between sleeping with someone and falling asleep with someone. The last person I fell asleep with was my ex-fiancée."

"What about all your girlfriends of the month?"

"I bolted after sex. Said I had to feed a neighbor's cat."

Had Raleigh used that excuse on me, I would've made myself believe him. Sometimes, it was better to accept a lie than seek out the truth.

"I wish I stayed in bed with you." He shot me a good ole boy, crooked smile.

We ate our meals while watching TV. One of the *Fast & Furious* movies came on cable. Raleigh was giving me side commentary throughout, filling in plot holes that he thought I couldn't live without but had no bearing on enjoying the movie. It was good looking people doing crazy action stunts in cars. That it was all practical effects was impressive, and there was a visceral joy in watching Paul Walker and Vin Diesel drive a car through not one, but two skyscrapers.

"I get to pick what we watch next." Even though I was enjoying the movie, I had to stand my ground in this fake relationship.

Which wasn't feeling so fake.

But Jesus, I attacked Raleigh multiple times like an animal in a *National Geographic* special. This inborn drive to be with him superseded all of my common sense.

We pushed our empty plates to the end of the bed, then I slid deeper into Raleigh's touch, getting cocooned in his arm for the rest of the movie. I could stay like this forever. It was never easy like this with other guys.

All of Vin Diesel's talk about family got me thinking about something.

"What's the deal with your family, Raleigh?" I looked up at him.

His jaw tensed. I needed to shut up and watch the movie, but once I asked the question, I didn't want to let it go.

"You don't have to share, but you've dodged every question about them. I'm curious."

"In case anyone asks?"

"No."

His breath hitched. I worried I had pushed too hard, but he began to soften.

"It's not pretty," he said.

"I'd like to hear." I wanted to learn all I could about this guy who I had so completely misjudged on nearly every occasion.

"My mom was an alcoholic, dad was always screwing around, not even trying to hide it, which made my mom drink more. And my brother was a drug addict. I hit every box on the shitty family checklist."

"Raleigh." I pulled him close to me and nuzzled into his chest.

My heart broke for him, and he needed to know I was here for him. "I'm so sorry."

Never in a million years would I have guessed he came from such a fraught background. He hid it well behind a flashy smile. He was used to hiding his pain from the world.

"It's okay. It is what it is."

"You didn't deserve that. How did you wind up..."

"Normal?"

I blushed in embarrassment for such an asshole question, but I was curious. How could he survive a household like that and seem so well-adjusted?

"Football," he said. "We moved around a lot. Dad was always losing his job, trying something else. We didn't make friends in the neighborhood easily. We kept moving until we wound up in upstate New York. I was throwing the football around in a park with my brother. This guy noticed and said I had a good arm. He was a coach in a kids football league. It saved me." His voice shook for the first time since I've known him.

"It got me out of my house. I poured all my energy into football and made my high school team. It was a small miracle that we didn't move while I was in high school. I wonder if my parents were able to get out of their fog enough to notice that I had a chance and they didn't want to fuck it up. I kept playing, and I got a scholarship to a local college."

"That's wonderful." I used to think sports was the antichrist, but it saved him. How many other kids had sports saved? "Reminds me of my path a little. I found an outlet away from my family with theater."

"It was something that could be all yours."

"Exactly. And I got a partial scholarship. There aren't as many scholarships for drama kids."

"That's because you don't bring in the big donations," he said with a wry smile.

Sports drove crowds in a way theater never would, unfortunately.

"Sports. Theater. They're both great. They accomplish the same things, but in different ways," he said, another unexpected soulful comment.

"Do you talk to your family?"

"My parents passed away. Dad had a heart attack while screwing one of his girlfriends. And mom got cancer. I think dealing with my brother really wore her down. He's been in and out of rehab. As the older brother, he got the brunt of the shitstorm in our household. He didn't have anything like I had with football. The last time I saw him, he wound up stealing from me, and when I confronted him, it almost turned violent. I want to help him, but he has to want help. I consulted a therapist and other addiction specialists, and they said it was best to cut off contact with him."

That he said all of this in a pleasant monotone showed me how hard he worked to push it all down. How hard he worked to overcome his childhood. And here I thought that my annoying family was the worst. I didn't know how good I had it.

"I'm so sorry. I never thought I'd say this, but thank God for football."

"Thanks." His thumb caressed my upper arm in this natural way, like he'd been doing it for years. "Anyway, I don't think that's the backstory you wanted to share with your friends. It's not what people want in a fake boyfriend. It'd be a real downer."

"It's you. The fact that you were able to come out of that experience and be this positive, uplifting, caring person is astounding. Almost as astounding as the fact that I used those adjectives to describe you." What a wild turn of events. And the truth is, I could've said a lot more. There were so many wonderful facets of Raleigh that he chose to hide under his cocky exterior. But I realized now that was armor. "You're a good person."

"I don't know. I'm just trying to put some good into the world."

"And I'm trying to put sarcasm and pettiness out there. The world could always use more." I slid my hand into his boxers and grabbed his dick for no good reason.

"Did you want to go again?"

"No. I'm full of burger and fries. I just wanted to make sure it was still there."

His eyes creased at the corners with a hardy laugh. "You're weird, Ev."

"You're not so normal yourself, Coach." I pulled my hand away before I accidentally did start us up again. "Wait, if you're all about kindness, then why would you always give me a hard time at school?"

"Because it was fun getting a rise out of you."

"It was fun fighting with you," I admitted. "Sometimes, I looked forward to seeing you in school and hearing you say something dumb or obnoxious so I could bitch about you in the group chat. I thought I was just a sadist."

Maybe there wasn't one moment when I first noticed Raleigh, like Bethany had asked. Maybe it was lots of little moments that added up to me seeing the real him right now.

"You're not this bad person that you think you are. Don't take this the wrong way, but you can be really sweet."

"Gross," I said.

His magic hands circled my hair. I melted into his touch. "It's true. I see how loyal you are to your friends, how you'd do anything for them."

"Have you been legit spying on me?" My friends were like my family. Though I had no idea how the fuck to explain tonight to them. There were some things too big for the group chat. "I'm not that good. I concocted a whole fake boyfriend to impress an ex-boyfriend who was a total asshole."

"Yeah, Noah seems like a pretentious creep."

"Don't I have fabulous taste in men?" I had to laugh because it was funny in a sad kind of way. "He wasn't always like that. Or maybe he was, I just couldn't see. He made me feel less than, but that's on me. I let myself feel small." There I went rambling again, but Raleigh didn't seem to mind.

"You shouldn't dim yourself for others. We can all shine."

"That's such a teacher thing to say."

Raleigh practiced what he preached. I thought back to today when he kept praising my directing skills to high heaven. Even if it was for appearances, he really sounded like he meant it.

"What was it like dating Noah?"

"It was college. We were young. But I just remember how cool Noah was. He was the star of the program right from the start. He'd acted in a few off-Broadway productions in high school and came to college with this instant sheen. Even at freshman orientation, he already had this whole social network. People adore Noah. I was this fumbling partial scholarship kid. It was hard not to fawn over him, especially when he was on stage. Noah has a beautiful voice that makes you forget what kind of self-absorbed person he is when he's not singing."

"I don't think his current boyfriend Gavin is all too thrilled with him."

"I noticed that, too. I hate that I still feel less than around Noah, although that feeling diminished when you were there."

"You are more man than Noah will ever be." Raleigh gave me a pat on the ass, probably no different than the ones he gave his players on the field. Though I doubted it made his players all dizzy and bubbly.

I shook my head and laughed, still processing the wildness of these past few weeks.

"What?" Raleigh asked, all sun-kissed smiles.

"I just pegged you all wrong."

"We can make pegging happen. I need to work up to it."

No pegging would be happening tonight. We resumed watching the movie, *Furious 7*. Yes, somehow they made at least seven movies in this franchise. I snuggled against his chest; Raleigh skimmed his fingers on my scalp in a heavenly massage.

The movie ended with a scene of Dom and Bryan driving side by side as a melancholy song played. This was Paul Walker's final film, and despite the final shot being Bryan literally drag racing into heaven, I got choked up.

"I think it's time for bed," Raleigh said, turning off the TV.

"You can have the clean bed. I'll take the messy one. You're the guest." I fumbled through my words.

"I was hoping we could share the clean one."

My heart was doing a roller coaster loop in my chest, but on the outside, I gave a simple nod. "Okay."

I brushed my teeth and took a shower, then put on fresh pajamas. When I exited the bathroom, there was Raleigh on one side of the clean bed, with the covers folded over for another person to join.

That person being me.

I climbed into bed, and immediately, he encircled me with his arms, pulling me against him and pressing his lips to my back as if he hadn't seen me in ages.

"Good night, Ev." Raleigh clicked the light off.

I didn't drift off into a peaceful sleep. Feeling Raleigh's stiff cock against my ass got me horny all over again. So we had sex again, stared into each other's eyes as we came, and took a joint shower.

Then I drifted off into a peaceful sleep.

All questions about how fake this relationship was would have to wait till morning.

22

RALEIGH

The next morning, I woke up early and went for a run. Having to leave Everett in bed was tough. I had an amazing sleep with him somewhat in my arms. The man loved to move around in his sleep; his REM cycle was a HIIT workout. It was another challenge of Everett that I looked forward to conquering over many more sleeps.

Or not.

I shook my head and rounded a corner in my running path. There were trails through the woods around the hotel. The sun had just come up on a peaceful, cloudy morning. The gray sky peeked through a cluster of trees packed with vibrant reds, purples, and golden yellow leaves. Back at Sourwood, my runs through my neighborhood were never this pretty. I savored the solitude of nature. It allowed me to think.

About Everett.

About the way being with him made me feel.

About how I didn't want this feeling to stop once the brides swapped "I Do's" and we returned to our regular lives.

This whole feelings thing wasn't my jam. My heart ambushed

me. This weekend was supposed to be a favor for a colleague, not a cruel tease of a happily ever after.

I'd been burned badly in the past. An ex-fiancée who peaced out all of a sudden. A family who only knew how to hurt each other. Everett and I were on a fun mission this weekend. I had to get thoughts of wanting more out of my head.

I reached a gorgeous vista that overlooked a valley of a river dotted with more beautiful trees. Damn, nature really went there today. Why wasn't I living in a cabin in the woods to take full advantage of this?

But nature wasn't helping me solve my confusion.

I needed a coach.

"Yo," I said into my phone a minute later. "Did I wake you?"

"Yeah." Hutch yawned into the line.

"What happened to your morning run?" There was a period over the summer when I'd gotten Hutch into joining me for a regular run. We'd bumped into the mayor of Sourwood and his boyfriend Dusty a few times on our jogs. Sadly, once the school year started, Hutch couldn't keep it up.

"It's Saturday," he said.

"So?"

"So God rested on Saturday after building the world. I needed a day off after teaching hundreds of hormonal kids how to shoot a basketball."

"Exercise is rest!"

"That's Orwellian bullshit," Amos said through the phone.

"Amos says that's Orwellian bullshit," Hutch repeated.

"I don't know what Orwellian means, so I'm choosing to take that as a compliment." That was the downside of your best friend dating a nerd: an improved vocabulary.

"Buddy, I'm happy for you that you're running on a Saturday morning. But I'm sleeping in. You should, too. You have a busy day today."

I would've slept in, too. I had every reason to. I left a gorgeous guy in bed. Again.

"Hey, listen. Can we talk for a minute?" I asked.

"Yeah." Hutch sensed the shift in my voice instantly. He knew when to cut the bullshit. "Let me go onto the balcony for privacy."

Hutch and Amos's condo had a little balcony with a view almost as nice as my current one.

"What's going on? Is everything okay?" The light rustle of wind crinkled in his phone.

"Yeah. The wedding's...interesting. I'm performing."

"Performing?"

"Long story. Look, there's been some odd developments with me and Everett."

"Oh God. I knew it."

I felt my face turn red. "You knew what?"

"That you and Everett couldn't survive a weekend together without tearing each other's faces off."

If by faces, you mean clothes, then yes.

"Is it World War III up there?"

"Not quite."

Were Everett and I enemies once upon a time? That seemed like forever ago. It was crazy how fast things changed between us.

"How did you know that you were into Amos? Like really into him?" I crinkled a leaf in my hand, letting it turn to dust like I'd done as a kid.

"When did I realize I loved him?"

"Love? Let's not get carried away." I broke into a nervous laugh. "Baby steps. When did you realize 'Hey, I like this guy and I want to be around him like pretty much all the time.'"

Jesus, was that how I felt? Everett and I had been glued together for the past twenty-four hours, and it was the best day of my life.

"Huh. I see what's going on. You're in deep shit." Hutch let out a hearty laugh, an odd reaction to his friend being in deep shit. "You fell for someone else at the wedding, but you have to keep pretending you're in a fake relationship with Everett. Sounds like you really fell for someone hardcore."

"What makes you say any of that?"

"Dude, you wouldn't be calling me if this was just another Alicia or Svetlana or some other random hookup of the month. I can feel your cold sweat from Sourwood. You are *in* it, my friend."

"Am not?"

"Was that supposed to sound convincing?" Hutch was having too good of a time with this. "Sounds like you actually met someone you want to stick around. As for the Everett factor, you can tell this special someone that you and Everett recently broke up, but you're here as his date as one last favor."

"I could." If only it were that simple. "But the thing is, the Everett factor...is Everett."

"As in..."

I listened to the silence of Hutch connecting the dots in his head.

"Holy. Shit. You and Everett?"

"Me and Everett. The Reverett hashtag is real."

"What did you guys do?"

"Pretty much everything."

"Holy. Shit." Hutch let out a huge exhale, most likely releasing the excess smoke from having his mind being blown. "You should've let me have a cup of coffee before springing this on me. Shit."

I couldn't tell if this was a good shit or a bad shit. Did he think this was a terrible idea like it should have seemed? I hated being so confused. On the football field, the quarterback has to make several split-second decisions and act. I was stuck in overthinking limbo.

"Shit," he said again.

"It kinda just happened. Again and again." It was impossible not for me to grin at the thought of what Everett and I were up to. "He's not the snob I thought he was. He's just very passionate about the arts."

And passionate about having my dick inside him.

"Have you heard of a play called *Into the Woods*? It fucking rules, I think."

"*Into the Woods*? What? You're recommending a play to me?"

"It's a musical. Sondheim."

"Raleigh Marshall is recommending a musical to me. I'm going to need a lot of coffee. I should probably spike it, too."

"You gotta help me out, Hutch. I have no idea what the fuck is going on."

Last year, I gave him advice for wooing Amos at a party. Hopefully he could give some valuable advice and return the favor.

I heard Hutch go into the condo and pour himself a cup of coffee, then slide the balcony door open once more.

"How's the coffee?" I asked.

"So are you two like a real thing now?"

Hutch was definitely caffeinated. No time for segues.

"Uh, no, we're not. I don't think so. I'm kind of confused about all of it. That's why I was calling."

I sat down on a tree stump, fist under my chin like that thinker statue guy. He was probably dealing with romance shit, too.

"Is this just a prolonged hook up then?"

"I don't know. The past twenty-four hours. Hell, the past few days. No, actually, the past few weeks have been really, really good. We've been doing it like rabbits, but then there are times when we've just been hanging out, just talking, and it's so...easy." I wiped my brow with my shirt. The solitude of nature wasn't helping me figure things out. "Okay, it's like...so I love football season. I look forward to Sundays when it's wall-to-wall NFL. The previous week could be great, or it could be shitty, but no matter what, there was

Sunday waiting for me. It's the comforting feeling of hearing the NFL music and drinking good beer and watching quarter after quarter of exciting play. As soon as Monday morning comes around, I'm thinking about the next Sunday. Everett is like Sunday, but in person form. A really sarcastic Sunday that also has a dick."

Metaphors weren't my strong suit. I wish I could have Jordana open my brain and script what she saw.

"He makes me laugh, dude." A big ole smile spread across my face thinking about how much fun we were having. "Relationships are supposed to be hard. Mine have always been a constant negotiation. But being with Everett is..."

"Easy," Hutch said.

Fuck. I had it bad for Everett. I might as well bury myself in fall foliage and let myself decompose.

The line was too quiet.

"Say something."

"I...that was really sweet, dude," Hutch said. "You and Everett."

"Reverett."

"I'm not calling you that." Hutch sipped more of his coffee right next to his phone. I had to pull away from the static. "So what's the problem? Does Everett feel the same way?"

"I don't know. I hope he feels something or else he's a really good actor. But he's so focused on impressing his friends and ex-boyfriend. Maybe he just sees this as what it's supposed to be. A weekend of faking."

"There's only one way to find out."

I prayed for another way. My usual confidence was lacking here.

"I have an idea," Hutch said. "After the weekend, ask him on a date. The fake boyfriend stuff will be done, so you'll find out if he wants to actually date you."

"I don't know. He might think that I'm trying to keep the charade going. More posts for social media and all that."

"Then you have to be direct. You have to tell him that you want to go on a real date with him."

It sounded so simple, but what if he said no? The thought of hearing a no, having all this abruptly end, freaked the fuck out of me.

"I remember when I found Tori cheating on me. Everything was going well, and then I walked in on her screwing Donovan. It all ended in a blink. I thought things were rock solid between us."

"What do you tell your players? Fear and hesitation have no place on the field. If it's a no, then find out now."

He had a point. The more I built this up, the more paralyzed I would be. I couldn't sit in these woods forever.

"Look, you're a good guy, Raleigh. You have a good heart. If Everett doesn't care about that, then he's not worth your time."

A warm smile spread through my chest. I always missed the relationship with my brother, but I was able to find a replacement in good friends. Hutch and I had only known each other for a few months, but we had that instant brotherly love spark.

"Thanks, dude."

"I gotcha," Hutch said.

"Okay, well I'm gonna go back to my hotel room." To tell Everett that I like him.

Holy. Shit.

I continued my run back to the hotel. Nervous energy put an extra fast spring in my step.

When I got to our floor, the sounds of a shower could be heard from outside the room. I got inside and stripped off my sweaty shirt. I ducked my head into the bathroom.

"Hey. How was the run?" Everett called from behind the curtain.

My dick began to swell in my shorts.

"It was good. It's nice out." I hovered in the doorway. *Listen, can we talk?*

Everett peeked from behind the curtain, his hair matted down from the water, giving him an edgy look. "You want to join me?"

He bit his lip, the cherry on top of this sexy scene.

"Oh." My shorts went from a regular tent to a megachurch revival.

It wasn't urgent that I talk to him. There were more important things at hand. Like Everett, soaped up and naked.

The conversation in my head could be tabled. Why make things weird before the wedding, right?

"Make room then." I stripped off my shorts and underwear, kicked my shoes and socks under the sink, and joined my fake boyfriend for a scrub down.

23

EVERETT

Later that morning, I met up with my friends for wedding day mimosas in the bridal suite. Just the core friends, no partners. It gave us the time and space to catch up, and more importantly, rehash tons of old college stories and speculate about what other kids from our class were up to. I hoped that we were still telling these stories and online stalking these kids when we're seventy.

Despite it being their wedding day and the opening night of their one-night-only play, Jordana and Bethany were relaxed and in good spirits. They were being sweet on each other, but no different from any other day.

"Where's Noah?" Danita asked.

We were having such a good time that I hadn't noticed he was the odd man missing.

"He had to take a call with his agent," Jordana said with a little eye roll.

"I'm surprised his agent would call on a weekend," I said. It must've been big news, good or bad. *Ugh, get out of my head, Noah.*

Jordana shrugged. "I'm honestly surprised he's here at all. He should've brought his laptop. He could've gone ahead and completely rewritten my script."

"Jordy." Bethany put her hand on her fiancée's knee. "Noah is a perfectionist. We know this about him. This is nothing new."

"We're not putting on an off-Broadway show. It's our story for our friends and family. He really thinks he knows these characters better? They're us." Jordana rolled her eyes.

"You know Noah. It's his way or the Cross Bronx Expressway," Danita said.

I gave a groan of acknowledgement, and to my surprise, so did everyone else.

"I shouldn't dump on Noah. I'm grateful that he was able to come and participate. I'm still feeling salty about the ticket thing." Jordana drained her mimosa.

"What?" I asked. I was the little kid that picked at scabs; it seemed that habit never truly went away.

"It's nothing," Bethany said, the peacemaker that she is. "The last time we were in New York, we asked him for tickets to his show, but he couldn't hook us up."

"He wouldn't," Jordana interjected. "He said he couldn't go around giving everyone freebies. We would've bought tickets, but it was sold out."

"I see his point. He probably only has a limited amount of comped tickets he can give out." Bethany shrugged.

"Was there anyone else he comped that night?" I asked. Once I started picking, I couldn't stop.

"Not that we know of. So he had the tickets." Jordana refilled her glass with a fizzy mimosa. She was generous with the champagne.

"It's not a big deal. We managed to get nosebleed tickets for the next night, and we met him for a drink after. It was a good night," Bethany said.

The tension in the room said otherwise.

Jordana strummed her fingers against her glass. "It's just how he said it, though. *I can't go around comping everyone's tickets.* He made it sound like we were freebie seekers leeching off our friend. We would've gotten tickets, but they were sold out. Two tickets is not some huge ask when your friend is the star of a hit show. I've done it all the time for my plays, which are in much smaller theaters. We're not leeches."

Bethany wasn't disagreeing with her. She was more diplomatic. "I love Noah, but I think he sometimes gets off on the power trip."

"I guess being a bonafide Broadway star and one pesky Oscar away from an EGOT will do that to a person," I said with a bitchy swirl of my mimosa.

Bethany seesawed her head, *really* trying to stay diplomatic.

"This isn't a new development," she said. "Like I said, we all love Noah. He's always had his quirks."

She and Jordana shared an amused look, and when I glanced over at Danita, she seemed to have the same expression. Before I could follow-up, because I now had lots of follow up questions, Bethany slapped my knee, and the moment passed.

"Everett!" She squealed.

"Bethany," I squealed back.

"We love Raleigh!" Her head bobbed up and down. "Danita said he was cool, but he far surpassed expectations."

"You two are so cute." Jordana wasn't one to squeal, but her high-pitched voice was getting there. "So cute. It's disgusting and ridiculous and I love every second of it. And your scene yesterday was straight fire. Well, not *straight* fire. But you know what I mean."

"Raleigh is a better actor than I thought," I said, meaning that in multiple ways. At this point, he had me fooled.

"You two had chemistry." Bethany mashed her fists together to demonstrate. "We're talking the premium Tom Hanks-Meg Ryan variety."

I found myself blushing, and I could just imagine what Raleigh would say about the color of my cheeks and the ego boost my friends were providing. He'd think he was king shit. But he'd also make this perfectly pleased grin that I thought way too much about.

"And the way he looks at you, like you walk on air. I never had a guy look at me like that," Danita said.

I...never had either. Raleigh made me feel special, like what I did and what I said was worth paying attention to.

But was he just a good actor?

He played to win. Was he merely competitive, or was he feeling the weird mix of emotions I was feeling after last night?

I could feel myself falling for him, getting vulnerable again. What if we returned to Sourwood, he gave me a mission accomplished fist bump, and we went our separate ways?

"You are so into him," Bethany said. I wish I had a mirror to see what I looked like. "Don't let this guy go."

"I won't," I said, even though technically, I didn't have him to begin with.

———

I took the long way back before returning to the room. I ambled through the hotel grounds, taking in the lovely fall weather and fresh air. I had to clear my thoughts.

Was I so into Raleigh, as Bethany suggested?

I rounded a corner past the parking lot and found myself wandering onto the tennis court. This hotel had a tennis court? It was officially the nicest place I'd ever stayed in. Did guests know to bring their own rackets and balls, or did the hotels provide them? I had so many questions.

I went to center court and ran my finger over the top of the net.

The wind blew stray leaves into a circle, a mini tornado in the making.

"Hey, Everett."

Noah appeared by the gate. He wore a stylish peacoat and jeans, like he stepped out of a catalog. He sidled up the court and joined me at the net.

"Hey."

"Did you come here to play?" he asked.

"Oh yeah. You know me. Nothing I love more than playing sports in coldish weather," I said.

Noah peered at me with his golden eyes that had the power to transfix. Immediately, there was a vibe happening.

"It's been good seeing you, Everett." Noah put his hand on the net and moved closer to me, a train barreling into the station. "It'd been too long."

"It's been a while."

"I'm glad we could all get together this weekend. So much has changed, but so much hasn't, y'know."

It'd been years since we were all together, but my college friends and I slipped right back into our same jokes and banter.

"Congratulations on all your success. You made it."

"Yeah." Noah nodded, looked down at his shoes. Then, the golden eyes were on me again. "I miss you, Everett."

I'd spent years wanting to hear those words. The moment took on a surreal quality. In a word: whoa.

"I've been thinking about you for a while, and seeing you here has brought back all these memories." Noah's voice had an inherently melodic quality that made it easy to listen to. "We were magic back then. I've been kicking myself for how things ended. I let you go."

"You kicked me to the curb. On graduation day."

"I was born with a flair for the dramatic." He managed a weak smile. "That was a bad joke."

"I'm not laughing. I thought things were going well, and you up and dumped me. You hurt me. If you cared about me, you wouldn't have been so cruel."

"I was scared. And confused. I was a big fish at school, but when I moved back to New York, I was going to be a nobody."

"It didn't work out that way."

"I didn't know that at the time. And it took me a good three years to break through. Everybody had all these expectations for me to succeed. I was the star of the drama program. You admired me, Everett. I couldn't bear for you to see me as a nobody. It was easier for me to run."

He was right, unfortunately. I did admire him. That was part of our relationship dynamic. He was the one on stage, and I was perpetually looking up at him from the audience.

"I don't want to run anymore." He moved closer, his hand dragging over the net until his fingers touched mine. "What if we could have another chance? Do it right this time?"

My stomach leapt up into my throat. I pulled my hand away. "I have a boyfriend."

I'd relished the chance to say that to him, and now that I did, I didn't feel the expected sense of glee.

"And so do you!"

"No, I don't," he said quietly.

"Is Gavin your actual twin?" I snarked.

"We broke up a month ago. I asked him to pretend to be boyfriends again for the wedding so I could save face."

I tried not to act shocked, but I was not that good of an actor, hence why I'd shifted to directing. My fake relationship was motivated by his, which was fake. It was a fake boyfriend ouroboros.

"Are you serious right now?"

"It was a long time coming. Gavin and I are headed in different directions. I think we're too similar. I want someone who can balance me out."

I tried to look away, but his eyes locked on me like a missile about to launch. He stepped closer, proudly invading my personal space. I was confused, flabbergasted, and overwhelmed by nostalgia.

"Everett." He put a hand under my chin, his touch as soft as ever. "Am I crazy for feeling this?"

"Crazy in the clinical sense or the romantic sense? Because crazy has a different connotation, and mental illness isn't something to joke about lightly. Then there's the whole crazy ex-girlfriend trope where women are always thought of as crazy, which is such blatant misogyny. And I guess that isn't germane to our situation since we're both guys. And I'm rambling."

"Everett, stop talking," he said with a sharp smile.

He leaned in to kiss me. I pulled back just before our lips met.

"I have a boyfriend," I said.

"What is your heart saying?" He put his hand over said heart, which was racing like his words were laced with meth.

"It's saying..."

A phone buzz broke the moment. I grabbed at my pocket, but it wasn't my phone.

"Shit," Noah said, looking at his phone. "It's my film agent. I have to take this." He turned away and launched into a conversation with his agent about points and backend.

I stood there, processing all this whiplash.

Noah turned back to me. He squeezed my hand. "Can we talk later? Before the ceremony?"

I nodded and left him to discuss agent things. My brain went into a fog that I didn't come to until I was in the elevator.

What just happened?

What the fuck just happened?

I got to my room by sheer muscle memory, the click of the key card unlocking the door. Raleigh was laying on the mess bed in a

Huskies Football branded T-shirt and matching gym shorts. *A Midsummer's Night's Dream* played on TV.

"You're watching Shakespeare?"

"It's pretty good. I had no idea what they're saying, but I still get what's going on?"

Raleigh was at his most charming when he wasn't trying. Who else could make quasi understanding Shakespeare endearing?

"How was mimosas with everyone?"

"Good." I sat on the edge of the bed. "You won't believe what happened."

"Hit me."

"I was taking a walk through the grounds—there's a tennis court here, BTW."

"Shit, for real? That's some fancy pants shit."

"I know! Anyway, I was walking by the court, and all of a sudden, Noah comes up to me."

I could feel Raleigh tense up across the bed. He muted the TV.

My mouth was going a mile a minute before my brain could catch up. I was still processing everything that had transpired. Usually, I saved the drama for the stage.

"He and Gavin broke up a month ago. Gavin's here as a favor. They're faking it. Ironic, huh?"

"Yeah. Very."

"He says he regrets breaking up, and he still thinks about me, and he misses me."

"Huh."

"I know. It's all so wild. I'm still trying to make sense of everything. My goal this weekend was to save face in front of Noah and make him regret dumping me. But apparently, I didn't need to do all that because he already regretted it?"

Raleigh sat up, his back in a rigid perpendicular angle with the bed. "Guess I didn't need to be here."

"I'm glad you are. Seeing me with you made Noah have this

realization. And my friends are all obsessed with you." And their opinions of Noah weren't as high as I suspected, but that wasn't pertinent right now.

"So, are you going to get back with him?" Raleigh asked, cutting through all my confused bullshit. His voice was drained of his usual affable charm.

"I don't know. I–"

"You should."

"Oh."

Raleigh sounded dead confident. A chill entered the room. He flicked his eyes back to the TV.

"You should go for it. That's what you've wanted the whole time. You wouldn't have wanted to save face in front of Noah if you weren't still into him. He likes you, you like him. Boom. Touchdown." Raleigh unmuted the TV, and to underline his disinterest, he pulled out his phone and scrolled.

That was that. Whatever I thought was happening here was all in my head. Served me right for thinking differently.

"Okay then. Thanks for the pep talk."

"Yep."

I gave a half-wave and left the room without saying goodbye.

24

EVERETT

Back to the tennis court I went. It was my personal Walden Pond. I pulled out my phone and regretted not investing in fingerless gloves.

Everett: What in the name of fuck.

Amos: What happened?

Everett: Everything.

Chase: In a philosophical sense, I suppose you're right. Everything is constantly happening.

Everett: Chase. Don't.

Julian: What's going on?

Everett: Noah wants to get back together. But I don't know if I want to because I can't stop thinking about Raleigh, who I've been having epic sex with which apparently has been epic MEANING-LESS sex for him.

I clamped my eyes shut after re-reading the text. The past hour was a roller coaster of emotional whiplash. One of those old, wooden roller coasters that really threw you around. Hopefully my friends had some wisdom because I was all out.

I opened my eyes. No response. No three dots even.

Everett: Hello? Is this thing on?

Chase: Sorry. We're at Amos's place watching *Heartstopper* again. All of our heads just exploded.

Chase: Metaphorically, of course.

Amos: I don't think it's metaphorical. I think my brain is actually going to explode.

Julian: I second that. What?!

Amos: Can we call you?

Julian: Correction. We need to call you.

Everett: Yes! Here for it.

I set my phone up on a stray folding chair in the corner and sat against the fence. Very emo. The screen came alive with my friends, my sorely missed friends, all hunched around Amos's laptop.

"Hey! What's up?" I asked.

"Uh, you tell us, Everett," Amos said.

Sadly, my emo pose made it impossible to pace. My body needed to exorcize all this bundled up nervous energy. I found a grimy tennis ball and tossed it in my hands.

"Since when did you think about Raleigh in a way that wasn't pure dislike?" Chase asked.

"I knew you guys were going on too many fake dates." Julian smiled victoriously.

Amos wore a stern look; he'd probably kill me for holding back all this juicy gossip. "Make like a china set and dish."

And dish I did. In a whirlwind of talking, I told them everything. About Raleigh and me getting to know each other better and hanging out. About Raleigh and me dicking each other wild. About Noah's apology and his semi-grand, semi-romantic gesture on this very tennis court. I talked so much that I also regretted not bringing lip balm. Master storyteller that I was, my friends were transfixed, barely blinking.

But at the end, I exhaled and remained as torn as ever.

"Raleigh told me to go for it. He didn't hesitate." That part, that final part, stewed in my gut. "He didn't even care. For him, this really has been all for show, a grand facade."

My friends didn't have a fast answer. They looked at each other, as stumped as I was.

"What were you hoping he'd say?" Amos asked.

"That he didn't want to lose me to Noah. That he and I are a better match than Noah and I ever were. And maybe some dramatic setup where I'm walking to the door, but Raleigh jumps up from the bed and slams it shut. He spins me around and pulls me into a kiss. The audience goes wild."

Even when I was spiraling, I couldn't turn my director brain off.

"I got nothing from him except callous disinterest. Like none of this mattered."

The blank expression on his face, the way he kept watching TV as if this development meant nothing, as if I meant nothing, hurt the most.

"But it's okay. Because Noah likes me. He's finally realized that he made a mistake."

"That's good," said Amos. "That's what you've wanted."

"Yeah. This weekend was a huge success. It exceeded all of my expectations." I nodded my head, hoping my heart would catch up. "Noah and I can continue to be the power couple that we were in college."

The couple where I felt invisible and constantly unsure of myself. None of that insecurity would come back now that he was a famous star, right?

The guys had no supportive smiles for me, only furrowed, concerned brows.

"Sounds wonderful," Julian said, the vocal equivalent of a deflated balloon.

"It is. It's great," I protested.

"Is that what you want?" Chase, the most literal of our four-some, asked

"Yes!"

Hearing myself scream *yes* instantly made every part inside me scream back *no.* My gut would not be ignored. Noah was expired milk that I was forcing myself to drink. I slammed my head into the fence, the links jangling behind me. This weekend was not going how I had envisioned in multiple ways. Raleigh was supposed to be an elevated plus one. My friends and Noah would see us and see that I was doing well. It was a simple mission that got needlessly complicated.

I peeked open one eye at the screen. "Can I change my answer?"

Amos, Chase, and Julian all perked up. There were those supportive smiles I was missing.

"What do you want to change it to?" Amos asked, like a teacher trying to get his student to come to a realization.

"Raleigh," I grumbled.

"Do you like him?" Julian asked. His eyes were impossibly soulful. How I wound up friends with someone so goodhearted was beyond me, but very welcome.

"I...that's a complex question."

"It's not. It can be answered yes or no," Chase said.

"There are shades. I mean, he's a jock. Who likes football. And thinks *Mamma Mia!* is the height of the theatrical experience. But he's also thoughtful. And sweet. And he thinks I'm the greatest director who's ever walked the earth."

"I'm with Chase. Yes or no?" Julian asked. "Sometimes, the binary works."

"If I say yes, then that means I'm putting myself out there for disappointment because he's already shown that he doesn't like me in that way. We were just having fun and getting carried away. He doesn't feel how I feel."

"Yes, he does."

A muffled voice from off camera piped up. The guys all turned around.

"Who was that?" I asked.

Julian tilted the camera to show Hutch by the front door, his eyes bulging in panic at everyone looking at him.

"Honey, did you say something?" Amos asked.

"Uh, what? Me? No. I just got back from the gym." He held up his gym bag for proof. His face was fifty shades of white.

"I'm pretty sure you said something," I said.

"I heard it, too," said Chase. Julian raised his hand as if to say me three. I was me four.

"That's what you and Raleigh were talking about this morning!" Amos said.

"What? No. We were talking about football."

"Is that why you had to go onto the balcony and shut the door? You needed to have a private conversation about football?" Amos arched an eye, leaving no detail unturned.

Raleigh didn't strike me as the guy who randomly called up friends to chat. And he was running this morning. Why did he need to call Hutch in the middle of his run? My instinct was to assume he had buyer's remorse about sleeping with me, and he needed advice from his friend to slither away.

Hutch put down his bag lightly and tentatively approached the guys. "Look, Raleigh and I just talked about stuff. Maybe Everett came up. I overheard your call, and I shouldn't have said anything."

"But you said something. 'Yes,' to be exact." Chase's inquisitive tone would not be reasoned with.

"That was a cough?"

"Hutch," I said. "so you know, Amos is willing to go on a sex strike if you don't tell us what this conversation was about."

Hutch's mouth dropped open in panic. "Seriously?"

"No!" Amos piped in. Traitor. "I appreciate that you're holding your conversation in confidence. You're a good friend to Raleigh. But Everett likes Raleigh, and if there's something you know that could help them be together, then you shouldn't hold back."

"Or if Raleigh admitted that he's not into me, that's cool, too," I said.

"Ignore him," Amos said to his boyfriend.

Hutch did the mental calculation, then pulled up a chair and adjusted the screen to face me. "Raleigh likes you, too. He really likes you. He was thinking about telling you how he feels."

Fuck. I banged my head against the fence again. "And then I barged in and opened my stupid mouth about Noah."

Fucking Noah. No matter what, he always managed to be the center of attention.

But more importantly: *Raleigh likes me! He really likes me!*

I could dance on air and walk on the ceiling. Knowing that Raleigh Marshall liked me was one trillion times more awesome than knowing Noah did.

Annoying, cocky, sweet, thoughtful Raleigh liked me.

I blinked and returned to the present, where everyone got a kick out of watching me.

"What?" I asked.

They laughed. *How funny. A person head over heels for their fake boyfriend.*

"Are you one hundred percent certain, Hutch?" I needed total confirmation so I could keep my expectations in check.

"Yes, sir."

"Because he's a little bit of a manwhore, in a good, sex-positive way. Maybe he just really likes me the way he liked those other girls. A big burst of excitement, and then he was over it. Next week, after the high of the wedding and fakery, he could be like 'whatever' and onto the next. Which is fine. You know, it's his life.

Because to say you really like somebody is a big deal, at least for me, and I don't take those words lightly."

"Everett," Amos cut in.

"Yeah?"

"You're rambling," everyone said in unison.

"Chase, you're the most logical, reasonable one of all of us," I said. "What do you think?"

A huge smile curled on his lips as if he discovered that alchemy was real. "Go get 'em."

———

MY LEGS WERE like pogo sticks boinging me back to the hotel. My heart was racing, every pore on my skin was prickling with life. I kept picturing being with Raleigh.

Maybe we could hang out more.

Maybe we could help each other scavenge for deals.

Maybe he'd be there opening night for *Into the Woods*, which somehow I could maybe pull off.

Maybe he could convince me to watch all the remaining films in the *Fast & Furious* franchise.

It was all possible. I thought I was going to be sassy and single for the rest of my life. But I could still be sassy with a boyfriend.

The wedding was set to start in an hour. I had stage fright, but not for the play. For telling Raleigh how I felt. The high of the call with my friends was quickly wearing off, and now I needed to summon my courage and bare my soul and all that. I could bare my soul on stage, so long as it was someone else's words and someone else's character. But Everett Calloway baring his own soul?

Terrifying.

First, I had to make a pit stop at Noah's room. It was only right to tell him that I didn't want to be together. It wouldn't be right to leave him wondering and dangling.

But also, I was looking forward to dropping him the way he dropped me. I could be a petty bitch when I wanted to.

I knocked on his door, all pumped up on adrenaline.

"Hey." Noah was still in the middle of getting ready. His shirt was unbuttoned at the top with his tie hanging around his neck undone.

"Hi!" I said with a kindergartener's enthusiasm. "Can we talk?"

"Yeah. You can help me run my lines." Noah nodded for me to come inside. He was alone. He handed me an extra script.

"Where's Gavin?" I asked.

"Bethany and Jordana needed some last minute help setting up the stage, and I still needed to get ready so I sent Gavin to help. You're not dressed."

"I also need to get ready, but I can be quick."

"You can shower here." Noah put his hands on my hips. Where I once would've been turned on, I was now full-on repulsed.

"I'm good." There was only one man I wanted to shower with. And unlike the loser in front of me, my guy washed my hair and massaged my scalp.

Noah sat on the bed. He patted the space next to him, but like peeing, I had to do this standing up.

I crinkled his script in my hand. "Noah, I've been thinking about our conversation earlier. We've been through a lot. We had our time back in college, but I'm a different person now. It's not going to work out this time. I've grown. We've both grown. We've evolved. Humans are always evolving. My friend is a science teacher, and he said that theoretically the X-Men scenario could be real, because living organisms are always evolving."

"Jesus, must you always ramble?"

It hit me just then that for an actor, he was not a good listener.

I was quiet when we dated because he didn't want me to speak. I was quiet until I became invisible. Not anymore.

"How about I cut to the chase: in the words of Ms. Swift, we are never ever getting back together. But maybe you could have a three-way with your ego and your receding hairline."

Noah's face turned to stone. A bitter smile took over his lips, as if it were hilarious that someone would turn down an award-winning actor. "Are you sure about this, Everett? You and I make sense. You and your airhead gym teacher don't."

"I could see why you think that. I used to think that. But I've never made so much sense with one person before. It's wild."

"Everett, come on. Sit down with me. You're not giving a mono-logue. Let's talk about this. I really felt something between us."

Noah reached for my hand, but I moved back.

"Well I didn't! What about me? Don't I have a say? I never had a say in our relationship. That's why you liked me."

He rolled his eyes, annoyed that I was talking and taking up space. "This is bullshit. I don't know why you choose to make me the villain in your life. That's a conversation you need to have with yourself. But fine, why don't we have one last roll in the hay. Get it out of our systems. I know you've been thinking about it."

Noah leaned back in a sexy come hither pose. And sorry pal, but now that I've seen Raleigh naked, I might as well have been looking at cold spaghetti.

"Pass."

"Fine. Then give me my script back. I need to prepare." He ripped it out of my hand, giving me a nasty paper cut in the process. And right in the space between my thumb and index finger, too. I put my hand to my mouth.

"Do you have a tissue?"

"Careful, Everett." Noah leapt back. "I'm wearing a white shirt."

He pointed to the box of tissues on the nightstand. "You have to get ready. It'd be rude of you to hold up the ceremony."

I put my cut to my mouth to help clean up the mess, which only made things worse. I glommed a bunch of tissues on the wound.

"Do you have a band-aid?" I asked.

"I don't. The front desk should." Noah adjusted his tie in the mirror, keeping his distance for the sake of his white shirt. "Just go."

I opened his door with my free, unsliced hand. "I was wrong."

"How so?"

"I thought fame changed you. But it didn't. You've always been an asshole."

25

RALEIGH

When I was a kid, I promised myself that I'd never make myself wear a tie as an adult. They were the most unnecessary clothing item invented, only useful when needing to tie someone to the bed.

I looked at my umpteenth uneven tie in the bathroom mirror. The skinny part came down to my crotch, and the fat part stopped at my chest. I ripped it off and threw it on the floor. On a good day, I couldn't tie a tie. But today, feeling like shit after my conversation with Everett, it was damn near impossible.

Why was I so upset? I should've known he still had the hots for the ex-boyfriend. Hell, the whole reason I was here was to make Noah jealous. It wasn't to save face. It was to get him back. In that case, touchdown Everett. It was my fault for thinking this was something it wasn't.

At least I didn't have to walk in on Noah's pale ass humping my fake boyfriend.

This was why I didn't put myself out there. There was no soft landing with romance. You were either on top of the world or kicked to the curb.

The only reason I wasn't bolting for Sourwood was because I didn't leave teammates in the lurch. Jordana and Bethany were counting on me to act in their wedding ceremony. I'd played football with sprained ankles and broken fingers. I could get through this wedding.

Then I'd bolt. Tell Everett something came up at home. He wouldn't miss me. He was probably going to spend the night with Noah tonight.

They were probably going to do it on the clean bed.

I scrolled through my phone, going through my list of ex-lovers and one night stands. One of these lucky numbers could take my mind off Everett tonight via late night booty call.

I tried one more time to do my tie.

Ah, fuck it.

I threw it on the bathroom floor and tossed on my blazer.

My stomach seized into knots when I heard the door unlock.

"Wow," Everett said, staring at me. "You look really good. You clean up well."

"Thanks. I wasn't going to half-ass my fake boyfriend role, even if I'm not technically needed anymore."

"About that...can we talk?"

"The wedding's starting soon. You need to get dressed. We can talk after." I was dreading the conversation to come. *Raleigh, it was just hate sex. That's all this was.* Maybe I could slip out of the wedding before Everett had a chance to officially break my heart.

"I'll be quick." Everett kept a hand awkwardly in his pocket while the free one scrambled through his garment bag for his wedding outfit.

"You're going to wrinkle your whole outfit." I unzipped the garment bag for him.

"Thanks. You're really thoughtful, Raleigh." He had a sweet tone and gazed up at me, his green eyes almost fooling me into thinking he meant it.

"Let's go. You have to get dressed. Everyone's waiting for you. Including Noah."

"Noah can go fuck himself."

I had whiplash, unless he meant for Noah to fuck *him*.

"Huh," was all I could muster.

"Noah's an asshole." Everett tried removing his suit from the garment bag one-handed. This was five seconds away from turning into a #weddingfail.

"You might have more success if you took your hand out of your pocket."

He removed his hand, which was wrapped in layers of bloodied tissues.

"Jesus Christ. What the hell happened?"

"It's not bad. I think the bleeding has stopped. I'll get dressed and then ask the front desk for a band-aid."

"You need to wash it out. Come with me." I took him by the tissue clump and led him to the bathroom. I turned on the warm water and pulled a washcloth from the stack of clean towels, one of the only towels left that we hadn't used.

"Thanks. I get frazzled when I know I'm going to be late."

"You won't be late. You might've prepared for this weekend by bringing lube and condoms. I prepared by packing band-aids in my dopp kit." It was a lesson learned after too many shaving incidents.

I grabbed a band-aid and cleaned out the cut. It wasn't bad. Just a slice.

"You don't have to do this," he said.

He was right. I wasn't his boyfriend. He had a free hand. He could clean his own wound, apply his own bandage. But I told myself it was the fastest way.

"So what happened?" I asked.

"Noah ripped the script out of my hand too fast, and it–"

I looked up, my jaw going tight. "Noah did this?"

"Yeah. It was an accident."

"He made you bleed?"

"I guess technically yeah. It's just a paper cut. It'll be fine."

"He hurt you?" My blood ran cold with a pure, cleansing fury.

"I mean, it stings."

"He hurt you." That fucking prick. He made Everett bleed, then left him to deal with the mess. What the hell did Everett see in him?

I bandaged Everett, then stared at him with single-minded focus. "Put on your suit and meet me downstairs."

"What are you doing?"

"He made my boyfriend bleed," I growled as I charged into the hall.

"It was a paper cut, and it clotted fast!" Everett yelled through the closing door.

I clomped to the elevator, my legs taking hulking strides. I pressed the down arrow, but I didn't want to wait. I sprinted down four flights of stairs to the main floor, adrenaline pumping through me. My vision was white and hot as I charged across the lobby.

The automatic doors practically jumped out of the way to let me out of the hotel. I was like the Terminator on a course that could not be stopped.

In the parking lot were golf carts ready to take guests to the amphitheater.

"Hello, sir. Are you going to the wedding?" the golf cart chauffeur, a pockmarked kid all of eighteen, asked me.

"I can drive." I grunted out. The kid turned white, sensing that I wasn't going to take no for an answer. He hopped out of the driver's seat.

Everett's yells behind me were a blur.

Noah hurt the man I care about.

I sped down the path that led to the amphitheater. I slammed on the accelerator.

The *Fast & Furious* movies never had a chase scene with a golf cart for good reason: they could only go so fast. I pushed the cart's limits as I zoomed through the wooded path into the park, swerving around other carts merrily making their way to the festivities.

Were this a *Fast* movie, I'd jump from the cart as it crashed into strategically placed oil barrels, which would explode in an orgy of fire.

In the real world, I parked it with the other carts and made a beeline for Noah.

He held court in the field at the back of the amphitheater with the brides and their college friends. Without saying a word, I grabbed him by his collar and pushed him up against a tree.

"What the hell?" he squealed out. His friends crowded around us.

"Raleigh!" Everett yelled behind me, catching his breath. He got off a cart driven by the pockmarked kid. He was still in his regular clothes.

"Apologize to Everett," I said slowly and calmly. "Now."

"For what?"

I pointed to his bandaged hand.

"Are you serious? It was a paper cut! Everett, are you being serious right now?" Noah looked from me to Everett. I pressed him harder against the tree until he winced in pain.

"You hurt my boyfriend. Apologize now."

"I'm sorry."

I shoved him harder until tree bark molded into his suit jacket. "Like you mean it."

"I'm sorry. It was an accident, Everett."

"Now apologize for being a dirtbag boyfriend in college."

"What?" he asked in a high-pitched crack.

"You heard me. You were mean to him then, making him feel small. And if you two are going to give it another go, you better not hurt him again. Because I'll find out. And if I do, then your acting skills will help you out in witness protection."

"Raleigh, we're not getting back together!" Everett exclaimed. "I don't want to be with him."

"You don't?" I asked.

"I don't. Just because he and Gavin are broken up doesn't mean he can slot me in."

"This is news to me." Gavin came forward and approached his squirming boyfriend. "When did we break up?"

"Wait, what?" Everett asked.

"We're not broken up. We're booked for a couples cruise in the spring." Gavin folded his arms and stared confused daggers at his boyfriend.

"I thought we were in an open relationship," Noah said, now no longer in a hurry to be put down.

"Just because you fool around with chorus boys behind my back doesn't mean this is an open relationship." Gavin shook his head and rolled his eyes. He tried to act nonchalant, but nobody could act their way through this betrayal. I felt bad for the guy. At least Everett and I knew what the deal was.

"Baby, let's talk about it."

"Noah, you want to be broken up? Your wish is my command." Gavin punched his boyfriend square in the stomach. Noah doubled over in my hands, and the force of Gavin's fist was so strong that I couldn't hold Noah up. He slumped to the ground.

"I'm so glad I took that stage combat workshop." Gavin walked away, leaving us all in his dust.

"What the hell is going on?" Bethany asked, visibly angry, her arm around her shaken fiancée. They were dressed in beautiful white suits, reminding me that this night was about them, not this bullshit.

"I'm sorry. I'm so sorry." I felt like shit. I was surrounded by theatrical types, and yet I was the one who made a scene. Some of the adult guests looked our way as they found their seats.

I helped Noah up and wiped off dirt and bark from his suit. He gave a quick, appreciative nod then got the fuck away from me.

"I'm sorry about all of this," Everett said to his friends.

"Jordana and I are getting married in eight minutes. Can everyone save their motherfucking drama until after we step on the glass?"

Danita came forward, her stage manager personality coming through. "Everett, get changed ASAP. Everyone else, take your places. The show will go on."

Everett wouldn't meet my eyes. I cursed myself as I drove us back to the hotel, not a word said between us.

26

RALEIGH

I decided to wait outside our room for Everett to get ready. The guy was already pissed at me. The wedding was starting in less than five minutes, and I knew it was killing Everett that we wouldn't be there on time.

The door whooshed open. Everett bolted into the hallway in such a rush that I didn't have time to admire how friggin' sexy he looked in his plaid suit and Gucci loafers. He should be on the cover of *GQ*. Or in bed with me.

Well, those days are over.

I jogged to catch up to him at the elevator.

"You look amazing."

"I know. I wasn't coming to this wedding wearing anything less than a fuck-you-I'm-sexy suit."

The elevator dinged open. It took its sweet time getting to the lobby, leaving me, Everett, and a huge gap of strained silence between us.

"How's your hand?" I asked.

"It's fine. It was literally just a paper cut."

"Look, Ev–"

"Raleigh." He turned to me, his eyes laser-focused, his body jumpy with the time crunch. "Because the wedding is starting in —" he checked his phone. "—two minutes, I'm going to cut to the chase: Noah is dogshit. I like you. And you like me."

I did an epic double take. "Wait, what? You like me?"

"Yes. I'm a fucking goopy mess over you. Keep up."

The elevator dinged open. Everett and I cut a line straight through the lobby like we were on a runway.

"The second Noah said he wanted to get back together, this big red abort button went off in my head. It was a hard no from me. Because I want to be with you."

Hearing him say that melted my heart and everything else inside me.

"I'm just as shocked as you are," he said with a smile that I would be committing to memory. He swung through the revolving door with me right behind.

"I thought you ultimately wanted to get back together with Noah. You seemed into it."

"Noah ambushed me and told me he wanted to get back together. I was in shock. And maybe at one point I did dream about reconciling, but that was before I fell for my fake boyfriend and became the aforementioned goopy mess." He slid into the golf cart's passenger seat while I turned the ignition.

We raced through the path almost as fast as my heart was racing.

"If you hadn't shut down earlier in the hotel room, then I could've mustered up the courage to tell you this back then, and we could've had pre-wedding sex. Again. I swear, sometimes you can be infuriating, and not in the sexy way."

The rushed confession was freeing. We were able to lay it all out there.

"I'm sorry for shutting down so fast. I really like you, Ev. I'm not used to feeling this way about someone. The people I've cared about the most have done the most damage, so I was trying to protect myself."

"I get it. You're the offensive guard protecting his quarterback from getting sacked."

Did he just use football lingo accurately? "That was the hottest thing anyone's ever said."

"You didn't need to do that macho histrionic bullshit with Noah earlier. I want you to know that just because we're officially dating doesn't mean I'm going to be this damsel in distress who needs his man to defend his honor."

"So we're officially dating?"

"Yes. I can't stop thinking about you. Jesus. Keep up. And go faster."

I went full Diesel and put the pedal to the metal, flooring it through the forest.

"I can't stop thinking about you either. You've gotten under my skin. You made me go see a play about Albert Einstein."

"And you made me watch a football game."

"But getting to know you has been one of the great experiences of my life. I've never been happier than when I'm with you."

"Ugh, same. I'm five seconds away from doodling your name in the margins of my script. It's so annoying." Everett rolled his eyes.

"And here I thought you hated me."

"Don't misunderstand me. You're an overly confident, exasperating jock who admitted that he finds sadistic pleasure in antagonizing me."

"And you're still an uptight, judgmental snob."

"I'm glad we cleared the air."

I drove past where the other golf carts were stationed and parked just behind the back row. On stage, the first scene of the play was being acted out. We snuck down the side row to the back-stage area.

"Hold up." Everett whispered in the wings offstage. He spun around and planted a sweet kiss that promised much more to come. "Of all the people out there, it had to be you, huh?"

"Sucks to be you."

"No, it doesn't."

I pulled him to me and squeezed his ass. He wrapped one leg around my waist before we pulled away from each other. We had a show to put on.

I took Everett's hand and led us to our seats on stage.

———

I WAS USED to being stared at, but having an audience here to listen to me recite words was a whole new frightening experience.

I kept stealing shameless glances of Everett through the play. He was fucking dashing in his suit, which was fitted on his slim body.

Noah's scene bombed. Nobody laughed at his punchlines, and the audience seemed apathetic to his more earnest readings. Because Gavin left, Jordana took the role, and they didn't have the same spark. Jordana didn't act like someone in love with her scene partner.

My palms got sweaty as the pages in the script turned. Everett rubbed a soothing hand on my leg and gave me a lazy grin that put me at ease. We got this.

I infused my lines with every ounce of meaning until my soul was wrung dry. I left it all on the staged reading field. I imbued my character's dialogue with heart and longing and need, everything I'd given him during our amazing weekend together. Everett acted the fuck out of his final monologue, stirring a feeling in my heart that made my throat go dry.

The audience gave us a rousing round of applause.
Touchdown.

———————

EVERETT PULLED me onto the dance floor. "It's time to put this body to use, Marshall."

The night turned into one of the most fun of my life. I'd been to fun weddings, but this one took the cake. Oh, and it had good cake, too.

"Let's see if you can dance," he said.

Fake Boyfriend Skill #3: Be a great dancer.

Monuments should be erected to my wedding dance skills. It was another arrow in my quiver for being an impressive fake boyfriend. Speaking of...

"So you really meant what you said before, about us being real boyfriends?" I asked.

Before Everett could answer, ABBA's "Dancing Queen" came on, and the entire wedding lost their shit, as people do when "Dancing Queen" comes on.

"See? What'd I tell you? People love *Mamma Mia!*"

Everett tugged me by the blazer flush against his body. The mix of sweat and cologne in his scent was more intoxicating than the open bar.

"No," he said with a confusing smile.

"No, you don't want to be real boyfriends?" I asked.

"No, not everyone loves *Mamma Mia!*"

"So that's a yes?"

"No."

"No?"

"I'm messing with you, ya dumb jock. We already have a hashtag. Might as well use it."

I tipped his chin to meet me in a kiss that set me on fire. We were threatening to pull focus from the women of the hour. We were in romantic bliss, backed by an ABBA soundtrack.

"Ugh." Everett rolled his eyes and nodded at the corner of the room. I followed his disgusted glance to where Noah was flirting with a server. All he wanted was someone to feel superior to. Gross. "Why was I ever into that loser?"

"Beats the heck out of me. That man is the dumbest person I've ever met. He had the opportunity to be with you, the soon-to-be director of *Into the Woods*, and he fumbled on the one-yard line."

"I have no idea how the hell I can pull together *Into the Woods* in eight weeks. We don't have the cast, or the budget, or the..."

I put a finger to his mouth. "Ev, we'll get it done."

Everett and I danced and danced. We chatted and laughed with his friends at table nine, making it the place to be. Bethany and Jordana kept leaving their newlywed table to join us. Everett's friends considered me their friend. We went to the bar and did shots. Lots of shots. More shots than I expected from this crew. Actors loved to drink, Danita told me.

"You are glowing," she said to Everett during a round of shots toasting to their old acting professor who'd passed away. Bethany, Jordana, and the rest of our friends nodded in agreement. Noah ducked out after the first dance. He claimed he had an early morning meeting with his agent.

"I feel like you've come into your own, y'know?" Danita said as the bartender filled a line of shot glasses. "When you were with Noah, it was like you were afraid to shine."

She threw an arm around me, as much as she could since I was very broad shouldered. "You guys make the best couple."

"Can I let you in on a little secret? We're not really dating," Everett said. "Raleigh's here as a favor to me. We're fake boyfriends."

His friends shared confused looks and got alarmingly quiet.

Then they burst out laughing.

"You expect us to believe that bullshit?" Jordana passed around shot glasses.

Bethany chuckled to herself. "You almost had us, Everett."

"Nice try, Ev." I pulled him against me, and we shared our final kiss as fake boyfriends.

27

EVERETT

TWO MONTHS LATER

Amos: Tonight's the night. Nervous?

    Everett: If the play you watch tonight is a hideous, dumpster fire disaster, just keep it to yourself and lie to me. Kthanxbye.

    Julian: It's going to be great! I heard it was sold out.

    Everett: A dumpster fire in front of a full audience.

    Amos: Stop!

    Chase: My students have been buzzing about it all week. I wish they talked about amino acids with the same excitement as *Into the Woods*.

    Amos: I don't think that's gonna happen, dude.

    Julian: You've been dating a jock for a few months and you're already resorting to calling us Dude? What's next - bro?

    Everett: Can we focus on what's important here?

    Everett: Me.

    Amos: You got this. You're the best theater director I know.

    Chase: Isn't he the only theater director you know?

    Everett: What if everything is all off and the audience bails after the first act?

Julian: We won't.

Julian: We'll be there till the end.

Everett: You say that now...

Amos: We are your closest friends, Everett. We're like family. If the play sucked, we'd happily say it to your face. :)

Chase: Raleigh is already convinced this is the best play in history. He's been talking it up nonstop. How many football players are in the show?

Everett: Two! And they can actually sing.

Amos: You have a very sweet boyfriend.

Everett: I do, don't I?

———

"ENOUGH TEXTING." The muscley arm of my half-asleep boyfriend reached across and grabbed my phone. He tossed it on his bedroom floor, then resumed holding me in place like I was about to ride a roller coaster.

"My friends were wishing me good luck tonight."

"Shouldn't they be wishing that you break a leg?"

Touché. And what was I looking at a screen for? I had a gorgeous, shirtless man in bed with me. And that man was my boyfriend.

Raleigh, eyes still closed, dragged his hand up to my face. What might have started as a caress ended with him clamping his hand on my cheek as if he were reading braille.

"This isn't sexy," I said as an errant finger slipped into my mouth.

Raleigh grunted. It was unnatural how hot he looked first thing in the morning. It was making me reconsider my coffee before sex philosophy. He looked up at me, his eyes squinty and cute.

"How'd you sleep?"

"I've been up for an hour, staring at the ceiling."

"Chill. It's going to be an awecess," he said, brushing golden locks from his eyes. "An awesome success."

It sounded too much like abscess, but I didn't have the heart to tell him.

"The Huskies victory over North Point was an awecess. This could be a ragesaster, a raging disaster."

Yes, as a dutiful boyfriend, I attended every single one of the Huskies' playoff games. And yes, I got really into it. It was drama! Each week had greater stakes, evolving storylines, shocking twists, and characters to root for. I cheered the loudest for our matchup with North Point High, where we trounced Coach Pancake Ass's team. Jackson the quarterback was the MVP of that game, connecting with nearly every pass, shutting up everyone in town who doubted his ability.

Would I find the same level of victory tonight?

For the past few weeks, I've been working to get *Into the Woods* off the ground. Rehearsals every day after school, coordinating with our student crew and student orchestra, organizing fundraisers to pad our meager budget.

The week we returned home from the wedding, Raleigh made several loud, vocal pitches for kids to audition. On the morning announcements, in his gym classes, during the football pep rally. That wiped away the stigma surrounding the school musical, as did a few athletes auditioning. When I posted a fresh sign-up sheet, it quickly filled up with real names. I never found out who defaced the original sheet, but it didn't matter anymore. As Amos would say, it was ancient history.

And it was all thanks to Raleigh.

I turned to him and rubbed a hand over his chest, just because that was something I could do now. When dating a guy with a hot bod, one must take advantage at all times.

"What if my directions weren't clear? What if all these first-time actors get stage fright? What if the smoke machines don't work? For a play to be a success, hundreds of little things have to go right. God, what if one of the students accidentally utters Macbeth in the theater and curses the production? We're not doing Shakespeare, but it could still come up somehow. Somebody could try and tempt fate."

Raleigh yanked me on top of him. Our lips met in a sensational kiss.

"I'm rambling."

"You are. I love your rambling."

"You're just saying that to get in my pants."

"It's not that hard to do." He slid both hands down the back of my boxers and grabbed my ass. "Relax, Ev."

He kneaded his fists into my ass cheeks, which felt surprisingly good. His strong hands moved up my back and gave my shoulders a rub.

"Here's what's going to happen. *Into the Woods* will go off without a hitch. Everybody is going to love it. The end."

I let out a moan, from his hands and his pie-in-the-sky vision. I didn't think my mind was capable of positive thinking. I preferred to live on the brink of perpetual disaster. It was good for the metabolism.

His hands moved back down to my ass, kneading and massaging.

"It's sold out. The opening is playing to a packed house," I said.

"There's only one opening I care about right now." His fingers slid over my crack, coating me in shivers. "Ev, we're about to hit a point of no return."

My ass moved to meet his fingers, hoping they'd slip further and hit the jackpot. "Aren't you a holesexual?"

"That's w-h-o-l-e."

I thrust back against his fingers to end this spelling lesson.

Raleigh let out a low groan. He spread me open and rubbed his finger against my hole. A swell of need surged in me.

"Get on your back." Raleigh pushed me backwards, and I spread out on the bed, legs automatically shooting into the air.

He yanked my underwear off in one smooth, ravenous motion. My hard cock stuck straight up. He slid his thumb, slick with spit, inside me. Then he added his tongue, the two tag-teaming my ass until I nearly lost consciousness.

"Fuck me, Raleigh."

"What about foreplay?"

"I won't last."

"You want to cut Act One and go right into Act Two?"

"While I think it's hot that you just used a theater metaphor, if you don't rush my end zone now, I'm going to have you ejected from the game, and I'll hit the showers by myself."

A wave of lust clenched me at the sound of him pulling off his boxers and slapping his engorged cock on my opening. He dribbled lube on my hole, then slid another powerful finger inside me.

I fucked against his fingers.

"So needy," he said in a low tone. I opened my mouth for his middle finger, which he slipped inside for a coat of saliva, then seconds later drove into my hole.

"You...quarterback."

"Quarterback isn't an insult."

"Shit." I loved our fun banter, but I couldn't come up with a witty retort when half his hand was inside me making me see stars.

Raleigh pulled out. He was loving having this control over me. I tried to act nonchalant, but that was hard to do when I was leaking pre-cum and moaning at the sight of him ripping open a condom.

He threaded his hand in my hair and kissed my neck as his

thick cock entered me. I went full pins and needles, overwhelmed by the masculine force of him.

I was a moaning mess, playing for the imaginary rafters. Raleigh made me want to be loud. I wanted the world to know how good it was to be fucked by this man.

He grunted above me, his chest sweaty, nibbling at my ear, meeting me for hungry kisses as he stretched me open. I was cocooned in his embrace.

"You drive me fucking wild," he whispered in my ear.

"Don't stop." I held on for dear life, wanting so badly to erupt but not wanting this moment to end.

He lifted me up and moved us to his dresser, all while staying inside me. The power of being hung.

The dresser was remarkably solid, taking our thrusting with minimal rattling.

"Where'd you get this?" I asked between moans.

"Facebook Marketplace. It was originally 800 bucks. They were selling it for 150. I bargained them down to 100."

Hot.

"Oh my God, I think I'm gonna come!" I jerked myself off, getting off on watching him, hot white jets filling the sweaty space between us.

Color flushed Raleigh's cheeks as he shot his load inside me.

He planted a sweet kiss on my lips, as if we were engaged in a wholesome romance.

"I'll go put on a pot." He went to detach, but I held him in place.

It was another moment I wanted to lock into memory. I thought I wasn't built for romance. I was glad to be wrong. Raleigh carried us back to bed.

"Sorry. I wasn't ready for this to end," I said.

"Relax. I'm not going anywhere, Ev."

———

"Curtain's up in fifteen minutes." Dean, hockey player by day and stage manager tonight, made the announcement backstage. He repeated it into his microphone, which sent the message to the lighting crew.

I knew that I used to give athletes shit for not being able to do anything but play with a ball, but they turned out to be incredibly creative and responsible young adults.

Backstage looked like a locker room. Athletes from different sports mingled in the wings. They'd built sets and took on roles.

Carson, a massive block of a teenager and one of Raleigh's linebackers, charged up to me. I had a feeling charging was his default mode. He was decked out in his Big Bad Wolf costume complete with makeup. It made him a very scary wolf, who also happened to have wonderful pipes.

"Mr. Calloway, I'm still confused on my motivation."

"You're the Big Bad Wolf."

"But am I, though? What if I see Little Red Riding Hood as my sister, and I'm not trying to eat her. What if I'm just trying to get us to hang out again?"

Actors.

"Carson, you're the Big Bad Wolf. You like to lure children into the woods and eat them."

"But what if I don't? Maybe Big Bad Wolf is just, like, a label put on my character by society. What if I'm just Wolf?"

I put my hands on his shoulders, which was difficult considering he was a human obelisk. "*Into the Woods* is deconstructing fairy tales. The Big Bad Wolf likes being big and bad. He is the one who chose that name for himself. He has agency here. Some of us eat a Snickers bar, some of us eat children. That's the circle of life."

"Isn't that from *The Lion King*?"

"The point still stands. Do you know what all actors love to play? The bad guy. They love playing villains. It's so much fun. Playing good people is boring. You have the most coveted role in the play."

A smile slid onto his lips, his made-up face getting extra animated. "I like that."

"Good. You're going to do great."

"Thanks, Mr. Calloway. I don't know what the old coach was thinking. Theater is cool!"

"We should get that printed on a T-shirt." I watched him run back to his starting place, the theater shaking in his wake.

I went over the plans with Dean one final time. The theater director wasn't backstage during the performance. The stage manager was the one in charge during showtime, making sure people remembered their cues. I got to watch from the audience, which was a blessing and an anxiety-filled curse.

After my talk with Dean, I returned to the wings to find it empty. Where had the actors and crew gone? My nerves were already on a razor thin edge. Having forty students vanish was not helping.

I heard a familiar voice coming from the dressing rooms. I poked my head in to find Raleigh in the center of a circle surrounded by actors and crew.

He had everyone take a knee.

"Ev, I was giving a last minute pep talk. Would you like to say something?"

"Directors don't really give pep talks."

"Well, don't you want to wish them well before the play goes up?"

He had a point. I looked around at the actors, a mix of social groups. Freshman, seniors, jocks, nerds, theater types, bookish types. It was a beautiful sight, what every drama teacher wanted to see. These kids were the best of South Rock High, showing what we could accomplish when we came together.

"So here we are. After weeks of rehearsals, we are about to mount the biggest, most elaborate musical in South Rock's history. Ever since I saw *Into the Woods* on Broadway, I wanted to put it up here. People told me it couldn't be done. There were too many sets, too many actors, too many songs, too many costumes. But I never lost hope. And now here you all are. Every person in this room has blown me away. I have been dazzled by the touches to your performances, to the details in your sets, to how much you care. It's cool to care about things, isn't it?

"I'm looking out on athletes, and drama nerds, and AP kids, people who live and breathe theater, and those who'd never sung a bar before. You are all more powerful than you realize. What you are about to accomplish is incredible. And fun! Don't forget to have fun out there! You're getting to play pretend. When we work together, we can do anything."

I gazed at Raleigh by the door, hanging on my words.

"Anything you wanted to add, Coach Marshall?"

"Yeah." Raleigh stomped forward. "Nobody comes into our house and pushes us around."

"Nobody's pushing us around," I said.

"Oh. That works a lot better for football games. But no, actually, it works here. The audience isn't going to push us around. Don't let them get inside your head. Now I want you to go out there and drive to the end zone. Ugh, metaphorically. Drive to the climax?"

Some of the actors giggled. They were still teenagers, after all.

"You got this. Now let's get out there and kick some Sondheim ass! Bring it in!" Raleigh had everyone put their hand in the center. He pulled me close to him. "Get in on this, director."

I slapped my hand on top.

"Go Huskies on the count of three," I said. "One...two...three."

GO HUSKIES!

28

RALEIGH

Tonight was the faculty Christmas party, which was being held at Stone's Throw Tavern. Aka, shots with co-workers!

I held up my shot glass to our small circle of friends. "Happy holidays! Best year ever!"

I clinked my glass against Everett's. We downed them instantly.

It was worth noting that Everett was wearing candy cane suspenders. I would be tying him up in them later tonight.

"Seriously, though. This year has been one of the best ever. I found a new best friend." I nodded at Hutch. "And made new friends." I nodded at Amos, Chase, and Julian. "We defeated North Point."

"Anything else?" Everett asked with an impatient eyebrow raise.

"Oh yeah. How could I forget? I PR'd on the bench press."

"Funny," he said.

"And of course, Everett finally admitted his long-simmering feelings for me."

On cue, Red Hulk joined the party.

"Long-simmering? You wish!"

"Let's be honest. You've had the hots for me since the second you met me. It was glaringly obvious. It was globvious."

"The only thing that's been 'globvious' is your blatant obsession with me."

Even though we were dating, I could still bust his chops. I pulled my cute Red Hulk by the suspenders into a kiss.

"As if anything could top being with you?" I whispered between us. I snapped a suspender against his slender chest.

"Gross." Hutch threw popcorn at us. "No PDA. This is a work event."

Principal Aguilar swung by and looked over our gathering. "Don't get too drunk, guys. I brought the karaoke machine."

He pointed at his prized possession, plugged in and center stage, waiting to be used.

"Karaoke is better the drunker you are," Amos said.

"Will you boys do another rendition of 'I Want it That Way'?" he asked.

"Another?" I asked. Was there video evidence of the previous time. The four nerdy teachers looked at each other, the idea seeming like a real possibility.

"We'll see," Everett said. "Maybe we'll do One Direction's 'You and I.'" He nudged Amos in the elbow. His friend turned red at the mention of that song. It was his and Hutch's song for adorable, personal reasons.

"I just want to say how much I love having all of you at school. You make South Rock a pleasure to lead," Aguilar said.

The man liked us almost as much as his cacti.

Oh, and his actual boyfriend.

Clint, said boyfriend, stopped by and held mistletoe above his and Aguilar's heads.

"Merry Christmas, fellas," Clint said. He was a fortysomething gruff construction worker, but whenever he got near his boyfriend, he turned into a fluffy stuffed animal.

Aguilar turned and pecked Clint on the lips.

"Is that all you got?" I asked, goading them on.

"This is still technically a work function," Aguilar said.

"C'mere, babe." Clint pulled him closer and smacked a big, honking kiss on his boyfriend. No tongue, though. It was over the top and corny.

"Are you and I gonna get like that one day when we're old?" Everett asked.

"Nah," I lied.

Aguilar turned to my boyfriend. "Everett, I just want to say again what a great job you did with the fall musical. It was very well done."

"Thank you, but the real praise goes to the student actors and tech crew who all crushed it." He beamed with pride. South Rock was chock full of student talent that had been awakened by *Into the Woods*.

"I can't believe the entire run was sold out." Aguilar laughed to himself. Cal, the scout leader who we'd met in the rest stop, recorded slick radio ads for free, which helped drive excitement beyond the school. All of Everett's college friends came to catch a performance, too.

"I'm going to review the budget for next year to ensure we have two play productions," Aguilar said.

"Really?"

"And we may open up another theater arts class next year depending on enrollment demand. Great work all around, Everett,"

Aguilar left Everett speechless. Speechless was a cute look on him.

"Way to go, Ev," I said.

"I couldn't have done it without you. You are the world's best boyfriend, Raleigh. You're saving arts education in public schools by day, and delivering earth-rattling orgasms by night. And early morning."

We listened to the younger English teachers do a medley of old school Destiny's Child songs. The older English teachers cut out an hour ago. Evidently, it was past their bedtime.

The teachers hogged the mic for a bit, but they were fun to listen to. We created a mini dance floor as they sang. I hugged Everett tight as we danced. I thought about how far we'd all come, how destiny had pulled us together.

After more dancing, I got us refills, and Everett found us a high-top.

"Can I tell you something that will make this night even better?" Everett looked up at me with a dopey smile as he sipped his vodka and Sprite.

"Shoot."

"You know how Noah was cast to star in the film adaptation of his hit Broadway musical? Well, the producers fired him after two days of shooting. They said he didn't play a high school student convincingly. He looked too old. I could only imagine how crushed Noah is feeling right now. Don't you just love the holidays?"

"What happened to goodwill toward men?" I asked.

"I have lots of goodwill toward men, with one exception."

I felt a little bad for Noah. After all, being a self-absorbed piece of dogshit had its downsides.

I slapped my hand on the high-top, ready to change topics away from ex-boyfriends. "Does this table look familiar?"

"I mean, it's a table, and I've been to this establishment many a time."

"It's the table where we watched football and had our first kiss."

"Seriously?"

I held a piece of mistletoe above our heads that I'd swiped from the entrance. "Shall we recreate the moment?"

"We don't need mistletoe for that. If I were directing this, I'd cut this scene because it's terribly cliché."

I did one of my favorite things: I shut him up with a kiss.

"Then again, people love clichés for a reason," he said.

———

LATER IN THE NIGHT, I mingled with teachers and danced some more. The holidays were weird because it was technically the end of the calendar year, but only halfway through the school year. So really, I was mostly celebrating getting two weeks off.

My holiday joy, though, was put on hold when I spotted Julian hanging by himself in the corner. Earlier in the night, he'd been chatting on the balcony with Seamus.

I sidled up to him.

"Hey, pal." I cheers'd his drink. "You okay?"

"Yeah. Just taking a breather." He shrugged into his mixed drink.

"Cool. Did Seamus go home?"

"How would I know?" he said with a hard edge. "We're not joined at the hip, despite what Everett thinks."

Everett had shared with me that Julian was globviously into Seamus. Once he mentioned it, it wasn't that hard to see.

Julian's face was an open book and devoid of holiday cheer.

"You're right. I'm sorry," I said.

"We're just friends," he said, more flustered than usual. Even nice guys had limits. "We teach in the same department. There's nothing more to talk about."

"Hey, I get that. if you ever want to talk...we're not friends through Everett. You're my friend too, J."

Being a football coach, I had developed the skill of getting grunty, non-verbal guys to open up. I was able to be their sounding board if they needed one.

After a moment where Julian seemed to be in deliberation, he peered at me with hopeful eyes. "If I tell you something, would you promise not to tell Everett?"

"Of course! Here." I pulled out a crumpled ticket. "This is the ticket to the first game I played at college. I found it on the ground outside the stadium and decided to save it as a memento. It's the closest thing I have to a bible." I put my hand over the ticket. "On behalf of this ticket, you have my word that I would never tell a soul. Unless my boyfriend or my friends are in danger. Are they in danger?"

"No." He cracked a smile.

"Excellent. Then we're good." I returned the ticket to its sleeve in my wallet.

He heaved out a breath. "Seamus and I have gotten close this year. I consider him one of my best friends. However I feel about him...it doesn't matter."

"Why?"

He rubbed his hands on his jeans. The guy was more nervous than my players before the game.

"I've been lying to my friends." He looked at the floor. "I'm a virgin."

Fortunately, Mr. Luka and Mrs. Larson, the art teachers, were in the middle of very loud rendition of "Love Will Keep Us Together." Their voices drowned out Julian's confession from being heard by anyone else.

He hung his head, and I could tell he was seconds away from tearing up.

"Hey, that's cool, J. That's nothing to be embarrassed about." I put a hand on his shoulder. "That's your choice."

"It's not a choice. I'm going to be thirty-five at the end of March, and I've never had sex. I've never even given or received a blow job."

"That's okay. Really, it is."

"And yeah, I do like Seamus as more than a friend, but he's straight. And even if there were some flexibility there, I have zero experience. If he found out his friend was a middle-aged virgin, he'd never talk to me again."

"No, he wouldn't. Seamus is a good guy. And you're not middle-aged!"

"I'd probably suck at sex."

"You won't. You're a smart guy. Stupid gay guys have sex all the time."

"That makes me feel even worse." He rubbed his forehead, the shame coming off him in waves. "I'm so embarrassed."

"Don't be."

"Most of the student population of South Rock High has gotten more action than me."

"Not as many as you think. It'd shock you to hear about how nervous my players are about having sex with their partners. They talk a big game in the locker room, but privately, quite a few of them are freaking out."

"At least they're having sex."

"If you really wanted to cash in your v-card, you could've found some random person on the internet to do the deed. But you want something more. You want it to be with someone special. I think that's worth waiting for."

I wondered how straight Seamus was. We once went to a Major League Baseball game, and maybe I was seeing things, but it looked like he was checking out the third baseman's ass for half the game.

To be fair, it was a nice ass.

"Look on the brightside. At least you haven't had to suffer through a bad blow job. Those are...beyond painful."

We started laughing, and slowly got back into the holiday spirit.

"Here." I handed him a cocktail napkin to wipe away the tears until his face was clear. We stayed in our corner until the redness left Julian's face.

"Thanks, Raleigh. I'm sorry for spilling my guts like this. I usually tell my friends everything, but…"

"Anytime. Let's get back out there," I said.

We rejoined the crowd trying to politely cover their ears during a version of "Love Will Keep Us Together" that just wouldn't end. I found Everett in the crowd. My arms automatically wrapped around his solid waist. I breathed in his scent through his crisp white shirt. I'd found a peace with Everett that I didn't know was possible. Someone wanted to chill with me in my corner of the sandbox. He was snobby, sarcastic, and I couldn't imagine my life without him.

Touchdown all the way.

"What were you and Julian talking about?"

"How out of tune our English department is."

The song ended, and Mr. Luka and Mrs. Larson finally relinquished the microphone. Everett and I swayed to the song in our heads.

"What are you thinking?" I asked of the serene smile on his face.

"That things are good. In this moment, things are good."

"Yeah. There's singing, dancing, friends hanging out together, two people falling in love. Oh man. This is just like the ending of *Mamma Mia!*"

EPILOGUE

A FEW YEARS LATER

Everett

I ran my hand along the smooth white wood checking for any substantial damage. I ignored the nicks in the piece. Those I could live with.

"It hasn't been used in a few years, but it's still in great condition," the guy said, anxiously watching me from the doorway.

Raleigh squatted down on the other side doing a similar check. His eyes combed over the piece of furniture as if he were an appraiser on *Antiques Roadshow*.

I'd gotten used to all of Raleigh's facial expressions over the years, but the ultra-serious stare he gave when looking over used furniture had to be one of my favorites. For a guy who loved to have fun, thrifting was a joke-free zone for him.

"What do you think?" The seller let out a nervous laugh, probably not used to being around hardcore thrifters. The guy just wanted to make some extra cash.

Raleigh and I caught each other's attention. We never shared our opinions in front of the seller. That would give them leverage.

"Can my husband and I have a minute to chat?" Raleigh tapped his ring finger against the frame.

"Yeah, sure! I'll just be in the kitchen." The seller pointed to the room behind him before exiting.

As soon as he was gone, Raleigh and I huddled.

"It's nice," I whispered.

"Yeah. Great condition."

"Really great condition." For once, the seller wasn't bull-shitting.

"It's a good brand, too. I Googled the model, and it has good reviews." He scratched at his light beard. It was graduated stubble. I thought I wouldn't like Raleigh with facial hair.

I was very wrong.

It gave him an air of maturity like a college professor. And I wanted to be his slutty student offering my body in exchange for an A.

"Should we get this new, though?" he asked. "It's a big deal piece of furniture."

"Raleigh, you're falling into the trap."

"The trap. Right." He nodded and gave his distracting beard another pensive scratch.

"We've been over this. People think they have to get brand new everything. They don't. We've been picking up things that are practically brand new. She won't know the difference."

"But we want her to be safe and comfortable." Concern creased his forehead. Raleigh's thoughtfulness was a guaranteed swoon from me. The man had a huge heart.

"She will be." I squeezed his hand. "She will be."

"Okay." He heaved out a breath and put on his game face. "What about the price? He's asking 300."

"He's living in fantasy land."

"Offer 150?" Raleigh asked.

"He'll counter with 200. We can probably get him to 175. Perfect."

Raleigh put his hand between us. "175 on the count of three."

He insisted on doing this whenever we were able to make an offer. I put my hand in the center.

"One, two, three. 175!" we whisper-yelled.

Raleigh called the seller back. He slapped on his social, gregarious grin, the kind that charmed everyone around him, including me.

"We love it. You've kept it in great condition. Would you take 150?" Raleigh asked.

"Yeah."

Raleigh and I exchanged a shocked look. So much for counteroffers.

"Really?" I asked.

"It's been taking up room in our basement for years. My wife is on me to get it out of here so we can turn this room into a bar. You probably could've gotten me lower."

"We'll remember that for next time," I said.

Raleigh handed over the cash. The seller tucked it into his front pocket. He assisted us in disassembling it and carrying the pieces to our car.

I stared at our new addition in the trunk. It was another gut punch of reality.

"It served us well," the seller said, a hint of wistfulness in his voice. "Enjoy."

We waved goodbye as he returned to his house. Raleigh joined me in staring into the trunk. He put an arm around me, and like I'd done for years, I sunk into his touch.

"We have a crib," I said.

"We have a crib," he repeated, just as shellshocked.

"This is happening."

"This is really happening." He took my chin in his strong hand.
"You ready, Dad?"

———————

LIFE WAS FUNNY.

There was a time in my life not that long ago when I didn't
want to get married, and I sure as hell didn't want kids. But once
Raleigh and I began dating, things snowballed. Being with him
opened me up to this new version of my life. I became someone
who had a serious boyfriend. And then I became someone who
talked about marriage with said boyfriend. And then I became
someone who entertained the idea of becoming a father. Looking
back, it seems crazy that any of this happened, but in the moment,
all these little steps forward made sense.

And it was all because of Raleigh. I was more excited about
watching him be a dad. He was fantastic with my nieces and neph-
ews: roughhousing with them, teaching them how to play football,
having tea parties. He could do it all. He loved everyone in my
family as if they were his. Any snide comments my siblings
might've uttered about us just being teachers and living in
Raleigh's modest house rolled off his back. Eventually, they
stopped. They saw how happy we were.

Watching Raleigh get close with my family filled my heart; he
finally had the big family he always wanted.

About two years into being married, Raleigh floated the idea of
starting a family. To my surprise, my gut response was excitement.
Raleigh had made life an adventure, and I wanted to see where it'd
take us next.

Raleigh was going to make an excellent father.

"Look at that." Raleigh screwed in the final piece of the crib. It
sat in the nursery, which I insisted we paint yellow. A pink nursery
for a girl felt too cliché.

The crib was beautiful. Soft white wood glowed in the sunlight streaming in.

"Wow," I said, at a loss for words.

"I can't wait to become a dad with you."

"You're going to be a great dad."

"I know." He flashed me his trademark cocky grin.

Raleigh not being modest? Some things never changed.

"Of course you're full of yourself about being a dad."

"I'm going to crush fatherhood. So are you." He shot me a wink, which even after all these years, and even in the privacy of our own home, still made me feel warm inside. "This kid is going to be so lucky. She'll get the best of both worlds. She's going to have a dad to teach her about the finer things in life."

I let myself play a future highlight reel in my mind.

"She's going to have a dad who'll coach her through all her little league games."

Raleigh tucked a lock of hair behind my ear. "She's going to have a dad who'll take her to see all these cool, interesting plays."

"She's going to have a dad who'll take her to football games and buy her overpriced concessions."

"She's going to have a dad who'll make sure she knows how to stand up for herself and not take shit from anyone."

"She'll have a dad who'll make sure she has a big heart and looks out for others."

"She's one lucky gal," he said.

"That she is."

Raleigh tipped my chin up and closed the gap with a soft kiss.

There was something about us watching the other ones become dads that was a weird kind of aphrodisiac. We were so excited and so happy that we inevitably became horny. There was probably a more scientific reason that I didn't feel like looking up, not when Raleigh was pushing me against the wall and turning up the heat between our lips.

"Hey," I said, catching my breath.

"Hey."

"We should probably take this to our own bedroom."

"Good call." Raleigh picked me up in one seamless move. I wrapped my legs around him, and he carried us to our bed.

Raleigh

I'm going to dad so hard.

I couldn't wait to start a family with Everett. I'd shower our daughter with love and corny dad jokes. I was excited to see a new side to Everett. Underneath his sarcastic comments was a big, tender heart that would reveal itself with our future kid. Everett liked to say that he was a petty bitch, but the guy was a big softie.

Although right now, he was very hard.

As was I.

I dropped him on the bed, and he got to work unbuttoning my jeans as I whipped off my shirt. He pulled down my boxers as I knelt on the bed, unleashing my rock hard dick.

Everett licked his lips before taking me, a dead sexy move that drove me wild.

I jutted my hips out, letting him take all of me.

"Fuck. Feels so good." A deep moan tore out of me. My days of being so loud were numbered. I threaded my fingers in his hair and pushed him down to my base. He bobbed up and down on my dick, hurtling me to the verge of spewing my load.

"Ev, you're gonna make me come."

"You say that every time." His tongue traveled down to my balls, taking them in his mouth. I rubbed my shaft and slick head across his cheeks. Everett was right. It felt awesome, manly, hot.

I pushed him back down on the bed and undid his pants. His cock popped straight up like a hand in class. I rubbed it against my beard. Everett arched his back, panting with need. He was a fan of the facial hair, though he didn't appreciate the occasional burn it left on his cheeks (and inner thighs).

I took him in my mouth, his hot length pulsing against my tongue. He writhed under me, lust possessing him. He fucked into my mouth. Drops of bitter pre-come hit the back of my throat.

"How much do you like that T-shirt?" I pointed to the I Heart NY white shirt he was wearing, which had to be several years old.

"It's fine. It's a shirt. It gets the job done."

"Do you have any sentimental attachment to it?"

"No."

"Good." I tore it off his body, the fabric ripping down the middle. I yanked the pieces off his frame and savored the sight of a stark naked Everett. Every cell in my body flooded with lust over his creamy skin and thick cock. "I need to have you now."

His hungry, heavy-lidded eyes agreed with me.

I flipped him over and yanked off his jeans and underwear, which had bunched at his ankles. Why did it feel like we were wearing seventy layers of clothing?

I gave his ass a hard slap, spread his cheeks, and spat on his pink opening. I swirled my tongue over his hole, feeling him clench under me. His pert cheek stuck in the air, practically begging to be fucked.

"Fuck I love the way your beard feels," he said, his face partially mashed into the bedspread. I rubbed my chin over his hole to set off more sparks for him.

Fortunately, we had some time before we needed to childproof our bedroom. For now, our lube could stay in my nightstand drawer easily accessible. I dribbled the liquid on Everett's hole, then coated my cock until it was nice and slick.

I pressed in slowly. Even after years of fucking, Everett still needed a few moments to get used to me inside him. Blame Mother Nature for blessing me.

"Holy fuck." He heaved out a thunderous sigh that vibrated against my dick.

"You fucking love it."

"Shut up. You're right, but shut up."

I laughed into his neck, loving that we could still crack each other up mid-fuck. Everett tightened under my lips.

"Shit. Sorry." I forgot he was super ticklish there. I'd save the tickling for post-sex.

Back to fucking.

I sunk all the way inside his tight ass, our grunts filling the air. Damn, Everett felt so good I was about to melt. Everett straightened up, his back going flush against my chest. I wrapped an arm across him to pull him close. I inhaled the salty sweat off his body.

"I want you so bad, Ev."

"You have me."

"I still want you. Over and over."

I reached around to stroke his cock. I pumped in time with our fucking. Everett quickly threw one of the ripped T-shirt pieces in front of him before he came. Hot white jets streaked across the shirt.

"Nice save." I gave his ass a soft pat. Then a hard slap because I was still fucking him like crazy.

"Come inside me," he said, still in a daze. "I want to feel you inside me."

Damn. Everett still knew how to drive me fucking wild. He was one sexy motherfucker. I filled his ass with my release.

I held him in silence, his skin tender and prickled with sweat.

"Wow," he said.

"Yeah."

"After all these years..."

"Yes?" I kissed his neck.

Everett turned to me. "...you are still a cocky shit. But at least you can fuck."

Once our heart rates came down, we showered off then returned to going about our day. There were chores to be done, dinner to make. Everett was putting together a budget for the spring production and narrowing down show choices. I had to devise lesson plans for the upcoming physical education units. We were busy, but we could be busy together, sitting on the couch together as we worked.

When night rolled around, I stopped by the nursery once more before going to our bedroom. I took in the sight. It was coming together. This was actually happening.

We got into bed. Before I could spoon Everett against me, he turned to face me.

"We're going to be dads," he said.

"We are? Since when?"

He smacked me playfully on the arm.

"What if we suck?" Everett brushed a finger over my beard, tracing my lips.

"Then we'll get better. I'm excited. Not just because I'm going to be a parent, but because I get to go on this crazy adventure with you."

Everett's wry smirk dropped for a moment to let a genuine smile light up his face. "Don't let this go to your head, but I love you, Raleigh Marshall."

"I know you do."

He gave me a classic eyeroll, which I treasured with every piece of my heart.

"And I love you, too, Everett Marshall."

———

Thanks for reading!

Can Julian finally shed his virgin status before his 35th birthday with the help of his straight best friend Seamus?

Find out in *Romance Languages*, a friends-to-lovers, virgin, nerd/jock romance and Book 3 in the South Rock High series. Start reading today.

Curious about Cal and Russ, the scout leaders from the rest stop? Before they were lovers, they were two single dads with one huge grudge. Their story can be found in *The Falcon and the Foe,* part of the Single Dads Club series.

Sign up for my newsletter to get the first scoop on new books, read bonus stories, and get exclusive access to other cool goodies. www.ajtruman.com/outsiders

Please consider leaving a review on the book's Amazon page or on Goodreads. Reviews are crucial in helping other readers find new books.

Join the party in my Facebook Group and on Instagram @ajtruman_author. Follow me at Bookbub to be alerted to new releases.

And then there's email. I love hearing from readers! Send me a note anytime at info@ajtruman.com. I always respond.

ALSO BY A.J. TRUMAN

South Rock High

Ancient History

Drama!

Romance Languages

Advanced Chemistry

Single Dads Club

The Falcon and the Foe

The Mayor and the Mystery Man

The Barkeep and the Bro

The Fireman and the Flirt

Browerton University Series

Out in the Open

Out on a Limb

Out of My Mind

Out for the Night

Out of This World

Outside Looking In

Out of Bounds

Seasonal Novellas

Fall for You

You Got Scrooged

Hot Mall Santa

Only One Coffin

<u>Written with M.A. Wardell</u>

Marshmallow Mountain

ABOUT THE AUTHOR

A.J. Truman writes books with **humor, heart, and hot guys.** What else does a story need? He lives in a very full house in Indiana with his husband, son, and cats.. He loves happily ever afters and sneaking off for an afternoon movie.

www.ajtruman.com
info@ajtruman.com
The Outsiders - Facebook Group

Printed in Great Britain
by Amazon

57874374R00158